A TRAVEL GUIDE TO THE SEVEN KINGDOMS OF

Westeros

DANIEL BETTRIDGE

JOHN BLAKE

Published by John Blake Publishing Ltd,
3 Bramber Court, 2 Bramber Road,
London W14 9PB, England

www.johnblakepublishing.co.uk

www.facebook.com/johnblakebooks ■
twitter.com/jblakebooks ■

This edition published in paperback in 2015

ISBN: 978 1 78418 372 1

British Library Cataloguing-in-Publication Data:

A catalogue record for this book is available from the British Library.

Design by www.envydesign.co.uk

Printed in Great Britain by CPI Group (UK) Ltd

3 5 7 9 10 8 6 4 2

Papers used by John Blake Publishing are natural, recyclable
products made from wood grown in sustainable forests.
The manufacturing processes conform to the
environmental regulations of the country of origin.

Every attempt has been made to contact the relevant
copyright-holders, but some were unobtainable. We would
be grateful if the appropriate people could contact us.

Contents

Welcome to Westeros

Welcome to Westeros: a land rich in ancient castles, stunning natural landscapes and Lannister gold. Known as the Seven Kingdoms – even though there are actually nine of them – the continent is vast, stretching about 900 miles at its widest point and 2,000 miles at its longest.

The geography varies immensely, often shifting drastically from kingdom to kingdom, from frozen, mountainous tundras in the north to the extensive river network of the Riverlands, the fertile farms of the Reach and all the way down to the arid deserts of Dorne.

Its people are almost as distinct as its landscape. While Targaryen rule united the continent, the Seven Kingdoms remain a hodgepodge of cultural influences, ethnicities and religious beliefs. Those differences have become even more pronounced over recent years as King Robert's rebellion has reopened the realm's old wounds, reviving quarrels that people had long since thought forgotten.

As a result, the question of what it means to be a Westerosi has become a major debate on the continent. While some stay loyal to the Crown, the power vacuum left by King Robert's untimely demise has led many to question the rule of the Iron Throne and rebellion is rife everywhere from the Iron Islands to the North.

For tourists, the conflict that continues to ravage the realm can be daunting and, indeed, safety is a principal concern for anyone who wants to leave the country with their head still attached to their shoulders. On the flip side, however, this renewed emphasis on cultural diversity is an exhilarating opportunity for tourists to truly experience the Seven Kingdoms' individual charms.

From the Rhoynish traditions and laid-back social structures of Dorne to the riches of the Westerlands via the pageantry of Highgarden and the ferocity of the Iron Islands, there's never been a better time to come and explore this conflicted and contrasting continent. Covering the Seven Kingdoms' main attractions (see below) will certainly get you started. But make sure you save time to scratch below the surface and get involved with the ever-growing assortment of attractions that have sprung up to cater for Westeros's burgeoning tourism industry.

FACT FILE

- Since the fall of the Valyrian Freehold, Westeros stands alone as the known world's largest centrally governed empire: a continuous landmass that runs from the Summer Sea, south of Dorne, to the Wall in the North.
- No one quite knows Westeros's exact population but the number is thought to stretch into the millions. Though more sparsely populated in the northern- and southern-most Kingdoms, the continent's central region is densely packed, as people flock to the fertile farmlands and forgiving climates.
- The most populous city in Westeros is the capital, King's Landing, which is home to more than 500,000 residents.
- The Seven Kingdoms were initially united by Aegon the Conqueror more than 300 years ago. The Iron Throne has ruled the continent ever since.
- The current monarch is King Tommen of the House Baratheon: the first of his name. Although, given the recent epidemic of mysterious royal deaths, whether he's still on the Iron Throne when you arrive remains to be seen.

Currency

Westeros's present currency was established shortly after the War of Conquest united the Seven Kingdoms more than 300 years ago. The currency is managed centrally in King's Landing, where the Master of Coin oversees matters such as the minting of new coins and the setting of exchange rates.

Coins are readily accepted throughout the continent although, typically, you'll find that higher denominations are used only by the wealthy, while coppers and silvers are preferred by the poor and lowborn. Bartering is also a common practice, particularly in rural areas such as those alongside the Wall, where the exchange of goods is more practical.

Common coinage includes **gold dragons**, which are printed with the Targaryen sigil on one side and the likeness of the King under whose sovereignty they were printed on the other; **silver**, often referred to as 'Stags', which came into existence some eighty years ago during the time of the Hedge Knight; and **copper**, which is the most commonly used currency in Westeros. There are several copper coins, including pennies, half-pennies, groats, half-groats and stars, all of which traditionally bear the seven-pointed star of the continent's religion.

Travellers will have to make provision to exchange their currency if they plan on making the journey across the Narrow Sea to Essos. Here, coinage varies from place to place, with each of the Free Cities using their own currency. As the name implies, slaves are the currency of choice in and around Slaver's Bay, while the Dothraki do not believe in money whatsoever and instead prefer to use an honour system where goods are exchanged as gifts.

Economy

Despite years of prosperity under the Targaryens, King Robert's rebellion and his subsequent rule have almost bankrupted the realm. In fact, the Crown is said to be more than 6 million gold dragons in debt, owing vast sums to the Lannister family, the Tyrells, the Iron Bank of Braavos and Tyroshi Trading Cartels.

Although trade continues to remain stable – particularly in commodities and luxury items – the recent War of the Five Kings, alongside extravagant tourneys, weddings and State funerals held in King's Landing, have only added to the financial deficit. Inflation is an inevitability that has led to common bartering replacing currency in many corners of the Seven Kingdoms.

Government and Politics

For most of Westeros's history, the continent's kingdoms were individually ruled and governed. Years of conflict meant that the number of kingdoms and their borders were constantly shifting with the balance of power until Aegon the Conqueror landed and unified everything north of Dorne under the rule of the Iron Throne.

Due to the vast size of his new empire, Aegon installed a feudal system whereby Westeros's Great Houses and their bannermen swore loyalty to him and ran their constituent kingdoms in his place. These Houses included the Starks, who were granted stewardship of the North; the Tullys, who took control of the Riverlands; the Greyjoys, who took the Iron Islands; the Tyrells, who took the Reach; the Arryns, who retained control of the Vale; and the Baratheons, who ruled over the Stormlands. Each of these lords was given autonomy over his own lands to wield his authority over the Kingdom's residents yet, ultimately, answering to the King.

That king was, for almost 300 years, a Targaryen, with rule passed down from generation to generation until King Robert Baratheon's rebellion. As well as claiming the throne for himself, King Robert and his followers all but exterminated the Targaryen line, replacing it with a marriage of convenience (and power) between the Baratheons and the Lannisters.

The suspicious deaths of King Robert and his son, King Joffrey, have caused chaos across the Seven Kingdoms, as have the repeated scandals and accusations of incest that have rocked the royal family over recent years. The end result is a kingdom in turmoil; a power vacuum which Houses once loyal to the Crown are attempting to fill.

Ultimately, the realm is a powder keg, with claims to the Iron Throne springing up in almost every corner of the continent. Tourists are advised to travel with caution and to stay abreast of the latest news from King's Landing throughout the duration of their trip.

Law and Order

Although the King's Peace is expected to be kept throughout the land, practices of law and order are largely based on local custom, with individual lords tasked with dispensing justice across the Seven Kingdoms.

While the King ultimately has the final authority, it is a lord's duty to keep the peace and dispense punishment in the name of the Iron Throne. Punishments are meted out at trials, where arguments will be heard, accusations levelled and sentences passed.

Lesser crimes are punishable by floggings and fines,

which are commonly handed out to the lower classes. However, offences such as rape, poaching and theft can lead to losing a limb (or a manhood), while the punishment for treason and oathbreaking is death. The accused are able to request a trial-by-combat if they want to place their fate in the hands of the Gods, or take the Black and join the Night's Watch on the Wall if they wish to avoid sentencing altogether.

Religion

Religious beliefs run deep in Westerosi culture, where the vast majority of the population adhere to their chosen faith. That faith is predominantly the Faith of the Seven, which was brought to these shores by the Andals. However, other religions are openly practiced on the continent. Here is a brief summary of the most common:

The Faith of the Seven – You'll find a Sept in almost every town in Westeros, where locals both noble and common practice their faith. In Westeros it is led by the High Septon, the leader of the faith, under whom operates scores of Septons and Septas alongside other orders, including the Silent Sisters, the Warrior's Sons and the Begging Brothers.

THE SEVEN

The faith worships the Seven: a single deity with seven separate facets, each representing a different virtue. People turn to different aspects of the Seven depending on what their prayer involves. The seven facets are:

Father – Personifies justice and is represented in most Septs by a figure of a bearded man who carries scales.

Mother – Represents nurturing. People pray to her for fertility, compassion and mercy.

Crone – Embodying wisdom, the Crone is prayed to for guidance. She is regularly depicted as a haggard figure who carries a lantern.

Smith – Always shown wielding a hammer, the Smith represents crafts, labour and strength.

Warrior – Prayed to for courage and strength in battle, soldiers ask the Warrior for victory on the battlefield.

Maiden – Symbolises virtue and innocence.

Stranger – Worshippers in the Seven Kingdoms rarely pray to the Stranger, who represents death and the unknown.

The Old Gods – Inextricably tied to the earth, the Old Gods are still followed in the North, where the locals hold a closer bond to the First Men and Children of the Forest, from whom the faith stems. The religion worships nameless deities who are tied to the land itself and who are represented by Weirwoods.

The Drowned God – A harsh religion followed only

by the Ironborn, followers of the faith are indoctrinated through drowning.

The Lord of the Light – Otherwise known as R'hllor, this foreign deity was originally worshipped across the Narrow Sea in Essos but has recently found a following in Westeros too. Followers worship fire alongside the Lord of Light himself, whom they see to be the one true god.

Climate

Westeros's climate shifts from the sub-zero wastelands beyond the Wall to the arid deserts south of the Red Mountains in Dorne. The belly of the country is more temperate, although temperatures fluctuate with the seasons.

The length of the seasons on the continent is unpredictable and often lasts for years at a time. The continent is currently enjoying an unusually long summer, which has lasted for nine years. However, White Ravens have been seen flying from the Citadel in Oldtown, suggesting that autumn is now around the corner.

Winter is coming and its arrival will have serious consequences for the continent. Much of Westeros lies north of the known world's equatorial regions, which means that the Seven Kingdoms and its people will have to endure winters that are far crueller than those of their near neighbours across the Narrow Sea. Snowfall and colder climates can extend as far south as King's Landing but the North will be particularly hard hit by the changing of the seasons and the people here can expect to endure a cold and cruel winter.

TEN THINGS NOT TO MISS

It's not possible to see everything Westeros has to offer in one trip – although we do suggest you try. However, here, in no particular order, are ten of the continent's highlights; a rundown of the landscapes, landmarks and life experiences that you won't want to miss.

The Wall (p. 42)

One of the wonders of the man-made world, the Wall and what lies beyond it simply have to be seen to be believed. A colossal structure forged of ice and rock, the Wall serves as the northernmost border of the Seven Kingdoms and gateway to the Wildling country that lies beyond.

Take in a tourney in King's Landing (p. 224)

Pomp, ceremony, pageantry and the continent's best knights charging at each other with lances dipped, a tourney in King's Landing has everything you could dream of and much, much more besides.

Journey to Dragonstone (p. 193)

Don't let the trip across the Blackwater Bay put you off. A journey to Dragonstone to see where the Seven Kingdoms first began is well worth it. Once the seat of power for the House of Targaryen, Dragonstone is crammed to the gills with history alongside Essos-inspired architecture that's like nothing else you'll see in all of the Seven Kingdoms.

Walk the streets of Oldtown (p. 132)

Of all Westeros's cities, Oldtown is possibly the prettiest and the best way to experience its dazzling architecture and cobbled streets is definitely on foot.

Drink the Arbor dry (p. 142)

See how wine is made and show them how wine is drunk with a trip to Westeros's premier wine-growing region.

Climb the Eyrie (p. 162)

The climb to the Eyrie is not for the faint of heart but those who make the trek skywards will be rewarded with stunning views from the loftiest castle in the land.

Follow in the footsteps of the First Men (p. 97)

Travel back in time with a trip to the ancient ringfort of Oldstones. Though today the ruined stronghold is little more than a collection of weathered rocks and mossy hummocks, in the age of the First Men the site was home to one of the most fearsome castles in the entire kingdom.

A night out in Sunspear (p. 264)

Enjoy a night out in Sunspear, where your every desire can be explored as you lose your inhibitions with the locals. A place where almost anything goes, Sunspear is famed for its hospitality, which perhaps goes some way to explain why so many revellers descend on the Dornish capital in search of an escape from the social constraints you'll find elsewhere in the Seven Kingdoms.

Hike the Ocean Road (p. 174)

Hiking is the best way to enjoy the superlative views over the Sunset Sea and the Shield Islands that are offered on this popular Westerlands trail.

Visit Essos (p. 269)

Take the short hop across the Narrow Sea to explore the neighbouring continent of Essos: a kaleidoscope of colours and contrasting cultures that is a world away from the Seven Kingdoms.

The North

The North is the largest of the Seven Kingdoms: a landmass that covers everything south of the Wall and north of the Neck. Barren, cold and unforgiving, it may not have the exotic charm of Dorne or the bountiful harvests of the Reach, yet, for many, this snow-strewn landscape is the beating heart of Westeros.

Presided over for centuries by the Starks of Winterfell, the North is so vast that it is almost as large as the rest of the Seven Kingdoms combined. Besides the two land barriers that represent its northern and southern borders, the North is bound on each side by major seas: the aptly named Shivering Sea to the east and the Sunset Sea in the west. In between these two oceans lie leagues of barren plains, pockmarked with forests, mountains and the occasional sign of civilisation.

Although there is a 'frontier' flavour to much of Westeros it

13

is only when you push further north that you truly experience what the edge of the world feels like. The kingdom is like a realm within a realm – in fact, it's easy to see why a king in the North presided over it until the War of Conquest. The popular imagination will tell you that the North is a perpetually frozen wasteland; an icy tundra of rocky outcrops and dense forests that is constantly blasted by ferocious weather, even in the height of summer. It's an exaggeration, of course, but not the most outlandish one you'll hear during your travels.

Though the landscape is wild, the North is not without its charms. There's beauty to the lakes, forests and icy tundra that make up the kingdom and if it's breathtaking landscapes you're after, you've come to the right place. There's also plenty of history here. As any Northerner will proudly tell you, the people up here can trace their lineage back to the First Men. It's not just the people who have stood the test of time either. From millennia-old landmarks like the Wall to ancient castles such as Winterfell, the North boasts one of the richest histories anywhere in the Seven Kingdoms.

The North is as much a state of mind as it is an actual place. On the surface, the people up here are as hard as the landscape they call home but get to know them and you'll quickly find out why they are proud to call themselves Northmen. There's a stoicism to those who've chosen to settle here, an inner strength and honour that is exemplified by the Starks, who have presided over these lands for centuries. But beyond the honour, there is also humour and a people who are as quick to laugh at themselves as they are the Southrons, whom they ceaselessly mock for their softness.

The main artery into the North is the Kingsroad, which

is well maintained and relatively safe for travellers. From here, popular attractions such as Moat Cailin, White Harbor and the Wall are easily accessible but many people choose to base themselves in the kingdom's capitol of Winterfell and explore the region from there.

HIGHLIGHTS

Winterfell (p. 18)

The kingdom's capital, this ancient seat of power serves up history and home comforts in equal measure. Ancient, atmospheric and filled with entertainment, it is one of Westeros's most compelling towns.

The Wall (p. 42)

One of the wonders of the man-made world, the Wall needs to be seen to be believed. As impressive as it is overbearing, it offers stunning sights and a fascinating insight into the rag-tag group of thieves and miscreants whose job it is to guard the Seven Kingdoms.

Moat Cailin (p. 63)

One of Westeros's more intriguing ruins, Moat Cailin has been the secret to the North's strength for generations, although these days you're just as likely to find Ironborn pirates along its battlements as you are true Northmen.

The Dreadfort (p. 66)

One of the kingdom's lesser-known castles, the seat of power for the House of Bolton houses an exhibition of flayed skin – one of the region's more macabre attractions.

Travel Essentials

Warm furs: It really is as cold as they say up North, where even the warmest of summers come complete with snow flurries. As such, it is not uncommon to see Northerners missing an extremity or two, with ears, fingers and toes considered luxuries by those who are just happy to survive the starvation that goes hand in hand with the region's ravaging winters.

Unless you want to join them, be sure to bring your thickest riding furs and your sturdiest boots. Don't worry if you forget to pack your thermal breeches, however – local traders will happily part with basic equipment and provisions for a few coins.

A sword: Ever since the uprising of young Robb Stark, the King's Peace has taken a leave of absence in this part of the realm. Raiders from the Iron Islands are a common blight and the War of the Five Kings has also led to an increased number of outlaws along the Kingsroad. At the time of writing, the best advice is to carry a sword – you won't get very far without one.

Gold: Although the North is distinct in many ways, it is still a part of the Seven Kingdoms so your currency is good in these parts. However, you may find that it doesn't go as far as in other parts of Westeros, as the onset of winter means that locals prize a storeroom full of grain over a purse full of coins.

Local Customs

Guest rights – The obligations of hospitality are taken very seriously in this part of the Seven Kingdoms, where both noble- and common-born people stick closely to the guest rights that were originally laid down during the time of the First Men.

The guest right is a sacred law of hospitality, which states that any guest who has eaten food and drunk wine from a host's table is safe for the duration of their stay. The practice is observed by the vast majority of Northerners and it is believed that breaking the pact is one of the foulest crimes imaginable and one that will invoke the wrath of gods, both old and new.

In many parts of the North, guest rites are typically extended to visitors through the ceremonial offer of bread and salt on your arrival and only end once you leave your host's protection.

'Winter is coming' – The words of the House of Stark serve as something of a mantra for all Northerners, who are more closely entwined with the surrounding climate than those who reside anywhere else in the Seven Kingdoms. Though it serves as a warning, don't be surprised to hear it used either as a greeting or form of farewell anywhere north of the Neck.

When to Visit

The best part of the year is during the long summer when the weather is milder and more palatable for those more used to southern climes. However, at the time of writing, news has reached us that the Maesters have dispatched their White Ravens from the Citadel. Yes, winter is coming, so book now before it's too late.

Famous Residents

Ancestral birthplace of the House of Stark, the North has long been home to some of Westeros's most noble noblemen. However, the recent actions of the 'alleged' traitor, Eddard Stark, have brought the House into disrepute and scattered the remaining offspring throughout the Seven Kingdoms. Today you're more likely to find a Bolton, or one of their bastards, in the North's more notable castles, with Lord Roose Bolton – the recently anointed Warden of the North – and his legitimatised son Ramsay among the more familiar faces you can expect to run into in this corner of the Seven Kingdoms.

WINTERFELL

A labyrinth of grey stone battlements and granite keeps, Winterfell is an oasis of civilisation that sits at the heart of the vast northern expanse of the Seven Kingdoms. Located on the Kingsroad, which runs from Storm's End to the Wall, this ancient seat of power lies on the confluence of the eastern fringes of the Wolfswood and the western branch of the White Knife.

The capital of the North, Winterfell is the seat of power for the House of Stark: a noble dynasty with a habit of putting honour before common sense, whose lineage extends back to the First Men themselves. Locals will tell you that there 'must always be a Stark in Winterfell': a mantra that goes some way to explaining how the family has presided over this remote settlement for some 8,000 years.

Like the land over which it presides, this stout fortress has weathered its fair share of adversity alongside a revolving door of inhabitants. But beyond resolute granite walls that have staved off long winters and wildling raiders lies the beating heart of the region; a capital that's filled with the down-to-earth hospitality for which Northerners are famed across the Seven Kingdoms.

Alongside Winter Town, a small local settlement made up of rustic wooden houses that extends beyond the castle's walls, Winterfell is a popular pit stop for the great and good of Westeros, from kings and queens to peasants and pirates. Its central location at the heart of the territory also makes it an ideal basecamp for those who are intent on exploring the wider northern area. Over recent years, however, the castle has also become a popular destination in its own right, with tourists flocking to the millennia-old fortress in order to soak up the history locked inside its stone walls or to soak away their troubles in the volcanic hot springs on which its foundations were built.

So whether you're passing through or staying for a few days, you'll quickly find yourself charmed by this ancient castle. It is a monument that never feels far away from the heart of the Seven Kingdoms, despite its isolated location.

THE KING WHO KNELT

For thousands of years, it was Winterfell and not King's Landing that ruled the northern kingdom. Presided over by the Starks of Winterfell, the North was the only kingdom to stand firm against the Andal invaders who sailed across the Narrow Sea from Essos millennia ago. The First Men defended their borders at the ancient fortress of Moat Cailin (see page 63), ensuring they maintained their sovereignty while the rest of the kingdom fell to their southern conquerors. The realm continued to be ruled by the King in the North – sometimes called the King of Winter – until Torrhen Stark swore fealty to Aegon I Targaryen during the War of Conquest.

After watching Targaryen and his dragons slowly topple the Southern Kings, Torrhen bravely marched south with an army of 30,000 northern men at his back. However, after seeing the Targaryen horde and its ferocious fire-breathing dragons, Torrhen relinquished his crown in order to save his people, submitting to Aegon at the spot where the Inn of the Kneeling Man (see page 79) now sits. Dubbed the King who Knelt, Torrhen was the last of the northern kings until Robb Stark's short-lived secession during the recent and bloody War of the Five Kings.

Getting There

By land: Winterfell is best approached by land, travelling via carriage or horseback along the bustling Kingsroad. The castle is around a month's ride from King's Landing, give or take time taken for hunting detours or fixing the occasional broken axle.

By sea: Those who don't fancy the idea of a month mounted in the saddle, or who are looking to avoid the prying eyes of the Kingsroad, can travel via sea. A ship following the Ice Dragon north from King's Landing can reach the city of White Harbor in roughly two weeks if the weather is fair. Trading vessels or Braavosi merchant ships are readily available along the Blackwater and will ferry you north for a handful of gold and a smattering of silver for their weary oarsmen. From White Harbor it's then just a short ride along the shores of the White Knife to Winterfell itself.

Dangers and Annoyances

Wildling raiders – As the capital of the North, Winterfell is by and large a safe destination for travellers, with the nearby garrison ensuring that the King's Peace is preserved. That doesn't mean that it's not without its dangers, however. The castle's proximity to the Wall means that Wildling gangs have been known to raid the nearby Wolfswood. Though few in number, the ever-depleting ranks of the Night's Watch mean that Wildlings have become an increasing concern, with one particular party even attempting to separate one of the young Stark lordlings from his possessions during a recent incident.

The Iron Islands – Relations with the nearby Iron Islands have also been strained since King Robert Baratheon's defeat of the Greyjoy rebellion. Although a recent insurrection at the hands of Theon Greyjoy – the onetime ward of Eddard Stark – was defeated, tourists should check for information before travelling to the area.

The weather – They're not called the Kings of Winter

for nothing. It's bleak up north, a desolate snow-strewn landscape that can chill you to the bone even in the height of the sunny season.

Where to Stay

Despite the influx of tourism over recent years, there's still a relative dearth of decent accommodation for travellers headed to Winterfell, so booking ahead is a smart move unless you want to sleep in the stables for the duration of your stay.

While there isn't much choice, Winterfell does at least cater for a variety of budgets, with rooms ranging from fully outfitted dwellings within the castle itself to modestly attired quarters at nearby inns. At the time of writing, regeneration work on the now-abandoned First Keep has yet to be completed. Plans to renovate the Burnt Tower, which has remained vacant since being set ablaze by lightning some 140 years ago, has been halted after safety concerns were raised by a tragic accident that left a young lordling crippled.

The best time to visit is during the summer when the weather conditions are more amenable to southern tourists, who take the place of locals, who themselves leave to tend nearby farms and homesteads. Harvest festivals are also a popular time to visit, although accommodation can fill up fast as local bannermen and their entourages come to town. Those looking for a bargain – and a very real risk of frostbite – can make huge savings during the winter months. But be warned: the winter weather conditions are not for the faint of heart.

Although royal visits to these parts of the kingdom are rare (who can blame them?), it's always best to check before you travel, as a visit from the King and his court will ensure that even the best-laid plans descend into chaos. While the opportunity to see the Iron Throne's latest incumbent might sound tempting, an official visit from King's Landing will typically test Winterfell to the limits, with quarters filled and stores bled dry to accommodate the imperial visitors. Our advice is to send a raven before making the journey north.

WHAT'S IN A NAME?

You'll find plenty of snow during your trip north and not all of it will be lying on the ground or falling from the skies. That's because Snow is the name given to bastards of the High Lords in this part of Westeros.

It is not uncommon for noblemen to share the beds of women other than their wives and so the Seven Kingdoms are strewn with illegitimate heirs who were born on the wrong side of the sheets. Though their highborn fathers are expected to support their upbringing or take them under their own charge, these unfortunate offspring are often saddled with a social stigma from the day of their birth.

Locals believe that bastards born of lust and lies grow up quicker than their trueborn kin and their nature is wanton and treacherous. As a result, bastards often exist on the fringes of society, taking up apprenticeships with local

---

tradesmen or entering the Order of the Maesters or the Night's Watch. Bastards are also given a separate surname to hold them apart from their father's Houses. This name is decreed by custom in each of the nine constituent regions of the Seven Kingdoms and often reflects the land into which the bastard is born. In the North it is Snow; in the Reach it is Flowers. Pykes are bastards from the Iron Islands, Rivers from the Riverland, Sand from Dorne, Stone from the Vale, Storm from the Stormlands and, finally, Waters from the Crownlands.

Winterfell (£££)

If you're more accustomed to swankier surroundings, why not stay in style by stopping within Winterfell itself? The large bedchambers, many of which boast panoramic views over the nearby Godswood and the castle grounds, are expertly appointed with antique furnishings and the softest feather beds the North has to offer. The last word in luxury, the walls of each bedchamber have hot water from the nearby thermal springs piped through them, which means you'll stay toasty even in the depths of winter. The system is so efficient that many visitors will find that they don't even need to light a fire to stave off the plummeting temperatures. On-site dining options include the highly recommended Great Hall: a cavernous eatery, where visitors can hang out by the great fire with a cup of wine and a sample of some of the North's signature dishes.

Godswood Guest Houses (£££)

If you're looking to get away from the hustle and bustle of castle life, Winterfell's Guest Houses, which are located on the fringes of the castle's Godswood, are well worth checking out. Situated within easy walking distance of the castle's ancient Weirwood and just a stone's throw from three of Winterfell's thermal pools, the Guest Houses are popular with punters wishing to beat their fellow travellers to an early-morning or late-night dip.

The Smoking Log (££)

Expect a lively atmosphere at this local alehouse; a good value, home-away-from-home located just a short ride from the castle keep in Winter Town. Tuck yourself into one of the modestly appointed rooms, all of which come with featherbeds, a warm fire and hearty welcome from the local serving wenches. Ask for a back room to avoid the worst of the noise, or head down to the alehouse to join the beery throng for yourself. Prices include a simple breakfast but it's well worth spending a little extra silver to sample the local beers and pies that the establishment is renowned for.

Winter Town Residences (£)

Winter Town is packed with commonfolk during winter but in the summer years it remains mostly deserted, as Northerners abandon Winterfell to tend to farms and homesteads scattered across the surrounding area. Only around one in five homes are occupied during the warmer weather, which means that a burgeoning industry in holiday rentals has cropped up, with locals letting out their homes for a modest price. Made from log and stone, the village is filled with row upon row of these rustically appointed houses that make ideal dwellings for budget-conscious travellers.

Eating and Drinking

While southern palates tend to favour more delicately flavoured feasts, travellers will find that northern tables are stocked with food that is as rustic as the kingdom's inhabitants. For generations locals have been living off the land surrounding Winterfell, with vegetables garnered from local homesteads and meats hunted from the nearby Wolfswood supplemented by a steady stream of produce from the castle's glass gardens.

The castle's location at the centre of the northern kingdom also makes it a busy hub for traders and merchants from across the North. Whether it's mutton from Deepwood Motte or fresh crabs from the Bay of Seals, Winterfell is a mecca crammed full of mouthwatering treats, local delicacies and some of the best craft beers in the Seven Kingdoms.

The castle and nearby Winter Town offer a smorgasbord of authentic northern fare, from the ubiquitous artisan pies that adorn alehouse menus to suckling pigs roasted to sizzling perfection on an open fire. For many visitors, one of the biggest holiday dilemmas is deciding where to indulge their tingling taste buds. Our advice? Ditch the diet and eat as much as you can – if nothing else, the extra calories might help you to stave off the bone-rattling cold for an hour or two.

Blackberry preserve

No trip to Winterfell would be complete without sampling

the castle's famed local delicacy, blackberry preserve. Grown year round in the castle's glasshouses (see page 30), the fruits are artificially ripened by the warmth of the volcanic springs beneath the castle foundations to bring a taste of spring to the land of winter.

Breakfast

The country around Winterfell can be a cold and energy-sapping land, so it's no surprise that breakfast is one of the most important meals for its northern residents. Locals typically break their fast with bread, cheeses, soft-boiled eggs and rashers of bacon served with locally sourced honey and blackberry preserves. A particular favourite in these parts are small fish from the nearby White Knife, which are lightly fried and washed down with a flagon of beer or a cup of mint tea. Delicious!

Alcohol

Winterfell residents enjoy their booze as much as the rest of the Seven Kingdoms, so don't be surprised to see a flagon of ale or a cup of wine served alongside your meal, even at breakfast. Visitors are welcome wherever the locals sup: the Smoking Log being one of the castle's most popular watering holes.

The local dark beer is particularly good. Brewed and stored in a cask house within the castle walls, it is renowned as one of Westeros's best brews and is even said to be a personal favourite of famous philanderer Tyrion Lannister. The castle cellars also stock a fine selection of wines, while mead and mulled drinks are popular with commonfolk seeking an escape from the biting winds that whistle down from atop the Wall.

Pie

Winterfell is famous for its pies. These pastry-encased treats are best enjoyed in the Great Hall or served up with a mug of ale at the Smoking Log. Fillings range from pigeon to beef and bacon, and the pies are traditionally served up alongside a plate of butter-soaked turnips to give them an extra calorific kick.

BRANDON THE BUILDER

The founder of the House of Stark and the first King in the North, Brandon the Builder is a legendary figure whose roots can be traced back to the Age of Heroes. While some men are renowned for their strength or swordplay, Brandon's brilliance came from his mind. Local lore states that it was he who laid the foundations of Winterfell some 8,000 years ago, using giants to help him raise the massive granite walls that still stand today.

Brandon's exploits didn't stop at the North's most impressive castle, however. It is also said that it is he who designed the Wall, setting its foundations into massive mountain ranges so that it might stand for millennia. It is also believed that when he was just a boy, the builder helped King Durran construct the formidable fortress at Storm's End — a fortification that has for centuries withstood the devastating weather of Shipbreaker Bay.

The Castle

The centrepiece of Winterfell is, of course, the castle itself: a granite stronghold that has stood since the time of the

First Men. Originally built 8,000 years ago, the structure has changed significantly over the centuries, with each incumbent expanding the sprawling complex. A maze of abandoned wings, long-forgotten rooms and hidden tunnels, it's said that even the castle's long-term residents haven't uncovered all of its secrets – a fact that only adds to the stout fortress's charm.

Whether you've stayed within its walls before or you're visiting for the first time, there's something about this northern outpost that pleases travellers. It's not as grotesquely huge as Harrenhal or as impregnable as Storm's End but Winterfell is, nevertheless, a formidable fortress and one that houses some of the richest (and, indeed, oldest) history in the Seven Kingdoms.

The entire castle is a hodgepodge of contradictions; a mixture of derelict towers and gleaming glasshouses, of summer snow flurries and warm waters sucked from the hot springs on which Winterfell is built. Even the architecture of the castle seems confused as the old hallways and occasional bridge visibly slant with the peaks and valleys that it was built upon.

Despite its size, however, Winterfell is still best explored on foot, where travellers are able to appreciate its subtle architectural changes and the rich history contained within every stone. Many of its attractions can be enjoyed in a single day (see below) but, to truly appreciate Winterfell's charm, it's worth spending the extra gold dragons to stay within its walls so that you can enjoy the surroundings (and the legendary northern hospitality) at a more relaxed pace.

A WALKING TOUR OF WINTERFELL

This invigorating walk will guide you through Winterfell's entire expanse, passing the famed fortification's oldest wings, taking in its assortment of architectural quirks.

Start: The North Gate
End: The First Keep
Distance: I league
Time: I day
Exertion: Easy
Points of interest: Glass Gardens, Godswood, Library Tower
Rest stop: Great Hall

I. The North Gate

Start your stroll at the North Gate: an imposing entrance that straddles the castle's defensive moat. Here, the moody granite walls stand 100ft high and 80ft deep. It is an imposing obstacle that has managed to withstand countless would-be invaders over the centuries.

2. The Glass Gardens

Head westwards from the North Gate and you will find yourself at Winterfell's famed Glass Gardens. Warmed by the hot springs on which the castle is built, these yellow-and-green glazed constructions are used to grow crops that would otherwise perish in the cold northern climate. Step inside to experience the humid atmosphere for yourself and perhaps enjoy a ripe blackberry fresh from the bush while you're at it.

3. The Godswood

Grab your furs and head south outside of the Glass

Gardens and through the iron-barred gate into Winterfell's Godswood: a pristine three-acre enclosure that's as old as the kingdom itself. This secluded spot is a nature lover's delight, littered with sentinels, ironwoods and soldier pines and filled with the sharp trilling of Snow Shrikes. It's also an opportunity to get in touch with your spiritual side and visit the Heart Tree that northerners have worshipped at since the time of the First Men.

4. Hunter's Gate

Beyond the Godswood you'll find the Hunter's Gate: the castle's western exit and a popular haunt with hunting parties. Here, you can explore the sights and smells of Winterfell's kitchen (the round building directly to the left of the gate), or visit the kennels, which are filled with all manner of hounds and even the odd Direwolf. Look up and you might also spy the occasional raven ferrying messages to the nearby Maester's Turret.

5. The Bell Tower

Just beyond the Hunter's Gate you'll stumble across the Bell Tower, which is host to one of Winterfell's strangest architectural phenomena. Look closely and you'll see that the bridge from the fourth floor of the Bell Tower connects with the second floor of the Rookery – an architectural quirk dating back to the castle's construction and Bran the Builder's decision not to level the land before laying Winterfell's foundations.

6. Library Tower

A short walk across the courtyard will bring you to

Winterfell's Library Tower, which was, unfortunately, damaged in a recent fire – a blaze which some say was started deliberately as part of a plot to take a young lordling's life. Though the climb up the Tower's steep and winding steps is not to be taken lightly, your perseverance – and perspiration – will be rewarded with one of the best-stocked archives in the Seven Kingdoms: a treasure trove that houses ancient Valyrian scrolls, rare tomes such as *A Life of the Lord Maester Aethelmure* and one of the last complete copies of Ayrmidon's *Engines of War* in existence.

7. The Great Hall

Keep the stables and the South Gate to your right as you make your way across the castle yard towards the giant iron-and-oak doors of the Great Hall. This cavernous room has played host to countless great feasts and can hold 500 lords, ladies and commonfolk at full capacity. Grab a trencher of bread and a skewer of roasted boar if your strength is flagging, or pay a visit to the raised platform at the end of the hall, where only the Starks and their most honoured guests are permitted to dine.

8. The Small Sept

When you've had your fill of the Great Hall, head back outside and make the short walk across the open yard towards the Small Sept. While northerners traditionally stick to the Old Gods, the late Lord Eddard Stark had this sacred structure constructed so that his wife might continue to practice her Faith of the Seven. Although it pales in comparison to the grandiose Septs you'll see in southern cities, this modestly appointed temple is a welcome break from the stark (no pun intended) surroundings you'll typically find in Winterfell. Carved masks hang on the seven walls to represent each of the seven.

9. The Great Keep

From the Small Sept you're just a stone's throw from the Great Keep: the inner sanctum that houses the ruling family as well as castle visitors. From here you can pay a visit to Winterfell's throne. Take a moment to admire the Direwolves carved into the throne's polished stone arms and to contemplate the long line of legendary northern kings who have ruled from this seat.

10. The Broken Tower and First Keep

Pass the Guard's Hall on your left – if you're lucky, a Stark pikeman might entertain you with a tale or two about his time in battle – and step back in history as you head towards the First Keep. This squat fortress is the oldest part of the castle and, although no longer in use, its rain-worn gargoyles still provide a fitting backdrop for the lichyard where the Kings of Winter lay their loyal servants to rest. Beyond the First Keep you'll see the Broken Tower. This ancient turret used to be Winterfell's primary watchtower until a lightning strike set it ablaze and caused the top third to collapse. Climbing the tower used to be a rite of passage for travellers, who would scale the outer walls in order to enjoy an unparalleled view of the castle below. However, a recent accident has put paid to that once popular pursuit.

Areas of Interest/What to Do When You're There

Whether you want to follow in the footsteps of the First Men or put your feet up and enjoy a deep and meaningful relationship with a mineral-rich hotspring, Winterfell has you covered. From history-soaked walking tours to shopping, via swordplay displays, spoken-word recitals and quiet contemplation, there's a cornucopia of attractions to entertain visitors.

Winterfell Hot Springs

Winterfell has long been a draw for history buffs and adventurous backpackers intent on exploring the northern realm but the granite labyrinth has recently experienced something of a renaissance as a new breed of traveller has ventured beyond the Neck to enjoy the health benefits offered by this millennia-old outpost.

Built on a series of natural thermal springs, the warm waters that were once the difference between life and death during the long winters of years past have become an attraction in their own right during the decade-long summer the continent is currently basking in. On any day you'll find a cross section of Westerosis, from highborn lords to hard-working stable boys, soaking away the stresses and strains of life in the Seven Kingdoms in the pools that spring up around the castle.

As one of only a handful of hot springs within Westeros, Winterfell's warm waters can attract quite a crowd, especially in peak season when swimming costumes are optional, despite the summer snowfall. If you're looking for some privacy, however, there are a dozen smoking pools built into secluded courtyards within the castle itself. But by far the most popular springs are those on the fringes of Winterfell's Godswood, where travellers can enjoy the regenerative waters surrounded by three acres of untouched woodland and a wall thick with lush green moss.

Godswood

Three acres of woodland that has stood for more than 10,000 years, the Godswood at Winterfell is like no other forest in Westeros. A dark, primal place, the woods lie at the heart of the castle, which was raised around the trees, many of which are as old as the realm itself.

Best enjoyed on foot, the Godswood is filled with sentinels, oaks, ironwoods, Hawthorns, ash and soldier pines, which fill the chilly air with the scent of sticky sweet sap. Look to your feet and you'll find a carpet of discarded needles and a network of tangled roots, while a glance skywards reveals a dense forest canopy that houses an ever-growing community of Snow Shrikes.

The Godswood isn't just a haven for nature lovers, however. Located at the centre of the forest on the banks of an icy dark pool lies Winterfell's Heart Tree: a picturesque setting frozen in time, which has remained practically untouched since the time of the First Men. With its distinctive bone-white bark and striking blood-red leaves, the ancient tree is one of only a handful of Weirwoods still standing in Westeros, and people make the pilgrimage across the Seven Kingdoms to worship in front of the melancholy face, which is said to have been carved out of the trunk by the Children of the Forest themselves.

A SACRED TREE

Weirwoods were once a common site across the Seven Kingdoms. Considered sacred by those who follow the Old Gods, the trees were first worshipped by the Children of the Forest, who carved faces into their bark, such as the one you'll find on Winterfell's heart tree. It is said that through these faces the Old Gods watch over men, and legend has it that the Seers once used the eyes to look back into the past.

When the First Men crossed the Narrow Sea more than 12,000 years ago, they too took up the faith of the Old Gods and began to adopt the practices passed down by the Children of the Forest. The first settlers planted Godswoods in their castles and villages, where a single Weirwood, known as the Heart Tree, was used for worship and to bear witness to important events such as marriages.

When the Andals invaded, however, they brought with them the Faith of the Seven and systematically destroyed the Weirwoods, which they believed represented the blasphemous Old Gods. But while Weirwoods are rare south of the Neck, the Andals never conquered the North, which is why Heart Trees such as Winterfells still stand to this day. Weirwoods also grow wild in the northern realm, especially beyond the wall, where Rangers of the Night's Watch have discovered whole groves of the sacred trees.

The Crypts

No matter where you look in Winterfell, you're reminded of the ancient history in which the House of Stark is steeped. It is a place alive with legend; a city in which you're surrounded by granite walls laid by Bran the Builder and Godswoods, where the First Men once worshipped. But to truly experience the history of this incredible fortress, you have to head below the surface to Winterfell's famed crypts: a subterranean mausoleum filled with Kings of Winter and Wardens of the North.

Accessed through a heavy ironwood door by the First Keep, a twisting stone staircase carries you below the frozen earth – bring your furs for it can get chilly down there – and into a long, narrow crypt. With its vauted ceilings and granite pillars, the tombs are an architectural marvel in their own right. But it's the long-deceased residents that are the real draw down here, as tourists flock from across the Seven Kingdoms to see the resting place of the legends of countless songs and stories.

In among the tombs of legendary lords, such as Brandon the Shipwright, Edrick the Snowbeard and Benjen the Bitter, you'll find more recent additions, like Lyanna Stark and former Hand Eddard Stark, alongside empty and unsealed tombs that are reserved for future members of the House of Stark.

While each tomb is different, ancient custom dictates that every sepulchre is adorned with a snarling Direwolf and an iron sword. The Direwolves are, of course, a tribute to the House of Stark's sigil, while the iron swords are set before the fallen Lords of Winterfell so that they might ward off vengeful spirits in the afterlife. Though many of these swords have rusted away over the centuries, the granite-etched likenesses of the long-dead lords are well preserved and are said by locals to offer an uncanny resemblance to their ancient inhabitants.

The crypts themselves are said to be larger than Winterfell itself. Split over many levels – some of which have partially collapsed over time – only the first floor is open to the public. The lower levels are closed off to travellers in order to preserve the family's privacy. Note that the crypts can get incredibly busy during peak season, so leave yourself extra time to explore the catacombs, otherwise you might miss something.

STATUE SPOTTING

Although you can easily while away hours exploring the entirety of Winterfell's crypts, there are a few iconic sepulchres that travellers simply mustn't miss. These include:

Jon Stark, who drove off early sea raiders and built a castle at White Harbor.

Theon Stark, also known as the 'Hungry Wolf' due to his appetite for armed conflict.

Brandon the Shipwright, so-called due to his love of the sea – his tomb remains empty after he tried to sail west across the Sunset Sea and was never heard of again.

Brandon the Burner, son of Brandon the Shipwright, who set fire to all of his father's ships out of grief.

Artos the Implacable, one of the few men buried in

the crypts not to be a lord of Winterfell – instead he is honoured for the part he played in the war against the Wildlings, north of the Wall in 184AC.

Torrhen Stark, whose tomb is one of Winterfell's most popular attractions, so you'll have to push past the crowds to see the 'King Who Knelt' (see page 20).

Lyanna Stark, whose kidnap by Rhaegar Targaryen sparked the rebellion that put Robert Baratheon on Mad King Aerys's throne.

Eddard Stark, the one-time Hand of the King and most recent Lord of Winterfell, who was executed in King's Landing under charges of treason – charges still hotly contested in this corner of the realm.

Spoken Word

From travelling Mummers troupes to silver-tongued singers, Winterfell's history has spurred the creative juices of many an artist. But by far the biggest draw on the local scene is an evening spent in the company of Old Nan, a longstanding Stark servant whose spoken word recitals are famed in these quarters. A toothless old woman who cannot even climb the stairs without assistance, Old Nan isn't much to look at but locked within her balding head is a cornucopia of tall tales that have entertained Winterfell's inhabitants for a generation. From stories about the derring-do of the Night's Watch to fearsome beasts that lie beyond the Wall, an hour spent in the company of this former wet nurse is an education in the history and folklore of the realm.

A FEAST FOR FOODIES

As the North's regional capital, Winterfell has played host to scores of harvest festivals over the centuries. A tradition almost as old as the castle itself, the festival celebrates the onset of autumn and dates back to when the Maesters of the Citadel would declare the end of summer, signalling houses to begin storing grain in preparation for winter.

In the recent decade-long summer, however, these festivals have become a fine excuse for a feast, with bannermen from across the North gathering to share stories and the finest produce their lands have to offer. Traditional harvest-festival fare includes boar, goose-in-berries, duck, salmon and lobster, with each dish offered first to the Lord in thanks for his hospitality. Songs are also an important part of the festivities, with spontaneous performances of old favourites like 'Iron Lances', 'The Burning of the Ships' and 'The Bear and the Maiden Fair' springing up among the din of the Great Hall.

It's not all feasts and frolics, however. Harvest festivals are often a pleasant pretext for the all important business of ruling the realm.

Weapons Practice

Lords and lordlings can regularly be found training at arms in the castle courtyards in preparation for future battles that may lie before them. Displays are often performed using wooden swords or blunted blades in order to protect the participants and while the weapons are dull, the action most certainly isn't, with tempers regularly boiling over among the boys at arms. The spectacle is open to the public but the action is best observed from the covered bridge that connects the Great Keep to the Armoury, where windows overlooking the courtyard offer a great vantage point to the action below.

Hunting

Hunting is a popular pursuit across the Seven Kingdoms and here it is no exception. Parties regularly range into the wilderness beyond Winterfell's walls in search of game that includes wild boar, deer and elk. Most meet at the aptly named Hunter's Gate, which is situated close to Winterfell's kennels and kitchens. From there, riders have easy access to the nearby Wolfswood and can come and go without having to cross through Winter Town.

Shopping

Although it pales in comparison to commercial capitals like King's Landing or over on Essos, shopaholics can still find an opportunity to spend some gold dragons during a visit to Winterfell. The marketplace in Winter Town is your best bet. Filled with little wooden stalls, it's where visitors can find local food, furs and northern steel forged by the castle's renowned armourer, Mikken. The market is ideal for souvenir hunters – especially those in search of replica Night's Watch garb or stocks of blackberry preserve – but it can also serve up the occasional steal, including Dragonglass from beyond the Wall.

HODOR

Hodor, Hodor, Hodor. Hodor. Hodor, Hodor, Hodor, Hodor, Hodor, Hodor. Hodor, Hodor. Hodor. HODOR.

THE GIFT AND THE WALL

Westeros is filled with impressive sights. From the towers of Harrenhal to the sprawling streets of King's Landing, via the High Tower at Oldtown or even the inside of one of Little Fingers' pleasure houses, there are many marvels that have been built by men over the millennia. All of them, however, pale into insignificance in contrast to the Wall. Named one of the Nine Wonders Made by Man by legendary explorer Lomas Longstrider, it's an awe-inspiring spectacle that can warm the hearts of travellers even as the temperatures around them plummet well below freezing.

Placed at the northernmost tip of the kingdom, it's a site worth going to the ends of the world for. Built more than 8,000 years ago, the structure stands 700ft high and runs from the Frostfang mountain range in the West to the Bay of Seals in the East, stretching unbroken across 300 miles of the Seven Kingdoms' northern border.

No matter how many tapestries you've witnessed or songs you've heard sung, its sheer scale needs to be seen to be believed, which is no doubt why so many travellers brace the freezing temperatures to make the dangerous pilgrimage north each year. While there are dozens of fortresses dotted along the Wall, most sightseers head straight for Castle Black: headquarters of the Sworn Brothers of the Night's

Watch – the men at arms who are sworn to protect the realm from what lies beyond the icy battlements.

Getting There

By land: The Wall is a two-week ride north from Winterfell. Travellers are advised to stick to the Kingsroad, where the going is good and a smattering of ramshackle inns line the way to provide a feather bed and a warm fire after a hard day's ride. These rude inns aren't the finest of establishments you'll ever stop in but you'll soon miss their lumpy mattresses and warming hearths once the sporadic villages and holdfasts lining the Kingsroad give way to the open expanse of the North. From then on, your only comfort will be a cold patch of dirt and an uninterrupted view of the stars until you finally reach Castle Black.

By sea: While it is possible to make the journey north by sea, it's not for the faint of heart. Ships to Eastwatch-by-the-Sea depart weekly from White Harbor but travellers shouldn't expect a comfortable journey. There are no pleasure barges to choose from; instead travellers must try their luck with merchants' vessels, sleeping in among the cargo and mucking in to pay their way. While the journey northwards is not without its charms – the uninterrupted views of the Grey Cliffs are a particular highlight – it's also fraught with dangers, especially in the Bay of Seals, where icebergs can sink even the sturdiest of ships. There have also been recent reports of a kraken pulling down an Ibbanese whaler in the region, so travellers are advised to be particularly cautious before setting sail.

A free ride: Most of the people you'll find journeying north are travelling to the Wall by choice but don't be surprised if you stumble upon a group who are being forcibly ferried to Castle Black. Once considered an honour, these days a large proportion of the Night's Watch's sworn brothers is made up of criminals who are rounded up from the dungeons of the Seven Kingdoms and sent north to serve their penitence. Often led by a Black Brother, these rag-tag troupes are easy to spot and can make a cost-effective option for those who lack the gold to make the journey themselves. However, be warned: although journeying with these Brothers-to-be may keep your purse intact, you might find that your stay on the Wall lasts considerably longer than you'd first planned.

Dangers and Annoyances

The cold – If you thought Winterfell was cold, wait till you get to the Wall! The weather here makes the rest of the North feel like a summer's eve in Dorne by comparison. Northerners say that the weather on the Wall is as cold and hard as the men who serve there and, if you've ever met a brother of the Night's Watch, you'll know that means to wrap up warm. Yes, it's cold up here – really cold, in fact. Even the thickest riding furs won't keep out the icy winds that whip off the wall and the staunchest boots can struggle to contend with snowdrifts which could swamp a small castle.

Wildlings – While the Wall was constructed to keep the Wildlings out, this hasn't stopped a steady stream of the Free Folk from risking life and limb to scale the icy battlements in order to seek out a new life in the Seven

Kingdoms. Though few in number, it's best to avoid these Wildling raiders, as even the kindest will put an arrow in your back, should the opportunity arise.

War – Although more and more visitors are making their way north to see this architectural marvel, it's important to remember that the Wall is still an active battlement and, as such, conflict is not uncommon. Ravens we've received from recent visitors suggest that tensions are high on the Wall at the moment, as a Wildling army intent on invasion has gathered at its base. Tourists are still being welcomed by the Brothers of the Night's Watch, who are open to any opportunity to boost their ailing coffers. However, given how thin the garrison has been spread after years of neglect, don't be surprised to have a spear thrust into your hand in the event of an attack.

Beyond the Wall – The Wall itself is a relative safe haven for travellers. However, the same cannot be said about what lies beyond it. The recent boom in tourism has led the Black Brothers to create a variety of tours and trips to enable travellers to explore the wilderness. But while the Night's Watch do their best to protect these parties, it's important to remember why the Wall is there in the first place. North of the Wall, Wildlings are the least of your troubles. Direwolves, Snow Bears the size of Aurochs and even Mammoths are a constant threat, and there have even been reports of attacks by White Walkers in recent moons. You have been warned!

Women travelling alone – Travelling alone can be a dangerous proposition for women in any part of the Seven Kingdoms but it's especially a problem on the Wall. Years of neglect have transformed the once proud order of the Night's Watch into a band of miscreants and, despite pledging to forsake relationships with women, many are known to break their vows. Women are advised against travelling alone.

SPEAKING TO THE BLACK BROTHERS

Unless you find yourself on the wrong side of a dungeon door, there's little reason why you'd ever come into contact with a Brother of the Night's Watch anywhere else in the Seven Kingdoms. It's a different story on the Wall, however, where every keep, castle and icy battlement comes complete with its own resident crow.

These sworn brothers are not there for your amusement, though. Although most are happy to pose for portraits or share stories of life beyond the Wall, they are there to serve the realm and not the burgeoning tourism industry that's blossomed around them.

Every Brother leaves his past behind him when he takes the Black but it's worth remembering who these men were before they came to the Wall. Many were plucked from the kingdom's darkest dungeons, criminals who'd just as happily turn on their own commanders, let alone a vulnerable tourist. Others might be bannermen sworn to your fiercest enemy. As such, there's an unwritten rule on the Wall that visitors won't share stories from the Seven Kingdoms lest they stir the old loyalties and lifestyles of the Brothers in Black.

The Wall

The foundations of the Wall were reputedly laid by Brandon the Builder after the Long Night to defend the realm from Wildlings and the Others. Built more than 8,000 years ago, the Wall stands 700ft high and stretches for some 300mi. Made of solid ice, its foundations were dug into the surrounding mountains and the huge structure was said to have been raised with the help of giants and long-forgotten sorcery – some say there are even spells woven into the ice to prevent magical beings from passing through it.

While today it's possible to see the Wall from miles off, the original structure was actually much smaller. Over the centuries the Night's Watch have built up the fortifications, quarrying huge blocks of ice from frozen lakes in order to raise the Wall higher. It's said that the Night's Watch would spend their summers building their defences, with each Lord Commander ensuring they left the Wall higher than they'd found it. However, the long summer has led to years of neglect and the greatly reduced garrison struggle to maintain the monstrous fortification, let alone raise it further.

You may have heard stories of the Wall but its sheer scale can only be appreciated when standing at its base. The icy expanse would dwarf even the great towers of Harrenhal and the blue line stretches along the horizon as far as the eye can see. Its size, however, is matched by its magnificence. For a structure designed to defend the realm, there's a strange beauty to the Wall. Best experienced on a clear day – though you don't get many of those in this part of the realm – it glistens in the sunlight with a kaleidoscope of blue crystalline colours.

While you won't want for ice and snow, you'll be pleased to hear that there are signs of civilisation even at the end of the world. In fact, there are 19 strongholds dotted along the 300-mile expanse of the Wall. However, due to the greatly diminished numbers of the Night's Watch, only three are regularly occupied. These are The Shadow Tower in the West, Eastwatch-by-the-Sea in the East and Castle Black at the centre. Castle Black is the Wall's tourism hub. Located at the end of the Kingsroad, it is easily accessible to travellers and offers the best assortment of dwellings and activities for intrepid explorers.

NIGHT FORT

Twice as old as Castle Black, the Night Fort was the first castle built upon the Wall but was abandoned by the order after it was deemed too costly to maintain. The castle lives long in the memory, however, as the setting for scare stories which northern nurses like to tell their charges.

It was here, for example, that the Rat King supposedly served an Andal king his son in a pie, where the sad song of Darry Flynt is set and where the brother called Mad Axe lost his mind and stalked the halls of the Night Fort, killing his fellow crows.

By far the most famous of these bedtime tales, however, is the 'Seventy-nine Sentinels'. According to the story, seventy-nine deserters abandoned their posts at the Night Fort. After they were captured and returned to the

> Wall, the Lord Commander punished the men by sealing them inside the Wall itself. There they stood with spears and horns, so that in death they may continue the watch they abandoned in life.

The Night's Watch

The Wall is protected by the Brothers of the Night's Watch, an ancient order who can trace their lineage back to the Age of Heroes. Originally formed to fight the Others over the centuries, the Night's Watch have fought many enemies but they never interfere with the affairs of the realm. Instead they have political immunity, serving only to protect the Seven Kingdoms from threats from the lands beyond the Wall.

The Brothers dress all in black, with black mail, furs and breeches the most common adornment. Their garb has earned them the nickname 'crow', particularly among the Wildlings, who call them 'black crows' – a derogatory term the brothers have adopted as their own. The black clothing, like their solid black banners, emphasises the brothers' sworn duty to put aside the petty squabbles of noble houses and erase any allegiance of their past in order to serve the kingdom in its entirety.

At the height of its power, the Night's Watch could call upon some 10,000 men-at-arms, half of which could be garrisoned at Castle Black. However, years of neglect by kings who have all but forgotten about the watch has seen that number fall dramatically, with recent figures suggesting the Night's Watch now only number a few hundred able men.

In days gone by it was an honour for the highborn – particularly those from the northern houses – to serve on the watch. Many younger sons who were low in the line of succession would be sent to take the Black and the shields of their houses were proudly displayed at Castle Black. Serving on the Night's Watch was once seen as an honour, with knights and noblemen heading to the Wall as a sign of their selfless devotion.

Today, however, the Watch is unrecognisable from its noble past. Service is seen as a punishment in the Seven Kingdoms, with the dregs of Westeros salvaged from dungeons across the kingdom to stand upon the icy battlements. While disgraced noblemen and bastard sons of highborn lords are not uncommon, the majority of the men you'll find at the Wall are peasants, thieves, murderers and rapists who chose to take the Black in place of corporal punishment for their crimes. As a result, the mood on the Wall is regularly dissatisfied and, more often than not, downright dangerous.

Those who've arrived at the Wall voluntarily are free to leave at any time during their training. However, once a Brother has said his vows – or, as the Brothers call it, taken the Black – desertion is punished with death. After taking their vows, the men of the Watch cannot own any land, marry, or father children. They are also encouraged to sever ties with the Seven Kingdoms and any family they may have there.

The Brothers of the Night's Watch are governed by the

Lord Commander: a leader who is democratically voted by the Brothers themselves – a process that can last for days or sometimes years. The rest of the order is divided into Rangers, Builders and Stewards. Rangers form the main fighting force of the Night's Watch. They are skilled warriors who are trained to survive the harsh conditions in the land beyond the battlements. Builders are tasked with maintaining the Wall itself, alongside the fortresses and defences that stretch along the hundred leagues of ice and rock. Finally, there are the Stewards – the largest of the three orders – who are responsible for providing day-to-day services such as cooking, cleaning or stewarding for the order's officers.

THE BLACK

When the recruits are considered ready to take the Black, they say their vows either in a Sept or before a Heart Tree if they stick to the Old Gods. The vows are as follows:

'Night gathers and now my watch begins. It shall not end until my death. I shall take no wife, hold no lands, father no children. I shall wear no crowns and win no glory. I shall live and die at my post. I am the sword in the darkness. I am the watcher on the walls. I am the fire that burns against the cold, the light that brings the dawn, the horn that wakes the sleepers, the shield that guards the realms of men. I pledge my life and honour to the Night's Watch, for this night and all the nights to come.'

Where to Stay

There are no inns at The Wall. Instead, accommodation options are altogether more rustic for travellers intent on spending a night or two at Castle Black. Given the ever-dwindling numbers of the Night's Watch, you'll find no shortage of vacant rooms to rest your weary legs in.

Travellers will find that their money goes a long way at the Wall, where the coffers of the Night's Watch have been bled dry by years of neglect. However, this far north, creature comforts are in scant supply so expect to rough it no matter how heavy your purse is. The Crows will tell you that rough-and-ready surroundings are part of the appeal of a visit to Castle Black, where lumpy straw beds and freezing-cold sleeping cells are part of an 'authentic' Wall experience. And while their tongues are lodged firmly in cheeks, there's some truth to the statement and those who want a glimpse into what life on the Wall is like will enjoy the opportunity to bed down with the Brothers of the Night's Watch.

The King's Tower (£££)

Given the disregard with which recent kings have treated The Wall, it perhaps comes as no surprise that royal excursions to this part of the realm are few and far between. In fact, a king hasn't visited the Wall in more than a hundred years. As such, the King's Tower, which was built to house honoured guests at Castle Black, had remained largely vacant until some enterprising brothers decided to open its doors to tourists.

Although the accommodations they've crafted from the King's quarters are hardly palaces, they do offer considerably more comfort than the other options available at the Wall. Located in the 100-ft tower that overlooks the wooden staircase leading up to the Wall's summit, the rooms are spacious and come complete with featherbeds, roaring hearths and a personal steward to attend to your every need. The warmth alone is enough to endear them to travellers who are happy to part with a few extra coins for the promise of a cosy night's sleep.

Mole's Town (££)

Located half a league south of the Wall along the Kingsroad lies Mole's Town, a ramshackle village where a thriving economy has sprung up to support the Wall and its burgeoning tourism industry. It's an ideal option for anyone looking to escape the clatter of swords and the chatter of the crows who man the battlements.

The most popular pit stop for travellers is the local brothel, a subterranean den where outsiders might find a crumb of comfort and a willing companion for the night. Built underground to escape the freezing temperatures, the entrance is located under a wooden shack with a red lantern slung outside to entice passing travellers. Beneath the surface lies a warm, damp cellar, where a common room full of ale and amorous companions greets guests. The atmosphere here is often raucous and almost always bawdy, especially when a Crow has come to spend some copper – or 'dig for buried treasure', as it's known on the Wall. The girls here are hardly Braavosi courtesans but if you're looking for a warm bed and a warm body to share it with, you won't leave disappointed.

Sleeping Cells (£)

At its height Castle Black used to house 5,000 Brothers of the Night's Watch. Today, however, the flock has been reduced to just 600 Crows, which means there's no shortage of sleeping cells available to the influx of tourists. Though modestly appointed – they were built to house men-at-arms, not holidaymakers – the cells are cheap and offer visitors the opportunity to spend a night in a Crow's boots.

Dank, cold and more uncomfortable than a wedding feast with the Freys, for many a single night is all that most travellers can stomach before they pack their bags and head for the relative comfort of the King's Tower. While the castle is vast, it's best to ask for a room near the garrison, where the added security of a sword-wielding Crow is essential in the event of a Wildling attack.

Eating and Drinking

Although their number has swelled in recent years, the facilities on offer for tourists heading to the Wall are still relatively threadbare. That's especially true when it comes to eating and drinking. There are no inns on The Wall. Instead, visitors are invited to sup at the Common Hall, sharing trestle tables with the Brothers of the Night's Watch. The company can often be unsavoury but the same cannot be said of the food. In fact, the black-clad Stewards do a fine job of serving visitors.

Hearty fare is always on offer, mutton stew thickened with barley, carrots and turnips being a particular favourite among the fighting men. On special occasions the rustic dishes give way to an altogether more elaborate spread. Try the set menu, where a hearty salad and a dessert of iced blueberries in sweet cream sit either side of a herb-encrusted rack of lamb, which visitors will tell you is almost worth taking the Black for. To wash it down, try Hot Wine, a Wall speciality made with cinnamon, nutmeg, honey, raisins, nuts and dried berries, which is made according to the Lord Commander's own recipe.

FORTY-EIGHT HOURS IN CASTLE BLACK

It's cold at the Wall and the nights are dark and full of terrors — or so they say — all of which means that you won't have to spend any longer at the end of the world than you absolutely have to. In fact, with a little planning, forty-eight hours is all you need for an authentic Wall experience. This itinerary offers a practical and enjoyable tour of the Wall, taking in some of the best attractions on offer. For more information, see the main entries:

DAY ONE

Morning: Spend your morning exploring Castle Black, home to the Brothers of the Night's Watch and the central hub of the Wall. Begin by exploring the castle's towers (The Silent Tower, King's Tower, Hardin's Tower, Lance and Lord Commander's Tower) before visiting the vaults (containing scores of ancient scrolls) and finally, the smith's, where you can see the castle's master-at-arms ply his trade. Donal Noye might not look like much but the one-armed armourer used to serve the Baratheons of Storm's End and reportedly forged the late King Robert's legendary warhammer before an accident crippled him. Before you stop for lunch, be sure to book your place on the **Top of the Wall Tour** because spaces fill up fast.

Afternoon: After sharing lunch (and a few stories) with the Black Brothers in the mess hall, wrap up warm and make your way to the Wall for your afternoon tour. On a good day they say you can see the whole of the Seven Kingdoms from the top or, at the very least, the gnarled Weirwoods of the Haunted Forest and the ever-growing Wildling horde beyond.

Evening: After a hard day of exploring, treat yourself to a trip to Mole's Town, where you can enjoy a horn of ale (and a lot more if you'd like) with the local wenches. Try to get some sleep, however, because tomorrow's going to be a busy day.

DAY TWO

Morning/Afternoon: Break your fast on some porridge and black bread at the mess hall before heading to the Flint Barracks to meet your guide for the day's excursion beyond the Wall. A day trip to the Haunted Forest to see the centuries-old Weirwood groves offers your nearest (not to mention safest) excursion or, if you're looking for an endorphin rush, grab a stone hammer and some wooden pegs for a day of climbing. Whatever you choose, make sure you're back at the castle before nightfall to enjoy the final weapon's practice of the evening. You might need it if the Others decide to come in the night.

Evening: There's just time to change into a fresh set of breeches and a new doublet before heading to the Common Hall, where you'll spend one final night with your newfound friends on the Wall. Be sure to enjoy some mead, as you'll need a full bladder (not to mention the warmth in your belly) as you head up to the Wall one final time, so that you can tell people that you, too, have 'pissed off the end of the world'.

Areas of Interest/What to Do When You're There

While the Wall itself is the biggest draw, a ramshackle industry of guided tours and excursions into Wildling territory have popped up to cater for travellers. From ice-climbing and giant-spotting safaris for adrenaline junkies to walking tours for those who want to stay safely behind the battlements, you'll find plenty of activities to help make your stay at Castle Black memorable.

Giant-Spotting Safari

Although the grumpkins and snarks you'll have heard about in children's tales are nowhere to be found, the wilds beyond the Wall still play host to some of the strangest creatures in the Seven Kingdoms. The Night's Watch run organised tours departing daily from Castle Black. Travelling with a garrison of Crows, the Ranger who leads your expedition will help you to explore your surroundings, offering an historical and ecological background to the environment and its inhabitants.

From Shadowcats and Direwolves to Snow Bears, giant Elk and even Mammoths, the lands beyond the Wall are home to several species you'll find nowhere else on the continent. The biggest draw for travellers, however, is giants. Standing 10–12ft in height, these colossal creatures have thick pelts that grow thicker around the waist. Though wild in appearance – even the women have beards, so telling the sexes apart can be difficult, even for a trained Ranger – the giants are a relatively civilised species who speak in the Old Tongue, ride mammoths and carry clubs made of boulders and tree trunks. Because nature is almost as unpredictable as the giants themselves, there's no guarantee you'll spot one, no matter how well your guide knows the land. But regardless of whether you see one or not, there's a tremendous experience waiting for you beyond the Wall.

Note: Travellers are expected to bring their own furs but the Brothers will provide you with mounts, guides and a rustic lunch of black bread and hard cheese.

Fist of the First Men

Another popular excursion from Castle Black is to the Fist of the First Men, an ancient ring fort built during the Dawn Age, long before the Andals first took Westeros. Located many days' ride north of the Wall, for centuries the Rangers have used the Fist to orientate their sorties into Wildling territory but have more recently taken to escorting adventurous tourists to this ancient landmark.

Located along the banks of the Milkwater, the steep climb to the top of the hill is worth it for the breathtaking views over the surrounding landscape. On top of the Fist lie a series of hip-high megalithic stones – the remains of an ancient ringfort initially raised by the First Men some 6,000 years ago.

Note: This is not an excursion for the faint of heart and

travellers are advised that they make the journey at their own risk. Wildlings and even Others have been known to attack parties on their way to the Fist and recently the Night's Watch lost a force of some of their best Rangers during a battle with the White Walkers. Pack some Dragon Glass and a spare set of breeches just in case.

Climbing the Wall

Adrenaline junkies can get their endorphin fix by climbing the Wall itself. The 700-ft expanse of ice is a formidable challenge for all but the most proficient of climbers. Stone hammers, pegs and a fully trained guide are all available for hire at Castle Black, but most climbers prefer to make the ascent closer to the recently re-garrisoned Greyguard. Due to an increasing number of Wildlings attempting to scale the Wall, climbers are advised to inform the Night's Watch before they set out in order to avoid being mistaken for a raider by the Brothers on the battlements.

Weapons Practice

This is held daily in the yard at Castle Black, where the master-at-arms puts new recruits through their paces. The induction to the Night's Watch is often a brutal process and no quarter is given to Brothers who are unable to wield a sword, even if they yield in the face of their attackers. But while the practice is anything but pleasurable for those taking part, it has become a popular attraction for tourists, who line the flagstone yard in order to see the new recruits put through their paces.

Wormwalks

Hourly tours through Castle Black's Wormwalks are offered by Brothers, who expect a copper or two in return for their time. The Wormwalks are a warren of subterranean tunnels that link the keeps and passages of the castle above. Though rarely used in the summer, in winter these passages are a lifeline when the deep snows and ice winds arrive, forcing the garrison below ground.

Top of the Wall Tour

The most popular excursion and the number-one attraction for tourists heading to Castle Black is the Top of the Wall Tour, an experience that draws visitors from across the Seven Kingdoms. Though popular with tourists, there's plenty of room once you're at the top of the Wall. In fact, at its peak the structure is wider than the Kingsroad and it's said that a dozen fully armoured knights are able to ride abreast atop of it, so you shouldn't have to worry about tripping over your fellow travellers.

There are two ways to climb the 700ft to The Wall's summit. The first is via a wooden stairway made of rough-hewn beams sunk directly into the ice. Alternatively, a mechanical iron cage provides an easier ascent for those looking to rest their weary limbs, and the ride also offers stunning views of Castle Black and nearby Mole's Town.

Once you reach the summit, you can enjoy commanding views of the wilderness north of the Wall and the realm south of it. Visitors are also able to take a tour of the defences while on top of the Wall. Alongside giant catapults and trebuchets, several straw men are also dotted along the battlements. These scarecrows (in a very literal sense) were put up to swell the dwindling ranks of the Night's Watch and draw the arrows of attacking armies.

While Wildling attacks are common, tourists are largely safe atop the Wall, as all but the strongest archers are unable to reach the summit. A bigger concern is slips and falls. The surface is slick underfoot and, although the Brothers are supposed to spread crushed stone to make safe walkways, they are often ill maintained, leading to the Wall's unfavourable reputation as an accident hotspot.

PISSING OFF THE END OF THE WORLD

For many travellers, a full bladder is as essential as warm furs and sturdy boots for their trip to the top of the Wall. 'Pissing off the end of the world' has become a popular rite of passage for visitors ever since Tyrion Lannister emptied his bladder off the side of the Wall on a recent visit and a steady stream of visitors now line the edge of the battlements in order to follow in his footsteps.

Souvenir Shopping

Replica black uniforms are a popular purchase for travellers looking to take a souvenir from Castle Black. By far the most valuable keepsake, however, is a piece of The Wall itself, although, depending on what time of year you visit, your prized possession may not last the journey home.

THE GIFT

Known as the Gift, the area stretching fifty leagues south of the Wall was given in perpetuity to the Brothers of the Night's Watch to help fund and preserve their order. Once a teeming mass of holdfasts, farms and settlements, today it's little more than a barren wasteland, with endless plains sprawling east to the Shivering Sea and rocky outcrops and wild forests extending westwards towards the Bay of Ice.

Often called Brandon's Gift, this area of land was first gifted to the Brotherhood by Bran the Builder, the legendary stark whose ingenuity is said to have helped shape some of the Seven Kingdom's most iconic landmarks. But Brandon wasn't the only noble to support the Crows. Thousands of years after the initial gift, Queen Alysanne visited the Wall with her brother, King Jaehaerys I Targaryen. The Queen was a prominent supporter of the Night's Watch and convinced her husband to extend the Gift by a further twenty-five leagues, giving the Night's Watch new lands to farm and villages to tax.

In recent years, however, dwindling numbers of the Black Brothers on the Wall have meant that the Gift has fallen into disrepair. The lands are now largely overgrown, its holdfasts unhoused and its farmlands untended. For years there have been plans to have the Gift resettled. Lord Eddard Stark sought to place new lords there before losing his head (quite literally) in King's Landing. However, the most recent and controversial plan proposes to settle

Wildling refugees on the Gift as they seek to escape the Others north of the Wall. The plan has the support of notable public figures, including Stannis Baratheon and Jon Snow, but has been met with outcry from both the Brothers of the Night's Watch and the Northern Mountain Clans.

MOAT CAILIN

Sitting in a commanding position over leagues of bog, quicksand and river, it's easy to see why so many people still say that Moat Cailin is the key to the North. The ancient stronghold of the First Men may not have been permanently manned for centuries but it still plays a vital part in the security of the kingdom. Raised roughly 10,000 years ago, the military base once consisted of twenty towers and a giant curtain wall that is said to have dwarfed even the great fortifications of Winterfell.

Located in a key defensive position, it was the last part of the Seven Kingdoms to fall to the Andals, who are said to have thrown themselves countless times against its walls before conquering the Children of the Forest through sheer weight of numbers.

Little of those formidable fortifications remains, however. Today the area is littered with basalt stones the size of cottages, which once made up the curtain wall, and only three of the twenty towers that previously stood here now remain. Nevertheless, it's a treasure trove for visitors, who can practically feel the weight of history bearing down on their shoulders as they walk among these ancient battlements.

Official Guides

Although Moat Cailin is open to the public, it is advisable not to explore the area without the assistance of a local Crannogman guide.

The ruined fortress is surrounded by quicksand and suckholes, alongside streams clogged with rotten trees. While rustic wooden planks have been laid to help guide walkers, it's easy to stray off the path and quickly find yourself chest-deep in the bog. Add in dangers such as snakes and lizard lions and you've a recipe for a holiday you'll never forget (or even return from).

So play it safe and explore with the aid of local experts from the nearby House Reed, who'll not only keep you alive but also informed about the fortress's rich history.

The three towers

Though the wooden keeps have long since rotted away, the three remaining towers of Moat Cailin offer a wealth of history and a surprising tactical advantage for defenders, even in their current ruinous state.

The remaining towers command the causeway from all sides, giving them an impeccable vantage over enemies who attempt to pass beneath them. Anyone who does try to storm the battlements would face constant fire from the other two, which is why it's possible for a hundred well-stocked archers to defend the ancient stronghold against forces of a far greater size.

Hopefully, however, you've come to Moat Cailin to

plunder its history rather than the lands that lay beyond its walls. That history is largely contained within the remaining towers, which provide ample entertainment for an afternoon of exploration. They include:

Children's Tower: Tall, slender and thick with moss, time has ravaged the Children's Tower so that only half of the crenulations of its crown now remain and the top looks like some giant beast has taken a bite out of it.

Legend has it that it was from here that the Children of the Forest attempted to drive back the Andals through the use of ancient magic. According to myth, when the Children could no longer hold Moat Cailin against the Andals' superior numbers, they summoned up a hammer of water in an effort to smash the Neck and separate the North from the South, much as they are said to have done with the Arm of Dorne. Their efforts obviously failed but the bogs and swamps that surround the battlements are said to be a testament to their endeavours.

Drunkard's Tower: So named due to the pronounced lean that's taken hold of the tower ever since its foundations started to fail, the Drunkard's Tower sits where the south and west walls once met.

Gatehouse Tower: The most complete of all Moat Cailin's towers, the Gatehouse Tower is still in fine repair and even retains some of its original outer walls. It's said that during his recent insurrection, Robb Stark took the Gatehouse Tower as his seat for his forays south.

> '*A naked man has few secrets; a flayed man, none.*'
> – Bolton family motto

DREADFORT

A few days' ride from Winterfell lies the Dreadfort, the ancestral home of the House of Bolton. While the rest of the Seven Kingdoms proudly proclaim their colours with animals, landscapes or monuments on their sigils, the Boltons have chosen the flayed man for their standard on account of the fact that they are famed for flaying the skin from their enemies.

The flayed man is not just meant to intimidate their opponents, however; it also serves as an advertisement for the North's latest attraction: a macabre exhibition showcasing the skins that the Boltons have separated from their enemies over the years. The brainchild of Ramsay Bolton – the bastard son of the presiding lord – the exhibition has only recently reopened after the death of Lord Eddard Stark, who had previously banned the practice under his rule.

The end result is not for the weak of constitution: a bloody spectacle that showcases tapestries and even cloaks made of the skin of Bolton enemies. Be sure to bring your strongest stomach, especially if you attend when the Lord is in residence and providing guests with one of the live torture-chamber demonstrations for which the Dreadfort is now notorious.

WHITE HARBOR

The largest settlement in the North – and one of only five cities in Westeros – White Harbor is the centre of trade for the kingdom. Located where the White Knife River flows into the Bite, it is a popular pit stop for merchants and a landing point for those travelling north by sea.

Originally built to maintain trade with the rest of Westeros while fighting off the advances of pirates from the Iron Islands, today White Harbor is a bustling travel hub, with merchants and travellers alike crowding its harbour walls and white cobbled streets.

Most tourists choose not to stay in the city, which is more of an industrial heartland than a destination in its own right. However, if you have time to kill while waiting for your horses to rest or your ship to re-supply, there are a handful of attractions to keep you entertained.

Where to Stay

Tourism hasn't yet reached White Harbor – a city more concerned with merchants than travellers – so accommodation opportunities are scarce for those who are looking to stay a night or two.

The Lazy Eel (£)

The vast majority of travellers spending the night in White Harbor head for the Lazy Eel, a local winesink-turned-hostel that's renowned for offering the oldest whores and vilest wine in all of White Harbor. Located by the Seal Gate and off Fishfoot Yard, you'll find the Eel (as it's known to locals) down a flight of steps by a sheepskin seller. It's not the most comfortable dwelling in the Seven Kingdoms but it might as well be Highgarden for all you'll care after a few cups of the local sour wine.

Eating and Drinking

Its proximity to the sea means that White Harbor is a veritable mecca for seafood lovers. With fresh catches brought in daily, it offers some of the finest and freshest fish in the Seven Kingdoms, alongside beers said to be so thick and tasty that a cask can fetch as much as a fine Arbor wine. In fact, your biggest decision will probably be where to park your taste buds.

The Lazy Eel (£)

For the light of purse, the Lazy Eel serves as an affordable eating option. However, don't go expecting Arbor wines and Highgarden feasts. The food here is little more than functional, with pies that are more lard and gristle than meat and pastry.

The Wolf's Den (£)

Once an ancient fortress, today the Wolf's Den serves as the city's prison and the inauspicious home of one of the finest brewhouses in town. This ramshackle establishment is little more than a hovel that clings to the castle's walls like a barnacle but that means little once you step inside, where you'll be greeted with a warm welcome, a fine mug of dark beer and a hot crab pie to die for.

Fish Market (£)

Located between the outer harbour and Seal Gate, the fish market is home to the day's freshest catch, including whitefish, winkles, crabs, mussels, clams, herring, cod, salmon, lobster and lampreys.

Areas of Interest/What to Do When You're There

Wherever you wander in White Harbor, the rest of the North seems to be calling you from just about every quarter, from ships headed for the Bay of Seals to horseriding to Winterfell or Moat Cailin. But those who choose to remain within the city walls will find a smorgasbord of attractions to distract their attention.

Fishfoot Yard

Located just inside the Seal Gate, this cobbled yard is a popular gathering spot for locals. Originally named for some dead lord, it's affectionately known as Fishfoot Yard by locals on account of the fountain that sits at its centre: an impressive 20ft sculpture of a merman known as Old Fishfoot. Surrounded by oil lamps, it is a popular spot for alfresco eating, with street vendors selling White Harbor's famous fried cod.

Seal Rock

This massive stone, which dominates the approach to the city's outer harbour, has long been a defensive outpost. It's crowned by an ancient stone ringfort said to have stood since the age of the First Men. But the history is just one reason why eager travellers will hand over a copper for a ferry ride there. The other is the local population of seals who have decided to call the rock home. Excursions are readily available and can be booked from your hostel or via representatives who set up stall at Seal Gate.

Sept of the Snows

Due to its links with the rest of Westeros, White Harbor is one of the only northern outposts to worship the Faith of the Seven. In the Faith's honour, the city built a large Sept with a dome roof surmounted by tall statues of the Seven.

Though similar to many of the kingdom's other spiritual sites, it's well worth even the most passing of visits.

Castle Stair

This famed street has adorned many a tapestry and as a result, it's the first place that many outsiders think to visit during a stay in White Harbor. It's easy to see why. The street is lined with white-stone steps and stunning white-marble mermaids, which lead up to a viewpoint offering unparalleled vistas of the town's two harbours. However, it's at night when the Castle Stair truly comes alive as whale-oil lamps cradled within the marble mermaids' arms are lit, transforming the stair into one of the most romantic settings in the Seven Kingdoms.

Merman's Court

The great hall of the New Castle, the Mermans Court, is where local Lord Wyman Manderly holds court and feasts. However, when the Lord isn't in residence, the hall is opened up to tourists who come to explore its ornate carvings and vibrant frescos, which depict a kaleidoscope of sea creatures ranging from cod to kraken.

The Riverlands

Rich, fertile and populous, the Riverlands are one of the heartlands of the Seven Kingdoms although, of course, the Riverlands weren't always part of the unified continent. Instead, during the time of Aegon's Conquest they were controlled by the Iron Islands to the east.

It's not the first time the Riverlands have been occupied. Because of their central position and a lack of natural boundaries, they have been the unwitting hosts of countless battles throughout the centuries.

Despite its war-torn heritage, however, this watery slice of the Seven Kingdoms is still a must-see for visitors to Westeros. Whether you approach from the North or from the South, it's an area of outstanding natural beauty; a lush green land that houses an idyllic assortment of endless plains and dense forests, criss-crossed by rivers and estuaries.

Both the forks of the Trident and the northernmost

portion of the Blackwater Rush run through the region, helping to shape the land and the people who live on it. In times of peace, the rivers are the lifeblood of the kingdom's economy. The Trident is the easiest way to move goods or men across the region and the aquatic arteries are regularly clogged with fisherfolk in skiffs and grain barges being poled downstream, merchants on floating ships, and even brightly painted mummer's boats with quilted sails of a hundred colours.

Recent conflicts may have ravaged the Riverlands but there's still plenty for hardy travellers to explore in this part of Westeros. Though the region doesn't boast any major towns or cities, the kingdom's key castles, alongside the historical sites that litter the landscape, still provide ample entertainment for those who choose to visit.

HIGHLIGHTS

Riverrun (page 81)

Historical seat of power of the House of Tully, Riverrun rules over the Riverlands and is an ideal basecamp for travellers looking to explore the Trident and the surrounding area.

Harrenhal (page 85)

One of Westeros's most compelling castles, this monstrous fortress is a testament to both the ingenuities and follies of men. Its colossal towers – warped and wrought by dragonfire – are just part of a surreal and stunning landscape that needs to be seen to be believed.

The Twins (page 85)

One of only two reliable river crossings in the region, this former hotspot for destination weddings has fallen out of fashion in recent years but is still one of the more prominent stops on any tour of the realm.

Oldstones (page 97)

One of Westeros's most compelling historical sites, Oldstones offers a glimpse into the kingdom's past and an opportunity to enjoy the company of a thriving alternative culture of outlaws.

Saltpans (page 98)

Part port town, part spiritual mecca, Saltpans offers an odd mixture of transcendence and travel opportunities for those passing through.

Getting There and Getting About

By land: Situated two weeks' ride from King's Landing, the Riverlands are easily accessible by the Kingsroad, which offers a safe passage for tourists. Its location at the heart of the realm also makes it easily accessible from nearby kingdoms such as The Vale, the Westerlands and the North.

By sea: The Trident and Blackwater Rush mean that travelling by sea is often the most efficient means of reaching the Riverlands. Port towns including Saltpans and Maidenpool offer excellent links to the North, King's Landing and the rest of the Seven Kingdoms, as well as destinations further afield, including Braavos.

River crossings: While the rivers that criss-cross the kingdom are part of the region's appeal, they can also be an annoyance to tourists travelling by land, especially when it comes to finding a safe crossing.

The Twins – controlled by the House of Frey – offers safer passage for larger groups, although crossing can prove to be expensive and travellers may have to marry off their eldest sons to get across.

Smaller parties can avoid the major crossings and catch a ferry from Harroway. The two-headed horse costs a gold dragon per passenger, though be warned: there are no discounts for children.

Dangers and Annoyances

Conflict – The Riverlands played host to some of the fiercest fighting during the recent battle for the Iron Throne. While travellers are still being welcomed, the area is yet to recover from the conflict, which left several villages burned or abandoned. Although some semblance of the King's Peace has recently been returned to the realm, tourists are still advised to travel with care.

Wolves – They have always been an annoyance in these parts but ravens from recent travellers suggest that packs of wolves are getting more numerous and increasingly dangerous. The War of the Five Kings has meant that their numbers have gone unchecked, particularly around the Gods Eye, where packs have become bolder, attacking sheep, cattle and even the occasional traveller.

Outlaws – Another by-product of the recent fighting is a band of outlaws who've taken to attacking travellers along the Kingsroad. The so-called Brotherhood Without Banners claims to be supporting the local community who have lost everything in the fighting. While their forays are typically focused on Lannister bannermen, the Brotherhood has been known to accost the occasional tourist. Bands are also said to be operating on the rivers, where they've been taking advantage of choke points created by sunken skiffs to harass unfortunate tourists.

Creatures, Flora and Fauna

Lizard lions: The Riverlands are one of only two regions in the Seven Kingdoms where it's possible to see lizard lions in the wild. These swamp-dwelling reptiles often resemble logs submerged in the murky waters until they bare their dagger-like teeth to scare away startled tourists.

Wild flowers: The Riverlands are famed for their flowers. In season, these blooms carpet the area around the Kingsroad as a patchwork of prettily coloured varieties vie for travellers' attention. Though tempting, don't try to pick the flowers, many of which grow around half-hidden bogs that can swallow a man in quicksand.

Poison kisses: These beautiful purple flowers are a common sight around the Riverlands and an even more common annoyance for tourists who ignore the local advice not to pick them. Contact with the skin will bring anyone foolish enough to touch them out in an uncomfortable rash. Children are often the worst affected so, if you're travelling with your family, be sure to keep them close at hand.

Top tip: if you do happen to come into contact with the harmful flora, a dollop of mud can help to ease the irritation.

When to Visit

Spring/summer is a popular time to visit, as the wild flowers are in bloom and the rivers teem with life. While there are good deals to be found during winter, the region can be prone to flooding, which makes river crossings more arduous than usual.

Famous Residents

Homeland of the House of Tully, one of the region's most famous former residents is Catelyn Stark, the maid of Riverrun who was married to Lord Eddard Stark before her unfortunate demise. A well-liked figure, she's still mourned by the smallfolk here. In popular culture, singers including Rymund the Rhymer and Tom of Sevenstreams are among the current crop of celebrities who fascinate smallfolk in this part of Westeros. Visitors can be all but assured to cross paths with them during their travels through the Riverlands but only a lucky few will catch a glimpse of Beric Dondarrion, the enigmatic Lightning Lord whose name has spread like wildfire across the realm in recent months.

Where to Stay

Rooms are readily available at the region's major castles (see relevant sections for details) but the Riverlands also houses a series of centrally located inns, which can offer more affordable accommodation for the duration of your stay.

AN INN OF MANY NAMES

One of the most famous Inns in all of the Seven Kingdoms – the Inn at the Crossroads – has a history almost as rich as the realm itself. Located at the crossroads of the Kingsroad, running north to south, and the Riverroad, running east to west, the inn has stood on the site for centuries, regularly changing its name to match its chequered history.

Originally called the Two Crowns, the inn used to be a favoured spot for King Jaehaerys I and Queen Alysanne during their frequent trips to the North. It then changed its name to the Bellringer Inn after its owner built a bell tower on the grounds, before it passed into the hands of a crippled old knight, 'Long' John Heddle. Heddle had taken up ironwork during his dotage and forged a new sign to hang above the door, which replicated the three-headed dragon of the House of Targaryen. After his work had been affixed, the inn changed names again, picking up the moniker of the Clanking Dragon in honour of the sound that Heddle's handiwork would make when the wind picked up.

After the sign was lost, locals simply began to refer to the dwelling as the River Inn, thanks to its proximity to the ferry. However, once the course of the river was diverted for agricultural purposes, it finally became known simply as the Inn at the Crossroads – a name it still carries today.

The Inn at the Crossroads (£)

A favourite of the late Tywin Lannister during his campaigns against the North, this large three-storey inn, located where the Kingsroad and Riverroad meet, is ideally situated for exploring the Riverlands. Close to popular attractions such as the Ruby Ford, it sits across from a picturesque small village of half a hundred whitewashed houses complete with a marketplace and small Sept offering all the amenities the average traveller could ask for.

With vacancies for some 120 people, you're bound to find space in one of the low dusty rooms that make up the bulk of the Inn's accommodation. Though a hodgepodge of cheap furnishings and cheaper beds – think hay-filled bunks and flea-ridden lounge furnishings – the rooms are adequately appointed and comfy enough after a hard day's ride. Ask for a room at the back to avoid the handful of bargain beds that are located directly above the din of the common room.

The bustling common room is rammed full of trestle tables and wooden nooks, where weary travellers converse over Masha Heddle's famed food. The large wood-panelled room has become a word-of-mouth favourite, thanks to its host's hospitality. The long, drafty space is exceptionally well maintained – thanks, in part, to the innkeeper's strictly observed 'no boots' policy – and is regularly packed with people from all walks of life.

While the prime seats soak up the warmth of the hearth, at the far end of the room the true inn experience can be found on the trestle tables, where it's elbow room-only among a throng of fellow travellers. Squeeze in and share bread and stories with your fellow travellers while bustling wenches serve you up a feast. The food here is fantastic. The house speciality comprises skewers of meat with tiny onions, fiery peppers and fat mushrooms, all served in trenchers of bread and washed down with local ale. Be sure to save some room for dessert, however, as the honey-soaked sweetcakes are particularly good.

With a cross section of the Seven Kingdoms sharing the same table, entertainment is never far away. And whether you're enjoying the ballads of a passing singer or a quarrel between two rival lords, your meal is sure to be served up with a side order of excitement and a tale or two to share with your newfound tablemates.

The Inn of the Kneeling Man (££)

Situated east of Riverrun, this historic inn is said to stand on the spot where Torrhen Stark knelt before Aegon the Conqueror. The inn itself sits on a bend in the Trident, with its whitewashed upper storeys leaning out over the river so far that you'd think it might dip into the water at any moment.

Don't let its unassuming entrance and hand-painted sign fool you: this inn boasts everything a weary traveller could need. From stables to a smithy, all practicalities are covered. The highlight of this unassuming hostelry, however, is its grounds: the inn boasts one of the best arbours this side of the Reach, with vines heavy with grapes, bulging apple trees and even a delightful garden. On sunny evenings the inn's tiny dock is also a popular spot with tourists packing its roughshod planks to sip an ale – brewed on site – while watching the sun set across the river.

Adventurous taste-trippers can also sample the ever-changing menu. From rabbit stew to horsesteak grilled with onions, all of the ingredients are foraged daily by the in-house cook. A range of artisanal breads is also now offered after a budding baker's boy was recently added to the kitchen staff.

The Ivy Inn (£)

Located along the Kingsroad, this tranquil family-friendly establishment offers a welcome respite from the rigours of the Riverlands. The on-site bathhouse is a particularly welcome sight for travellers who are looking to soak away the strains of their journey. Try the pork pies served with baked apples – a dollop of comfort food, that's just what the Maester ordered after a long day's ride!

THE RUBY FORD

A popular destination for tourists and treasure hunters, the Ruby Ford rests at the bend of the Green Fork of the Trident, a short ride from the Inn at the Crossroads. The spot won its name during the Battle of the Trident, where King Robert Baratheon defeated Prince Rhaegar in battle to win his crown.

As the battle between the two armies raged, the two men met in face-to-face combat in the waters of the ford – a duel that ended when King Robert slew the Crown Prince by crushing his chest with his mighty warhammer. The blow split the Targaryen heir's breastplate, which was encrusted with rubies forged into the shape of the three-headed dragon of his House.

Locals say that Rhaegar's rubies are still being discovered

> in the ford, which has led to a rush of treasure hunters
> and have-a-go holidaymakers intent on finding their
> own souvenir from one of the bloodiest chapters of the
> kingdom's more recent history.

RIVERRUN

Surrounded by rivers and rich lands, Riverrun is the centre
of the Riverlands, an ancient castle that's been the ancestral
home of the Tullys for centuries. Situated at the point where
the Tumblestone and Red Fork rivers meet, Riverrun is like
no other castle in the Seven Kingdoms.

Although not especially large, its location at the confluence
of two great rivers gives it a distinct tactical advantage,
while the defences have been specifically designed to make
it almost impregnable during the time of siege.

Built of sandstone, which rises almost majestically from
the river itself, Riverrun contains a magnificent wheelhouse,
a stunning Sept and a delightful Godswood that make up
an ideal itinerary for a day spent sightseeing. Despite the
lack of genuine attractions, many holidaymakers choose to
linger at the castle a little longer, taking an extra day or
two to bask in Riverrun's creature comforts and regain their
strength before continuing their trip.

Accommodation

Most people choose to stay in one of the nearby inns.
However, the castle itself also offers accommodation for
those who've got the gold.

The Lord's Solar (£££)

If you want to pretend you're king of the castle, this handsomely appointed accommodation in what used to be the Lord's Solar is well worth the gold. Situated high above the castle walls, the room opens out onto a charming veranda offering panoramic views of the rivers below. Inside you're greeted with a cavernous room complete with an exquisitely carved four-poster bed. There's even your own on-site master. A filling dinner of boars' ribs and stewed onions or boiled beef and horseradish is also included.

Eating and Drinking

Unless you want to ride out to an inn, there's only one option when it comes to eating and drinking at Riverrun. But boy, is it a good one...

The Great Hall (£££)

Offering some of the finest dining this side of King's Landing, an opportunity to feast in Riverrun's Great Hall is not to be missed. Famed for its bacon-wrapped trout and pease and onion soup, the Hall offers an elegant – if isolated – dining experience for two or more people. Be sure to book early and, if your purse is heavy, stump up the extra silver for a flight of ale from the castle's own brewhouse.

Areas of Interest/What to Do When You're There

From castle tours to pleasure-boat cruises, your days can be as busy or carefree as you want them to be.

A castle tour

From its red-rusted Watergates to its stunning sandstone Sept, those who take a guided tour through Riverrun's halls won't be disappointed. Tours depart daily from the keep and guides are on hand to help bring alive the castle's history, including that of the dungeon where Jaime Lannister was recently imprisoned after his capture at the Battle of the Whispering Wood; the Great Hall where Robb Stark was crowned King in the North; and the rooms where a young Petyr Baelish is said to have played with Lysa and Catelyn Tully as a child.

A river tour

The best way to see the Riverlands is from the water and Pleasure Barges depart daily from Riverrun, ferrying well-to-do travellers in style along the slow-moving waters of the Trident. These overnight cruises are available for a small purse of silver and offer every comfort of the castle, including privies, servants and security.

An audience with Rymund the Rhymer

Famed across Westeros for his silky-smooth vocals, no trip to Riverrun would be complete without seeing Rymund the Rhymer: one of the castle's most popular attractions. Riverrun's resident singer is known for renditions like 'Wolf in the Night' and his own arrangement of the 'Battle of Stone Mill'. He also takes requests, particularly after an afternoon spent serenading tourists in the brewhouse.

High Heart

One of the most popular day trips from Riverrun is a ride out to High Heart, a sacred site that once belonged to the Children of the Forest. Situated atop a tall hill a short distance from the castle gates, High Heart's crown is home to a ring of thirty-one Weirwood stumps and offers unobstructed views across the surrounding land.

Considered sacred by the smallfolk, who believe the

hill is still guarded by the Old Gods, the area was closed until recently due to the activities of a band of outlaws who preyed on hapless tourists. However, an agreement with the Brotherhood without Banners has ensured that the trip has reopened, enabling tourists to experience one of the Riverland's most ancient and most sacred sites. Not only has the Brotherhood ensured the safety of tourists, guaranteeing no harm will come to anyone who sleeps on the hill, they've also added their own attractions, including the so-called Ghost of High Heart: a withered old woman said to be descended from the Children of the Forest themselves who will tell your future for a few coins or a sweet song.

THE WHISPERING WOOD

A day's ride from Riverrun lies the Whispering Wood. At first glance it's difficult to see what all the fuss is about. But once you break through the forested canopy, you quickly realise why so many travellers make the trip each year to this seemingly unremarkable patch of land.

The backdrop for Robb Stark's stunning tactical victory over Jaime Lannister, the ambush at the Whispering Wood is one of the most famous chapters of the Northmen's recent uprising. Save for the attention of treasure hunters, the site itself has also remained largely untouched since then. In fact, the forest floor is littered with the spoils of war, from rusted helms to broken mail, shattered lances and even bones, all half-reclaimed by nature, making it a popular destination for tourists who want to relive the excitement of armed combat without any of the danger.

THE TWINS

Once a popular destination for bridal parties, the now infamous saga of the Red Wedding means that this fortified river crossing has fallen on lean times, making it little more than a pit stop on many people's tours of the Riverlands.

The castle, which is made up of two identical keeps on either side of the Green Fork of the Trident, took three generations to construct and forms the only crossing within a hundred leagues.

One of the major conduits between north and south, within its walls lays a cacophony of voices as travellers and bannermen from across the Seven Kingdoms gather. As such, it's a great spot for people spying or catching up on the latest gossip from across the Westeros. However, you may not want to stay long within its walls. The food isn't great (unless you're a fan of river pike and jellied calf's brains), the music's terrible and the ageing Lord Walder Frey is a notoriously dour host, who will just as readily lop off your head as marry you to one of his ever-growing brood of daughters, should the mood take him.

HARRENHAL

The largest castle in all of Westeros – not to mention the most ill-omened if you believe the legends – Harrenhal is a fearsome fortress; a maze of gargantuan towers, monstrous walls and colossal keeps.

Size matters across the Seven Kingdoms but that is especially true of Harrenhal. Everything here is big, from the kitchens to the forges and the accommodations to its bear pit. Even the holdings are vast. Situated on the northern bank of the Gods Eye lake, Harrenhal commands some of the richest tracts of land on the continent: a fertile tapestry of fields and woods that is as beautiful as it is bountiful. If you're looking for meandering streams, rolling hills and sunlit fields, you've come to the right place.

The sumptuous setting is, however, in stark contrast to Harrenhal itself and the bizarre, yet brilliant battlements that blight the otherwise beautiful landscape. The castle covers three times as much ground as Winterfell and its buildings are bigger than any other in the Seven Kingdoms. Its stables, for example, can house 1,000 horses, while its kitchens are as large as some castles' great halls. In fact, in the castle's pomp, Harrenhal is said to have been big enough to garrison a million men.

However, after it fell to Aegon during the War of Conquest, this colossal castle has fallen into disrepair and decay. Today, only about a third of its capacity is used, with the rest of the battlements left to rot and ruin. Don't let the battered towers and half-empty keeps put you off, though. Harrenhal is a must-see for any traveller. It is a testament to man's ingenuity that, thanks to an influx of men and money during the recent War of the Five Kings, Harrenhal is once again well on its way to becoming a booming tourist destination.

A CASTLE WITH A CHEQUERED HISTORY

Harrenhal was built by Harren the Black, the last Iron King to rule over both the Riverlands and the Iron Islands. Renowned as a vain and bloody tyrant, Harren built his castle as a monument to himself, intending it to be a fortress that would dwarf any other keep that came before or after it.

His plans took more than forty years to come to fruition and drained the Riverlands of cash and resources to finance the construction. Thousands of slaves from across the known world were killed during the process, with men freezing during winter and sweltering in summer as they toiled in quarries or laboured to build the castle's towers and walls. The environment took a hit too, with Weirwoods, which had stood for thousands of years, cut down to form beams and rafters.

Once it was finally complete, Harren boasted that his new home was impregnable. However, he hadn't accounted for Aegon the Conqueror and his dragons who, ironically, set foot on King's Landing the day Harren took up residence in his new seat of power. In the end, the battlements were no barrier to the dragons, who flew over the high walls and roasted Harren and his bloodline to death in their seemingly invincible towers.

To this day the castle bears the scars of their assault, with its melted and charred stone a testament to the fearsome beasts' power. Since it fell to Aegon, Harrenhal has become something of a white elephant for the Seven

Kingdoms. Too big to garrison and too expensive to properly maintain, it has fallen into disrepair as a series of lords have met with an unfortunate end after taking up residence within its walls.

The Castle

From its fissured and blackened stone walls to the colossal keeps and battlements, Harrenhal's size is almost beyond comprehension. Though much of it has fallen into disrepair, the gargantuan fortress still attracts visitors from across the Seven Kingdoms and beyond, as people flock to the area to see Harren's legacy for themselves.

The size is instantly apparent: you can see the towers rising from leagues away but only truly appreciate the enormity up close. For example, the gatehouse that greets visitors is as big as Winterfell's great keep, while the curtain walls protecting the castle are the size of mountain cliffs – so large, in fact, that you can only see the very top of Harrenhal's five great towers from outside.

Though the towers are not quite as wondrous as they once were, there is still a strange beauty to the gnarled and ruined state you'll find them in. When Harrenhal was attacked by Aegon and his dragons, their fiery dragon breath melted the stone as if it were candle wax, leaving the structure twisted and tempered.

The names Harren had once given to these towers have long been forgotten. Instead, they are now named after the various disasters that have befallen them. The tallest is the Kingspyre – so-called because it's where Harren and his sons were burnt alive. There's also the Widow's Tower, the Tower of Dread, the Tower of Ghosts and the Wailing Tower – which gets its name from the peculiar sound that the stone makes when the wind blows.

Though the upper floors of the towers have not been inhabited for more than eighty years, recent garrisons have worked tirelessly to prepare the gargantuan fortress for tourists who can now explore every inch of Harren's famed fortress. You can now actually stay within the walls themselves, giving visitors an opportunity to rest their weary limbs after a day exploring the colossal construction.

A WALKING TOUR OF HARRENHAL

Despite its enormity, the best way to experience Harrenhal is on foot. Visitors are encouraged to explore under their own steam and the entire building is open for tourists to meander around. Due to its sheer size, it can be easy to get lost within the castle walls. However, with a little forward planning it's possible to see everything Harrenhal has to offer and still get back to your chambers in time for a hearty meal and a well-earned rest.

Start: The Hall of a Hundred Hearths
End: The Godswood
Time: Full day
Exertion: Easy
Points of interest: The Towers, the Godswood
Rest stop: The Bathhouse

---

1. The Hall of a Hundred Hearths

Our tour begins in Harrenhal's Great Hall, which is commonly called the Hall of a Hundred Hearths due to its enormity. In reality there are only thirty-four hearths but it's easy to appreciate how it got its impressive moniker as you stroll around the smooth slate floors, enjoying surroundings that could feed and house an entire army. Take some time to soak it all in and head up to the galleries that ring the hall to get a bird's-eye view that will help you appreciate its sheer scale.

2. The Kitchens

You need some colossal kitchens to prepare food for a hall this vast and that's the next stop on our walking tour. Located in a round stone building just across from the great hall, Harrenhal's culinary heart is as big as Winterfell's Great Hall. Underneath its domed ceiling you'll find a vast preparation area, alongside gigantic ovens used to cook up eats and treats around the clock.

3. The Bathhouse

After taking in the sights and smells of Harrenhal's kitchens, it's time to step out into the flowstone yard and head towards the castle's famed Bathhouse. Built from stone and timber, like everything else in Harrenhal the baths here are big – huge, in fact. Built in the style of the free cities, the great stone tubs are large enough to hold six or seven people at once. There's no time to stop for a soak, however – after all, you've got a castle to see, but make a note of the location and stop by at the end of the day to soothe away the aches and pains of your day's exploring.

4. The Smithy/Armoury

A short walk from the Bathhouse lies Harrenhal's smithy and armoury. It's here that a team of master smiths works day and night to forge new weapons and armour. Take time to see the twenty furnaces lining the long hall alongside the vast stone troughs (used to ferry water to temper the glowing hot steel) that are built into the floor itself. If you're lucky, you may see a new helm being hammered into shape by one of the army of smiths who call this scalding building home.

5. Tour the towers

The main attraction of any tour is, of course, Harrenhal's colossal towers. The maze of storerooms, cells and sleeping quarters which lie within the towers aren't much to look at but the same cannot be said of the walls containing them.

Starting at The Tower of Ghosts – Harrenhal's most devastated structure – make your way past the ruins of the old Sept to the Widow's Tower, which adjoins the Kingspyre via a vast stone bridge. Take a moment to look up at the walls, which are gnarled and twisted from the dragon fire. Many say that the Kingspyre now resembles a melted candle, especially the uppermost third, which sags from the remaining structure.

As you pass through the hubbub of the flowstone yard, take a moment to enjoy the hive of activity, which often includes weapons practice and drills for the castle's garrison. Once you've had enough of the frenzied activity, finish your tour at the Wailing Tower to stop and listen to the haunting noise that's made as the wind rushes through the stones

6. The Godswood

Once you've finished with Harrenhal's fire-damaged towers, it's time to make one final stop at the castle's Godswood. Like everything else here, Harrenhal's Godswood is enormous. Spanning more than twenty acres, the air is thick with the sharp smell of pines and sentinels and filled with the ripple of water from the meandering stream that snakes through the trees. At its centre lies the heart tree, a huge Weirwood that has stood in this spot for thousands of years. While the Godswood is not so iconic as Winterfell's or as beautiful as Riverrun's, the sheer scale makes for an impressive sight and it's the perfect way to finish off a long day exploring the castle and grounds.

Accommodation

Given the size of this enormous castle, it is almost impossible to explore Harrenhal and the surrounding area in a day. Instead, most visitors choose to spend a night or two in order to fully appreciate the fortress and its surrounding lands. As such, there is a smattering of accommodation options available to suit almost every budget.

Kingspyre (£££)

If you're feeling particularly flush, or want to tempt fate

by pretending you're the lord of Harrenhal, a night or two spent in the Kingspyre is well worth the gold. Though the upper levels of the tower are now off limits, the lower cells have recently been renovated and played host to such nobleman as Lord Tywin Lannister and Roose Bolton. These cavernous sleeping cells come complete with featherbeds, a warm hearth and sweet-smelling reeds to line the floor. Also included is a daily fruit bowl and unlimited spiced wine, alongside other luxuries such as a cup-bearer and an in-house leecher, who will tend to your ailments through the ancient art of bloodsucking.

Harrentown (££)

Those looking to spend a few less coins can stay in nearby Harrentown, located just a short ride away from the castle itself. Here, you'll find an assortment of lodgings including the inn, which is set upon wooden stakes that rise directly out of the waters of the Gods Eye. With comfortable rooms and beautiful views out over the lake, it's a great base to explore the surrounding area and within easy reach of the castle too.

Wailing Tower (£)

If you're looking to save some gold, you can sleep in the workaday serving quarters located in the cavernous vaults beneath the Wailing Tower. Apart from the constant noise of the wind rushing through the stone – a haunting howl that might put off light sleepers – this accommodation is devoid of any pretension, with straw beds and furnishings more rough than ready. The good news is that the cramped conditions come cheap and for just a few coins – or an afternoon spent filling a lord's cup – you'll get your own bed, water and a chunk of soap. Board also includes a bowl of barley stew filled with carrots and turnips, as well as a breakfast of oatcakes. Yummy!

THE CURSE OF HARRENHAL

Since Harren the Black's fiery demise, Harrenhal has changed hands more times than the Iron Throne. A series of lords and noblemen have tried and failed to restore the monstrous fortress to its former glory, many of them meeting grizzly ends in the process.

The myriad of misfortunes has led many to believe the castle is cursed, thanks to Harren's tyrannical ways and the brutalities conducted during its construction. One school of thought is said to believe that Harren mixed the blood of slaves into the mortar used for the stonework – an old magic that forever cursed the castle to prevent any other lord from holding it.

Areas of Interest/What to Do When You're There

Whether you want to explore the natural beauty of the Gods Eye and the local holdings or make the most of the castle's mega-sized facilities, there's plenty to keep tourists entertained during their stay at Harrenhal.

Gods Eye

More of a sea than a lake, this vast expanse of water is so large that it's impossible to see the far shore from its edge. The water itself is stunning: a melting pot of blues and greens that looks like a sheet of beaten copper when the light shimmers off it.

The lake's surprisingly warm waters make it a destination for pleasure seekers, who splash around the shallows or set out on boats and barges to explore its shores. Rentals are readily available from the jetties at the nearby Harrentown.

Isle of Faces

Located in the centre of the Gods Eye is the Isle of Faces, one of the most sacred spots in all of the Seven Kingdoms. It was here that the First Men and the Children of the Forest are said to have signed a pact to cease their long-running war at the end of the Dawn Age. In celebration, every Weirwood on the island was given a face so that the gods could witness the pact. Those faces remain today and the island is home to the last remaining Weirwood groves in Southern Westeros. The sacred trees are tended to by the Green Men, an ancient order tasked with guarding this hallowed spot. Day trips run regularly from Harrentown, where boats and barges ferry eager travellers across to explore these millennia-old groves. Guides are also available to help you follow the footsteps of the First Men.

Hunting

The castle's rich holdings are filled with game, which, unsurprisingly, makes it a popular destination for hunters. Parties are held daily from Harrenhal's gatehouse, where horses and equipment are available to rent by the hour. The nearby woods are rich with deer and quails, while the local rabbits make a popular quarry for tourists, who can bring their catch home with them to cook up in the kitchens.

Bear Pit

King Harren was a big fan of bear baiting, so he had a colossal pit constructed alongside the rest of his castle.

This lavish arena stands ten yards across and five deep and is surrounded on all sides by six tiers of marble benches. Though considered barbaric in some quarters, it is still possible to see the practice at Harrenhal, where bears are regularly pitted against prisoners who are only armed with blunt-edged tourney swords for their protection.

Bathhouse

Whether you want to wash off the dust of the road or soak away your aches and pains after a hard day's exploring, an evening in the bathhouse might be just what the doctor ordered. Filled with cavernous stone tubs, the house is designed in the style of the Free Cities, which means that men and women alike share the waters. Each tub holds up to seven people and, while you may feel self-conscious undressing in front of your fellow travellers, your troubles will soon wash away once you're safely soaking underneath the warm waters.

Eating and Drinking

There's plenty for travellers to tuck into during a visit to Harrenhal. The fertile fields and game-rich groves surrounding the castle mean that great eats are never very far away, with the castle's cavernous kitchens cooking up a feast of hearty fare.

Rabbit stew

Harrenhal is famed for its rabbit stew, a heady, slow-cooked concoction filled with wild mushrooms and onions and served with fist-sized chunks of bread. The rabbit is caught and prepared fresh daily and travellers can even cook up their own quarry, caught on the hunting excursions that leave daily from the castle Gatehouse.

Bakery

The kitchens at Harrenhal are renowned for their baked dishes, with the cavernous ovens churning out freshly prepared pies, tarts and bread around the clock. The pies are a particular favourite. Filled with nuts, dried fruit and cheese, these pastry-encrusted treats are the ideal accompaniment for a day spent exploring the castle and its grounds.

Beer

The on-site brewhouse means a good flagon of ale is never far away. However, despite its reputation for great beer, make sure you find time to try the hot, spiced wine, a warming alternative that's quickly becoming the tipple of choice for Harrenhal's highborn visitors.

OLDSTONES

A popular destination for daytrippers, Oldstones is the aptly named ruins of an ancient castle. Once the stronghold of the House of Mudd, this ruined refuge sits high on a hill above the Blue Fork, like the crown on a king's head.

Though the local smallfolk long ago made off with the castle's masonry in order to build their barns and homes, the foundations still remain alongside the occasional pile of crumbling stones, which show where the walls and keeps once stood.

The ruins are extensive and offer a glimpse into just why this was one of the Dawn Age's most impregnable fortresses. Beyond its battlements, Oldstones' real attraction lies at its centre and the great carved sepulchre that's somehow survived the test of time. Half-hidden in waist-high brown grass, the sepulchre entombs Tristifer IV Mudd, one-time king of the Riverlands and a fearsome warrior who is said to have fought a hundred battles, winning ninety-nine and losing just one.

Though rain and wind have weathered the monument, it's still possible to make out the warrior king's likeness carved into the stone alongside the fearsome warhammer he still clutches in his hands. It's a sight that's well worth the ride. However, the ascent is not for everyone: the hill leading up to Oldstones is thickly forested with gorse, bracken, thistle and blackberry bushes and the road itself goes twice around the hill before reaching the summit. Though passable, the track is ill maintained and makes for slow going for all but the best of riders.

SALTPANS

This seaside town, located on the Bay of Crabs, east of Harrenhal, is a popular destination for tourists looking to escape the hustle and bustle of castle life and fill their lungs with the scent of sea air.

Whether you're taking in breakfast at the Stinking Goose (the sausages and fried bread aren't great but you're not exactly spoiled for choice in this part of the realm) or exploring the ancestral home of the House Cox, there's plenty to keep you occupied. Most travellers, however, choose to spend a day visiting the Septry, located on a small island half a mile across the bay.

Known as the Quiet Isle, on account of the penitent brothers who live there, the Septry is as stunning as it is sacred; a beautiful tapestry of terraced fields, fishponds and quaint cottages. At high tide a modestly priced ferry shuttles tourists across the bay. However, at low tide tourists have to contend with the muddy flats that surround the isle – an obstacle the locals like to call the Path of Faith. It is said that only the faithful can cross this soggy passage, while the wicked get sucked into the quicksand, so be careful!

Once at the Septry, you can tour the picturesque grounds, which include the Hermit's Hole – a cave said to be the site where the first Holy Man lived when he came to the island, more than 2,000 years ago. Don't let the name fool you, however. The Hermit's Hole is no ordinary cave. Instead, it is richly appointed with woollen carpets, tapestries and driftwood furnishings. There's also a windmill and a small wooden sept for visitors to stroll around. The island even has its own arbour, where small, tart grapes are grown, along with a brewhouse offering some welcome refreshment after a hard day's exploring.

Given the uncertain nature of the bay, the brothers have recently built modest accommodation to house visitors who are trapped by the local tides. These include basic cells in the cloisters for men, alongside more modest accommodation in cottages that have been built to house women. Both are well priced and offer a more-than-adequate option for those who want to wait until morning to make their return journey to Saltpans.

The Iron Islands

The Iron Islands are an archipelago located in the Sunset Sea off the coast of Westeros. Situated west of the Riverlands and northwest of the Westerlands, this holding is one of the smallest regions in the Seven Kingdoms, yet it's punched above its weight to play a very prominent role in the realm's history.

Made up of seven major landmasses – Pyke, Great Wyk, Old Wyk, Harlaw, Saltcliffe, Blacktyde and Orkmont – the Iron Islands are rocky, barren, barely fertile and frequently beset upon by high seas and storm winds. There are no precious metals to be mined here, no lands to farm, or animals to herd so locals spend their nights drinking ale and arguing over whose lot is the worst. All in all, it's not the most attractive of propositions, which is perhaps why the islands' residents have spent the best part of their history raiding the other regions of the Seven Kingdoms.

The Iron Islands are ruled from Pyke, the seat of House Greyjoy and home to an ancient fortress, also called Pyke, which sits precariously on several natural rocky towers which jut out of the sea like spears. Connected by roughshod rope bridges and surrounded by crashing waves, this outlandish outcrop is like no other castle in the Seven Kingdoms; which perhaps explains its appeal to the hardy tourists who brave rough seas and an even rougher welcome to see it with their own eyes.

That welcome is provided by the Ironborn, the rough and ready residents of this part of the realm. There are no farmers or merchants on the Iron Islands. Instead this is a fierce and proud people who take what they want from those around them. Known for their naval supremacy, the kingdom is sometimes called the Islands of Ten Thousand Kings on account of the fact that every man (or woman) who captains a vessel is king on their own ship.

Therein lies the appeal of a trip to the Iron Islands for many travellers. Given Westeros' propensity for order, duty and proper behaviour, this archipelago of outlaws offers a welcome break from the norm; even if it does come with the inherent risk of being made a longship captain's salt wife.

HIGHLIGHTS

Pyke (Page 112)

The heart of the Iron Islands and seat of power for House Greyjoy, Pyke is home to the castle of the same name; a precarious fortress built high along rocky outcrops that rise out of the stormy seas below.

Great Wyk (Page 117)

The largest landmass on the archipelago, Great Wyk is the only Iron Island where a handful of the holdfasts and villages don't face directly into the sea.

Old Wyk (Page 117)

The Ironborn consider Old Wyk to be the holiest of the Iron Islands, the location where legend tells the Grey King slew the sea dragon Nagga. It's here that the First Men are said to have found the Seastone Chair (see pg 115), the throne of the Iron Islands; and here that Kingsmoots (see pg 118) took place for thousands of years before the Greyjoy reign.

Religion

Unlike the majority of the rest of Westeros, the Iron Islanders don't worship the Faith of the Seven. Instead they worship the Drowned God, a brutal deity who is said to dwell in a great watery hall beneath the sea itself. The Iron Islanders believe that the Drowned God put them on the earth to take what they want from the weak, encouraging them to carve out their names in blood, steel and song.

The faithful say that they are born from the sea and that when they die they return to it; it's perhaps unsurprising then that drowning is a prominent part of the religion. Not only is it the method of choice of the Iron Islands' executioners, but it's also seen as a holy act. As such, new-born babies, young children and even grown men are ritually drowned before being quickly resuscitated, an act which commits their bodies to the sea as an offering to the Drowned God so that they may walk his halls once they die.

The clergymen of this religion are known as the Drowned Men. These spiritual leaders earn their place by being drowned for a second time in their lives before once again being resuscitated by their peers. Not all of those who undergo the ritual are revived however, but it is believed that those who do rise from their watery graves have been chosen to spread the word of the Drowned God. These priests are easily spotted thanks to their rough spun robes of mottled green, grey, and blue; the colours both of the sea and of the Drowned God. They also carry driftwood cudgels and skins full of saltwater with which they perform ritual anointments (or just swig from in order to strengthen their faith).

These Drowned Men are an important part of life on the Iron Islands. As well as anointing new-born babes, they also bless ships and offer spiritual guidance to noble lords and smallfolk alike.

Originally settled by the First Men many thousands of years ago, for much of their history each of the Iron Islands was its own individual realm, ruled over by two kings; one a rock king to rule the land and another a salt king to rule the seas.

This changed some 5,000 years ago when King Urron Redhand slaughtered the other kings and established a hereditary line that has ruled over the kingdom ever since. His dynasty led to the resurgence of the Iron Islands, and

---

even today men huddled around driftwood fires will tell you of the old days when Iron Islanders lived by the sword, raping and raiding their way across the Seven Kingdoms. At one time the Iron Islands managed to bring much of the west coast of Westeros under their rule and even conquered the Trident, which lead to the coronation of the first King of the Isles and Rivers.

However, their supremacy was crushed after Aegon's War of Conquest, which pushed the Ironborn back to their islands and brought them under the rule of the Iron Throne. Old habits die hard though and the Iron Islands have consistently proved to be a thorn in the kingdom's side. From raiding parties to outright rebellions, they continue to defy the Iron Throne, and though a previous insurrection was crushed by King Robert Baratheon, recent reports suggest that the islanders are once again intent on invading the mainland.

Local Customs

Whilst part of the Seven Kingdoms, the Iron Island's unique customs mean that this offbeat archipelago can feel a world away from the courts of King's Landing. Some practices to prepare yourself for ahead of time include:

Society – Whilst knights and highborn nobles are regularly referred to as 'Ser' or 'Lord' on the mainland, you'll find no such pretensions on the Iron Islands. Instead even the highest of lords are referred to by their House name.

The Iron Price – Currency can be confusing on the Iron

Islands where everything comes with two price tags. This is because the Old Ways are still highly regarded here and the locals firmly believe reaving and plundering to be the most honourable of pursuits. As such you'll find your money won't go very far on the Iron Islands where the locals believe in paying the Iron Price – relieving their fallen adversaries of their possessions – rather than buying and bartering for wares. From jewellery to weapons, it's actually frowned upon to have paid for your possessions (known locally as the Gold Price) and locals won't wear anything they haven't liberated from a dead enemy. It can be confusing for tourists, but the best advice is to leave your valuables at home – lest you want to defend them with your life.

Family ties – Families are close on the Iron Islands, very close in fact. Indeed the brothers and sisters have been known to be as friendly as Lannister siblings, if you catch our drift.

When to Visit

To be completely honest, life on the Iron Islands is bleak, no matter when you visit. As such travellers can book safe in the knowledge that they'll be getting a traditionally terrible experience no matter when they book.

Dangers and Annoyances

Piracy – Needless to say piracy is a common problem on the Iron Islands. The old ways die hard and even though the Islands have become safer for tourists in recent years, the political tide is constantly shifting and recent reports suggest the Ironborn are back to raiding and reaving on the mainland. Visitors are typically safe once within the

Islands themselves though travellers are advised to be on their guard just in case.

Bridges – Bridges are a way of life on the Iron Islands, particular on Pyke where rough rope bridges knot together the stone pillars on which the castle is built. Though well-maintained, these bridges can be perilous, particularly in high winds or high spirits; even Ironborn kings have been known to fall and dash their brains on the rocks below.

Travel Essentials

Sea legs: Land lubbers are not looked upon kindly in the Iron Islands where the sea is part of the way of life. The only way to get around the Islands is by boat. But be warned, the ride is rough. Squalls and high seas regularly toss and turn the boats so be sure to bring your sea legs lest you find yourself on the receiving end of some not-so-kind jests on behalf of your hosts.

Warm clothing: Wet, cold, windy; the Iron Islands are everything you'd normally avoid in a holiday destination. But for those completists who are intent on ticking off all Seven Kingdoms, warm clothing is essential. Sealskin robes are a favourite with locals – waterproof and warm, they're readily available from Port Downs, where a bargain can be struck if you're not willing to pay the Iron Price.

Famous Residents

Birthplace of House Greyjoy, which has been a constant thorn in the kingdom's side over the centuries; the Iron Islands have also been home to countless brigands, bandits and pirates over the years. Today its most notable residents include Asha Greyjoy, one time heir to the Seastone Chair and an attractive, well-built warrior princess who's immensely popular in these parts. Other famous faces include Euron Greyjoy, the tall, handsome and optically challenged captain of the *Silence* – a ship manned only by mutes who's tongues Euron himself had torn out. There's also Victarion Greyjoy, the bullish commander of the Iron Fleet and Damphair, the Drowned God priest, who travels the Iron Islands drowning people in the name of religion. All in all, they're not the most pleasant bunch of people. I would keep that opinion to myself while travelling anywhere near the Iron Islands though if I were you.

'We Do Not Sow' – Greyjoy family motto.

Getting There

By sea: Unsurprisingly the only way to approach the Iron Islands is by sea. A handful of gold will fetch you safe passage on a Southron merchant vessel from Seagard and a few extra coins will even secure use of the captain's quarters (and possibly his daughter) to boot.

If you're looking for a faster ride however then look out for a longship with an Ironborn captain. These skilled sailors depart regularly from along Ironman's Bay and can make the journey in half the time, so long as they're not distracted by any vessels unfortunate enough to cross their path.

Where to Stay

The tourism industry on the Iron Islands may still be in its infancy but there's a growing assortment of accommodation open to visitors, particularly when the Ironfleet has sailed for distant shores.

Pyke (£££)

One of the Iron Island's largest establishments, staying at Pyke may seem dingy compared to other castles in the Seven Kingdoms, but it's the lap of luxury as far as this offbeat archipelago is concerned. From the outside the castle can seem like a dreary, foreboding place, but within its walls are clean, cosy rooms, like the snug little sleeping cells located in the Sea Keep, ideal for budget-conscious visitors. Those with a little more gold to spend can obtain one of the large, furnished suites inside the Bloody Keep. Though the furnishings have seen better days, the suites have high vaulted ceilings and stunning seafront panoramas. If your room doesn't have a sea view then decamp to the Lord's Solar to nurse a drink and share stories with the locals as you watch the sun set.

Lordsport (££)

If you're headed for Pyke then your ship will most likely stop in at Lordsport, one of the few safe anchorages on the island and a hub for tourists coming to and from the Islands. Though this small harbour town was razed to the ground by Robert Baratheon during the Greyjoy Rebellion, it has since been rebuilt by the enterprising smallfolk who didn't just restore, but completely remodelled, the town's inn. Twice as large as its predecessor this charming three-storey hostel is made from reclaimed stones, some of which are still charred from the former king's assault. But whilst the outside still shows the scars of war, inside you'll find a warm snug hostel that's an ideal spot for travellers to spend the night before heading on to Pyke.

Ten Towers in Harlaw (£)

If you're looking to get away from the hustle and bustle of Pyke, why not head for the easternmost isle of Harlaw, which is located around a day's sail from the Iron Islands' capital. Famed for its shaggy ponies, which are used throughout the kingdom, the isle is home to Ten Towers, the seat of power for House Harlaw and the newest castle in the kingdom. With its distinct towers, the castle looks more like ten fortresses squashed together rather than one solitary structure, which is the appeal for many travellers who love to explore this hodgepodge hostelry's charms. Ten Towers is a popular destination for both would-be rulers and anglers, thanks to the fine fishing that can be found off of its Long Stone Quay.

Eating and Drinking

It's important to remember you're not staying at Highgarden or the Arbor. Indeed, given the lack of farming and pasture to raise herds, food on the Iron Islands can be functional at best. However, thanks to its setting, the Islands do have one thing going for them: great seafood. Peasant stews and rustic soups are popular with locals and are quickly gathering a reputation with tourists too.

Fish stew

The Iron Islands are famed for their fish stews, with each island, harbour and town specialising in their own concoction. From clams to cod you can't go far wrong anywhere on the islands. But for a truly authentic experience head to either the Inn at Lordsport, where the Peppercrab stew is said to be the best in the realm, or the Great Hall at Pyke, where they serve their rich creamy fish stews in trenchers of bread.

Bizarre breakfasts

Whilst porridge is a morning staple, to break your fast like a true Ironborn son try the local delicacy: a clam and seaweed broth served with black bread that's not nearly as bad as it sounds.

Areas of Interest/ What to Do When You're There

Life can be grim on the Iron Islands, but you wouldn't know it to look at the locals. The people here are a strange bunch, but they do know how to live. From finger dances to feasts via kraken-spotting tours and Kingsmoots there's plenty for adventurous travellers to explore on a trip off the west coast of Westeros.

Finger Dance

A favourite pastime of the Iron Islanders, the Finger Dance takes its name from the fact that the dance usually ends with one of the participants losing a digit. It's no surprise really, as it involves a reveller spinning a hand axe whilst another must catch or leap over it without missing a step. It may sound barbaric, but it's a strangely beautiful tradition that can be enjoyed in halls and inns across the Islands. The Ironborn make it look easy... but don't let peer pressure or a few horns of ale tempt you into taking part. The Finger Dance is a skill that needs to be mastered over many years. And yet, despite a protracted campaign to educate travellers, hundreds of tourists every year still leave the Iron Islands with missing digits as a permanent reminder of their visit.

Shopping

Tourists willing to pay the Iron Price can grab themselves a bargain on the Iron Islands, especially if they're willing to wipe away the blood of their opponents once they've haggled over the point of a long sword.

Boat tour

The Iron Islands boast some of the best ships in the land – although the folks at the Arbor may have something to say about that. The harbours around Islands such as Pyke, Great Wyk and Harlaw positively teem with the longships of the famed Ironfleet; expertly crafted vessels that are among the finest, and indeed fastest, in Westeros. So if you really want to get a feel for life on the Iron Islands it's best to take to the water. Tours can be arranged anywhere on the Islands, where captains will be able to show you around the area's stunning coastline. A skilled skipper will even sail you right underneath Pyke's iconic High Bridge and take you out into open waters where it's possible to spot a wild kraken if they're in season.

PYKE

The main attraction for many travellers heading for the Iron Islands, Pyke is the seat of power for House Greyjoy and the central hub of the kingdom – though you wouldn't know it to look upon it. Dark, desolate and dreary; it's not the most inviting of castles, and even family members are said to receive frosty welcomes in these parts. But whilst the reception can be as cold as the weather, Pyke is still one of the most formidable fortresses in the Seven Kingdoms; a seafront structure which looks like it's been cut out of the very cliff it rests upon.

In fact, that's partly true, because much of the castle was built with the same grey-black stone upon which it rests. What's more, being set so close to the sea means that the castle is festooned with lichen and speckled with seagull droppings, making it seem to the casual bystander like just another cliff on the Iron Islands.

Perhaps the most striking thing to note about this ancient castle is its construction. Pyke was originally built on a great cliff that shot out of the sea like a sword. However, thousands of years of erosion has worn away the rock, and all that remains today are three small outcrops along with dozens of small, barren rock stacks upon which the castle's keeps and towers stand. Today, these stacks are connected by a network of stone and rope bridges, perilous crossings which are the only way of travelling from building to building.

PYKE CLIFFTOP HOP

There's no safe anchorage at Pyke itself, so travellers are forced to stop at nearby Lordsport before making the short ride to the outer walls. It's from here that most of the organised tours run, but if you're looking to save some dosh it's just as easy to explore the castle under your own steam with the help of our handy walking tour.

Following a well-beaten path, this short walking tour will introduce you to this ancient castle and the many eccentricities that make it unique amongst all of the Seven Kingdoms.

Start: Castle Gatehouse
End: Sea Tower
Distance: One league
Time: Half a day
Exertion: Easy
Points of interest: Bloody Keep, Sea Tower, High Bridge
Rest stop: Great Hall

1. Castle Gatehouse

Beyond the gatehouse is a small expanse of headland before you reach the castle itself. These lands are taken up with many of the day-to-day functions of the castle. By far the most popular stop for travellers is the stables, where tourists stop to pet the shaggy Harlaw ponies which the Iron Islands are famous for. The stables can be popular so prepare to have to wait your turn.

2. Curtain Wall

Once you've had your fill of pony petting, take some time to examine the curtain wall itself. Pyke's outermost defences still bear the scars of Robert Baratheon's assault, which crushed the Greyjoy rebellion after the Baratheon's ascendance to the throne. There are three great towers guarding the wall. The southernmost however is considerably newer than its fellow fortifications – its paler stones belying the fact that it was here that Baratheon's siege machines broke through the Greyjoy defences.

3. High Bridge

Walk south across the headland and you'll eventually reach

the bridge to the Great Keep. The so-called High Bridge is an architectural marvel that spans the gap between the Gatehouse and the castle's Great Keep. This magnificent stone structure is so big that a skilled captain can sail any longboat beneath its arch. And, when winds and tides are fair, visitors crowd the crenellations in order to get a bird's-eye view of the ships passing below.

4. Great Keep

Once across the bridge you'll enter the Great Keep, the very heart of Pyke, which is located on the castle's largest islet. Here you'll find the smoky Great Hall, a popular pit stop that can seat up to 400 travellers looking to rest their feet and fill their bellies as they tour around the castle. You can sit and sup on fish-stew and roasted goat with your fellow travellers or take your place in the line-up at the dais to get a glimpse of the Seastone Chair, the throne from which the Iron Islands are ruled. Ornately carved into the shape of a kraken, legend has it that this oily blackstone chair was found by the First Men when they originally made land at Old Wyk.

5. Bloody Keep

Farther out from the Great Keep lies the Bloody Keep. Once again located on its own islet, the Bloody Keep is accessed via a long stone archway. This is one of the few covered bridges on Pyke and so it's a popular stop for tourists looking to shelter from the rain whilst admiring the sea views. Once you've had your fill of salt air and spectacular scenery, make your way inside the keep itself. The largest of the castle's structures, the Bloody Keep is where the Greyjoys house their guests, and its here that a smattering of comfortable, well-furnished suites have been opened to cater for well-to-do tourists.

For many however, the Bloody Keep's biggest draw comes not from its lodgings but it's macabre history. Many thousands of years ago it was here that the Greyjoys slaughtered the sons of Bernarr II Justman, the last King of the Trident. The boys were killed in their beds and pieces of them were sent back to the mainland as a message. Sick with grief, and intent on revenge, Justman died waging a fruitless war against the Ironborn.

6. Sea Tower

Once you've seen the spot where the boys were butchered in their sleep, make your way to the Sea Tower. Located on the outermost island of Pyke the Sea Keep is the oldest part of the castle. Round and tall, this sheer tower has slowly been eroded by the elements, and despite the best efforts of conservationists, will one day be sucked into the sea entirely. To get to the Sea Tower you must first navigate a series of ever-narrower rope bridges. *Be careful.* They are known to be perilous when slick with sea spray and can sway wildly in the storm winds. Several tourists, and even a few of the Ironborn, every year end up dashing their brains on the rocks below.

Once across, your dice with death will prove worth the risk. Many tourists choose to enjoy a drink in the Lord's Solar or, if the weather's nice, climb the castle stairs to the soot-stained watchtower to see some of the best sea views in all the Seven Kingdoms. The best time to visit is at dusk where the sun dips below the horizon, turning the sea into a patchwork of magnificent blues and purples.

GREAT WYK

The largest of the Iron Islands, Great Wyk is the only place in the kingdom where you can get away from the sea for an hour or two as you explore inland. Home to noble Houses Merlyn, Sparr and Farwynd, alongside some of the most affordable accommodations in the region, it's especially popular with tourists thanks to its proximity to the nearby Hammerhorn. It's also a popular destination for hikers with well-maintained trails tracing the battle lines where Stannis Baratheon subdued the isle during the rebellion.

OLD WYK

The holiest of all the Iron Islands, Old Wyk is home to sacred sites like Nagga's Cradle and the beach where the Seastone chair is said to have been discovered by the First Men. Home to noble houses such as Shatterstone, Stonehouse, Drumm and Goodbrother, Old Wyk is a popular daytrip for tourists who'd rather spend a day on the windy black mountains that make up much of the island, rather than their entire trip.

Nagga's Hill

Located on the island of Old Wyk, this site is sacred to the Ironborn; a holy bay where the remains of the Grey King's Hall rest. These remains, known as Nagga's Ribs, consist of forty-four monstrous white stone pillars that are, according to local legend, the ribs of a great sea dragon which was used to form the beams and pillars of the Grey King's Hall (see below).

A sacred place for the Ironborn, Nagga's Cradle also plays a significant role in the politics of the region. It was here that the Islanders would hold a Kingsmoot, an ancient ceremony where the captains of the longships met to vote on their new king. The practice was forgotten for more than four thousand years but was recently revived to elect Euron Greyjoy as the new Iron King. Nagga's Hill is open to the public and entry is free, but visitors are expected to bring a gift in exchange for entrance.

The Grey King

Almost as important as the Drowned God to the Ironborn is the Grey King, an ancestral ruler whose modern day heirs are said to be House Greyjoy. Legend has it that the Grey King was chosen by the Drowned God himself, who helped the king to kill the great sea dragon Nagga.

The story goes that Nagga was the first sea dragon, a monstrous creature that could feast on kraken and leviathan and would even flood islands in its anger. Yet, with the help of the Drowned God, the Grey King slayed her and turned her bones into the beams and pillars of his Great Hall and her jaws into his throne.

Legend has it that the hall was warmed by Nagga's fire and that the Grey King's men feasted at a table shaped like starfish, and sat on mother of pearl thrones. The Grey King is said to have reigned for a 1007 years and took a mermaid for his wife with whom he plotted war against the Storm God. However upon his death the Storm God snuffed out Nagga's fire and his great throne was sucked back into the depths of the ocean.

The Reach

The continent's second wealthiest region behind the Westerlands and its second largest behind the North, the Reach would be the Cinderella of the geographical ball if not for its rich soils, which make it the most bountiful realm in all of Westeros.

Famed for its fertile farmlands, which are watered by the River Mander and its tributaries, the Reach is the breadbasket of the Seven Kingdoms and a leading producer of the grains and fruits that feed this country.

Over the centuries a thriving economy has been built on these lands, attracting vast swathes of civilisation who've come to gorge themselves on the physical and financial nourishment served up by the soil – there's a reason why they say everyone is fat and drunk and rich in the Reach, you know. The end result is one of the most densely populated realms in all of Westeros and a kingdom where the culture is every bit as rich as the land from which it has sprung.

Ranging from the Red Mountains of Dorne in the south to the Westerlands in the north, and the Sunset Sea in the west to the Stormlands in the east, tourists could spend a lifetime falling in love with the kingdom. Many do. For visitors, however, a quick trip around the highlights serves to give them a feel for what the Reach is all about. Those highlights include Highgarden, the seat of power for the House of Tyrell and the heart of the kingdom. With its tiered walls, shaded groves and marble colonnades, the castle is more pleasure palace than fortification; a sumptuous citadel filled with the sound of singers and harpists rather than swordsmiths and men-at-arms.

Beyond Highgarden are the market town of Ashford and the historical hub of Oldtown – the oldest city in the Seven Kingdoms and home of the Maester's Citadel, while those looking to get away from the crush of civilisation can take a pleasure cruise up the River Mander or explore the outstanding natural beauty of the Ocean Road.

Of course, no trip to the region would be complete without making the journey southwest to explore the Arbor. If the Reach is the Westeros's breadbasket, this small island haven located a stone's throw from the mainland's shore is most certainly its wine cellar. Home to an exquisite array of wines that are considered by many to be the finest vintages in the entire known world, the Arbor is a must-see for any traveller making the journey to the region.

With its pretty picturesque towns, flower-filled fields and bustling markets, it's no surprise that thousands of tourists flock to the Reach every year to enjoy its spoils. No trip to Westeros would be complete without indulging in the particular delights served up by this plentiful kingdom.

HIGHLIGHTS

Highgarden (page 131)
The heart of the kingdom, filled with sun-soaked courtyards, groves and fountains, the castle is a feast for the senses and renowned for its endless gardens filled with golden roses.

Oldtown (page 132)
The oldest city in all of the Seven Kingdoms, Oldtown is a must-see for any traveller visiting Westeros. The home of the order of the Maesters, the place is steeped in history and filled with tourists pounding its cobbled streets in search of it.

The Arbor (page 142)
Famed throughout the known world for its fine vintages, every corner of the Arbor is filled with vines producing the kind of wines that will one day adorn the table of lords, ladies and even the occasional monarch.

Getting There and Getting About

By land: With borders to five other kingdoms, the Reach is easily accessible by land. The main artery of transport to and from the region is the Roseroad, a busy route running from Oldtown to King's Landing via Highgarden and Bitterbridge. Though it can be closed by the Tyrells during times of conflict, the Roseroad offers safe and secure transport for tourists looking to travel to the region from the country's capital. Those looking to travel via the Westerlands can take a scenic stroll along the Ocean Road, a popular course to explore some of Westeros's iconic coastal scenery.

By sea: The Sunset Sea located on its western coast means that travelling to the Reach via sea is increasingly preferred by tourists looking to save the time (and money) they'd spend on travelling by land. Port towns such as Old Oak, Blackcrown and Ryamsport provide hubs for tourism and trade alike. The *Myraham*, a fat-bellied merchants' vessel, also runs a regular service to and from Pyke from Oldtown. However, travellers are advised to send a raven before they set off, as recent raids by the Iron Islanders have made travel by sea precarious of late (see Dangers and Annoyances).

Creatures, Flora and Fauna

Roses

Famed across the Seven Kingdoms for its flora, the Reach is often called the flowerbed of Westeros, thanks to its abundant blooms. Everywhere you look there's a patchwork of colourful buds but perhaps the region's most unique offering are its roses, which adorn both the realm and the sigil of its ruling House. Nowhere are they more noticeable than around Highgarden itself, where fields of Golden Roses, unique to this part of the continent, stretch as far as the eye can see.

Produce

Its warm climate and rich soils mean that the Reach is filled with all manner of foods that you can't find anywhere else in the Seven Kingdoms. From succulent fireplums to melons, peaches and some of the best vines in the known world, you can pick the produce straight from the tree in just about every corner of the region.

Travel Essentials

Clothes: Thanks to its southerly location the Reach has a more temperate climate than every other kingdom in Westeros, save that of Dorne. Snowfall here is practically unheard of in all but the harshest of winters; instead the weather is warm and so hot you can barely move during the height of summer.

As a result, everything in this region of Westeros is a little more laid-back, including the dress code, which mirrors the climate. Short gowns made of silk are a must for women travelling to this part of the continent, while men will find that they must shed the wools and leathers that are common in other parts of the continent in favour of altogether more appropriate attire.

Dangers and Annoyances

Ironborn Raiders: The Ironborn's blood has been up ever since Euron Greyjoy's ascension to the Seastone Chair. Greyjoy has vowed to conquer the whole of Westeros and began his campaign with a surprise attack on the Reach. With their forces off fighting for the Crown in the Riverlands, the realm was left unprotected and suffered staggering losses on the Shield Islands, the defence outpost built to defend the kingdom from attack by sea. Though efforts are being made to stem the assaults, the Iron Islanders are becoming increasingly bold, attacking as far as the Arbor over recent moons. Tourists should seek advice before they visit, especially if they plan to travel by sea.

CHIVALRY

Knights both anointed and landed play an important role across Westeros. But nowhere are the sword-wielding Sers more celebrated than in the Reach – the self-styled home of chivalry for the Seven Kingdoms.

Knights are revered here and a lifetime spent with sword in hand is among the most esteemed of existences. While skills with sword or lance might be prized across the rest of the continent, it is honour above all else that is valued in the Reach. Chivalry is everything and knights from Oldtown to Highgarden are taught how to respect their opponents and their charges before even learning to swing a sword.

This deep-rooted sense of chivalry stems from the Faith of the Seven, the religion of choice for most residents of southern Westeros. The faith is strongest in the south, where the Andals first landed, and has permeated every aspect of the culture, particularly knighthood. Here, knights are celebrated like celebrities and tourneys are a particular favourite with locals, who come to cheer on the chivalrous Sers. In fact, it is in the Reach that Westeros's first ever tourney is said to have taken place. The event, which, according to legend, featured fifty lords competing for the hand of Maris the Maid, set in place the tourney traditions that are still strictly observed to this day.

Famous Residents

The Tyrells are by far the most famous faces in this part of Westeros. A formidable House whose military strength is matched only by its wealth, the younger siblings have become famed socialites who draw admirers from across the Seven Kingdoms. Despite her recent move to King's Landing, Margaery Tyrell, the only daughter of Lord Mace Tyrell, is well liked in these parts and, indeed, across Westeros. With her soft curled hair and shapely figure, it's easy to see why so many kings (three and counting) have fallen for her charms. Her brother, Loras Tyrell, is equally easy on the eye. The so-called Knight of Flowers is a skilled warrior whose talents with a lance and dazzling good looks have made him a fan favourite on the tourney circuit. Now a member of the King's Guard, it is said that half the girls in the Seven Kingdoms want to bed him and half the boys want to be him.

When to Visit

Its southerly location and temperate climate make the Reach a popular hotspot for tourists all year round. Even in the harshest of winters the region seems impervious to the snow that blights the rest of Westeros and so tourists might be able to find themselves an out-of-season bargain in the continent's breadbasket. By far the most popular time to travel is during the autumn, when the aroma of wild flowers and freshly cut vines fills the air and the temperatures have cooled from their stifling summer heights.

Where to Stay

From the high society of Highgarden to quaint thatched cottages in bustling market towns, there's accommodation aplenty for travellers visiting the Reach. Some highlights include:

Highgarden (£££)

If you're looking for luxury, search no further than the splendour of Highgarden, a castle famed throughout Westeros for its hospitality. Opulent, indulgent and unflinchingly extravagant, within its tiered walls lies a cornucopia of comforts, from shaded courtyards to ornate halls. Just off the marble colonnades that snake throughout the stone fortress there are scores of beautifully appointed rooms, each one filled with the aroma of fresh flowers cut daily from the fields surrounding the Tyrells' seat of power.

Alongside the accommodation, there's plenty of entertainment on offer, from the fiddlers, singers and harpists who seem to gravitate to Highgarden for the good times and the well-to-do guests. In fact, there's so much for you to do that your only problem will be trying to fit it all in.

Horn Hill (££)

Home to the Tarlys – an old family with rich lands, a strong keep and a curious way of treating their children – Horn Hill is a great bolthole for visitors looking to escape the hustle and bustle of the Reach. Set in hilly woodlands a hundred leagues northeast of Oldtown, this comfortable keep is filled with travellers supping on local game (ask the owner about hunting rights) and being regaled by tales of Lord Randyll's valour. Make sure you ask to see Heartsbane, the Valyrian sword that has been in the family for generations. But whatever you do, don't mention Lord Randyll's erstwhile son Sam, lest you want to wind up sleeping in the stables.

Ashford Castle (£)

A bustling market town that sits at a fording of the Cockleswent River, this affordable – if isolated – homestead is an ideal choice for travellers looking to save their gold for summerwine and spun sugar. Filled with row upon row of adorable whitewashed holiday homes, there's no shortage of accommodation, although those looking to stay in the town's triangular castle should book early to avoid disappointment.

Eating and Drinking

It should come as no surprise that the Reach offers some of the finest food anywhere in the Seven Kingdoms. From succulent produce to fine Arbor vintages, the chefs here have their pick of the best ingredients.

Summerwine

Cheap and plentiful, Summerwine is abundant in this part of the Seven Kingdoms, where the temperate climate and mineral-rich soils are perfect for growing the succulent sweet grapes essential for this vintage. Sold almost everywhere you'll find people, its affordability means that you can expect to see many a merry local who will happily dip their hand into their purse to buy a cup. Best enjoyed in an inn or straight from a skin during a ride to take in the Reach's stunning natural scenery, casks are also a popular souvenir for tourists looking to take a taste of the South home with them.

Sweets

Highgarden is famed for its food but while the savoury treats that are served from its kitchens will fill your belly, the sweets produced within the castle walls will delight even the most sophisticated of palates. From exquisitely crafted pastries and lemon cakes shaped like roses to spiced honey biscuits, blackberry tarts and apple crisps, there's a plethora of sugary treats on offer for visitors.

Sugar spinning is a local delicacy here and skilled chefs attempt to outdo each other by crafting ever more intricate sculptures, like unicorns and cream-filled swans almost as easy on the eye as they are in the mouth. The rich ingredients mean that these saccharine treats aren't to everyone's taste but it's impossible not to marvel at the craftsmanship involved in creating them.

Areas of Interest/What to Do When You're There

From wine tasting in the Arbor to pleasure cruises along the Mander, there are plenty of activities for travellers looking to pamper themselves during a trip to the Reach. Those looking for a little more excitement can take in a tourney or feed their sweet tooth with a sugar-spinning class.

Pleasure boat along the Mander

Departing daily from Highgarden and sailing along the Mander, pleasure-boat tours are popular with tourists and locals alike. Passengers can enjoy the cool breeze off the water as their barge carries them slowly south, taking in unobstructed views of the surrounding country from the comfort of the shaded decks. More like palaces than pleasure boats, these vessels are steeped in luxury, with

Dornish silk cushions adorning the decks and exquisitely carved furniture filling the bedchambers. Your every need will be taken care of by servants who will ensure your glass of summerwine never runs dry and your plate is always filled with freshly made pastries and produce from the on-board chef.

Though your waistline may be a little larger by the time you disembark, you can rest assured that your purse will be light enough to compensate for the extra pounds. After all, these tours don't come cheap but travellers with the purse to match their ambitions can expect to enjoy the experience of a lifetime: a lavish cruise through a landscape that they'll be talking about for years to come.

Wine tasting in the Arbor

No visit to the Reach would be complete without a trip to the Arbor, the wine-growing region famed throughout the known world. Separated from the mainland by the Redwyne Straits, boats depart regularly from the nearby towns of Blackcrown and Three Towers, ferrying thirsty tourists to the island. Most of these ferries put in at Ryamsport, where the dockside is filled with locals touting their tours.

Aside from the price – be sure to haggle for the best possible deal – there is very little difference between each of the operators. Most begin with a ride through the nearby vineyards, where your guide will educate you on the climate and clay-rich soil that make the Arbor ripe for wine growing. From there you'll head for Vinetown, where the real fun starts. After a tour of the facilities, where you'll see how the wine is produced and aged, it's time for the all-important business of tasting the local produce. From iconic Arbor golds to rich reds, summerwines and even the occasional sour wine, your cup will be filled with the finest the region has to offer. Once you've had your fill, there's just time to buy a skin of your favourite swill (or even a cask, if you're feeling particularly flush) before staggering back to the port to hitch your ferry ride home.

Learn to spin sugar

After sampling some of the local sugar-spun treats, why not take a course to attempt to master the skill for yourself? Pastry chefs in the Reach train for years in order to sculpt the exquisite treats that you'll find served up throughout the kingdom and while you won't be creating your own swans or unicorns on your first attempt, an afternoon spent in the company of these experts could have you forging your own cattle, or at least a tasty mess you can pretend is cattle.

Classes are offered at most of the region's major castles but the best place to try your hand at sugar spinning is in Highgarden, where the master confection craftsmen operate. Admission includes an afternoon's tuition alongside all of the equipment and ingredients you'll need. Tourists can even take freshly made treats home with them, provided they can resist them for that long.

Take in a tourney

It's impossible to swing a lance in the Reach without coming across a tourney or two. The self-styled centre of chivalry is renowned for its reverence for knighthood and regularly hosts competitions for locals looking to hone their skills with sword, mace and lance. Tourneys are a very serious business here, with stringent rules and regulations upheld by every entrant. But despite its fussiness over the finer details, the pageantry in the Reach is unparalleled within the Seven Kingdoms.

Participants in this part of the realm prize their appearance as much as their abilities. Expect elaborately enamelled armour and shining plates alongside some of the finest blades you'll ever see. It's not just the knights who are easy on the eye, either. The tourneys here are often edge-of-your-seat affairs, with knights jousting for glory or going toe-to-toe to defend a maiden's honour. For information on tourneys, head to the local castle and seek out the Master of Games, who will be able to update you on the very latest events.

HIGHGARDEN

The jewel in the Reach's crown is undoubtedly Highgarden, home to the House of Tyrell and administrative centre of the kingdom. Not that all that much administrating goes on beyond the castle walls, however. In fact, the fortress is famed throughout the Seven Kingdoms for the quality of life it offers.

The architecture here is almost as stunning as the fields of golden roses surrounding Highgarden. Filled with groves, fountains and shady courtyards, it is possible to lose hours wandering through the tiered walls and marble colonnades, picking fireplums from the trees or stopping to hear a harpist pluck a tune.

And it's not just the architecture that's stunning; the entertainment here is top notch too. While some castles are filled with men-at-arms, Highgarden is packed to the rafters with singers, fiddlers and pipers, who ensure the court remains one of the most civilised in all of Westeros. The wildlife is also A-grade. Local Lord Willas Tyrell is known to breed some of the finest animals in the Seven Kingdoms, including prize-winning hawks, hounds and horses. With sumptuous food and summerwine that runs like water, it's easy to see why so many people choose to spend the bulk of their stay at the castle. Others, of course, decide to take in Highgarden's unique pleasures in a single day and although it is possible to do a whistlestop tour of the grounds, the best solution for travellers is probably somewhere between the two extremes.

OLDTOWN

Built by the First Men, long before the Andal invasion, travellers have been making their way to Oldtown since records began. The oldest city in Westeros – and one of its largest – this ancient settlement in the mouth of the Honeywine was once the continent's capital until King Aegon I Targaryen's arrival and the establishment of King's Landing.

Runic records tell us that the city traces its roots back to the Dawn Age when the First Men and Maesters claim to have lived alongside the Children of the Forest. What started out as a small settlement quickly developed into a trading post where merchants from Valyria, Old Ghis and the Summer Isles put in to take on provisions and trade with the locals. As the city grew wealthy and powerful, so it attracted the attention of outsiders. In the early centuries pirates operated out of Oldtown, plundering passing ships – indeed, the building that currently operates as the Ravenry of the Citadel is said to have once been the stronghold of a pirate lord. Later, the city attracted the attention of outside powers. It was sacked three times in one century and only survived the Andal invasion by opening its doors to aggressors.

Today the city is a labyrinth of wynds, alleys and crooked backstreets, divided up by vast canals and criss-crossed with endless bridges. Its quaint cobbled streets are known throughout Westeros and the stunning stone mansions and guildhalls can rival even King's Landing's architectural marvels. The jewel in the city's crown is, of course, the Citadel: the centre for the order of Maesters who still serve lords throughout the Seven Kingdoms. The Maesters are not the only order to have adopted Oldtown, however. The city's Starry Sept was the base for the Faith of the Seven until the Great Sept of Baelor was constructed in King's Landing. By the water's edge you'll also find scores of temples dedicated to all manner of gods that are worshipped by the sailors who dock here from foreign shores.

The end result is a cacophony; a city full of culture clashes and contradictions, of old gods and new, familiar Westerosi customs and peculiar foreign practices. But therein lies its appeal for travellers. Whether you're exploring the architecture, sampling the local delights or shopping at one of the wharfside bazaars, it's almost impossible to fully experience everything that Oldtown has to offer. And that's what keeps people coming back.

Dangers and Annoyances

Slippery when wet: While the cobblestone streets that give Oldtown its picture-perfect charm are one of the city's biggest draws, they're also one of its greatest hazards, responsible for injuring scores of tourists each and every year. Slick after centuries of use, the streets can get slippery when the river mist descends on Oldtown. Travellers should be careful not to fall, especially if they've enjoyed an ale or two at the Quill and Tankard.

Alchemists: Don't trust alchemists. Sure, they can make coins dance across their knuckles but don't take their promises to heart. At best you could lose a few gold coins, at worse you might lose your life. If you are approached by an alchemist, be sure to seek out a member of Oldtown's City Watch, the city's formal policing and protection units currently run by Lord Moryn Tyrell.

Noise: While the clatter of hooves on the cobblestone roads may seem quaint at first, it can be a constant cause of irritation for light sleepers who struggle to get off without a dose of Dreamwine. If you do happen to drift off, you can be sure of a rude awakening. At dawn the bells from the Sept ring out across the city and first light is filled with the prayers and incantations of the Red Priests. Locals learn to sleep through the din, but for visitors, the noise can take time to adjust to.

Eating and Drinking

There's plenty to sink your teeth into in these ancient streets, with culinary havens seemingly tucked around every corner.

The Quill and Tankard (£)

An Oldtown institution, the Quill and Tankard is known for its fearsomely strong ciders and comely wenches, which have been drawing in the punters for more than six centuries now. They say the inn has never closed in all of that time and even today the place is filled around the clock with a cross section of society, from seamen, smiths and singers to rivermen and would-be Maesters. With its torch-lit terrace, which looks directly onto the lapping waters of the Honeywine, this sloping timber drinking den is a great spot for some alfresco drinking or to quench your thirst after a hard day exploring the city's streets.

The Checkered Hazard (££)

This upmarket gastro inn is a popular hotspot that's filled with well-to-do locals playing tiles while supping on expensive Arbor gold. However, it's the food here that attracts most people through the door, with suckling pig in plum sauce served with chestnuts and white truffles a house speciality.

Areas of Interest/What to Do When You're There

From ancient history to a spot of shopping, there's something for everyone on the ancient streets of Oldtown.

Climb the Hightower

At 800ft tall this colossal lighthouse, built to safely guide ships through the Whispering Sound, is the highest structure in all of Westeros, even eclipsing the Wall that stands leagues to the north. Its origins are unknown, with some scholars claiming the structure dates back to Old Valyria, while others suggest it was built by the Mazemakers much later. Whatever its history, the Hightower is, without question, one of the marvels of the modern world.

The tower stands so high that the locals say they can tell the time based on the shadow it casts across the city and while a vertigo-inducing stare from its base can give you some idea of the Hightower's size, you can only truly appreciate its scale from on high. Climbing the 800ft to its roof is no mean feat but those who hack up the Hightower are rewarded with jaw-dropping views of the surrounding country. On any given day travellers can enjoy staggering vistas of Oldtown, the Reach and the surrounding kingdoms. And when the weather is clear, it is said that you can see all the way to the Wall.

Visit the markets

Oldtown's place as a bustling trade post between the Seven Kingdoms and beyond means that the city is a shopper's paradise. The wharfside markets here are crammed to the gills with goods from all corners of the known world. Firepeppers from Dorne, fine Myrish carpets and exotic spiceflower perfumes from the Dothraki plains all fill the stalls here with foreign imports standing side-by-side with Westerosi favourites.

The best bargains can be found at the aptly named Thieves' Market, where wine and cloth (two of Oldtown's more popular exports) are in abundance. Those travellers looking to get their hands on one of Oldtown's now infamous Woodharps should head towards the city proper, where there is a burgeoning trade for these iconic and highly sought-after instruments.

See the glass candles

Originally brought to these shores from Old Valyria, these ancient candles are formed of obsidian, the glass-like substance more commonly referred to as Dragonglass. Tall and twisted, these razor-sharp objects aren't like normal candles; in fact, they haven't burned since the last of the Targaryen dragons died out. Yet that still doesn't stop tourists who flock to see these ancient artefacts every year in the hope that they might one day be reignited, signalling the return of sorcery to a realm that has almost forgotten what magic looks like.

Stroll through the Septs

Once the centre for the continent's spiritual leaders, it is perhaps no surprise that religious sites take up prime real estate in Oldtown, with temples and Septs occupying almost every major street. Most of these are reachable on foot and many travellers choose to take them in during a leisurely stroll through the city. The Starry Sept, once the seat of the High Septon until Aegon's landing, is a popular draw with tourists, as is the Lord's Sept in the centre of the city and the Sailor's Sept down by the dockside. Those looking for a little more solitude to go with their spirituality, however, should catch a ferry across the Honeywine to the Seven Shrines that fill the gardens on the opposite bank of the city.

WHAT'S IN A CHAIN?

Known as the Knights of the Mind, the Maesters are the pre-eminent scholars, healers and councillors of the Seven Kingdoms. No matter how small, almost every castle in the realm has its own Maester to help guide its lord, heal its sick and teach its children.

Every one of these Maesters has been trained at Oldtown's Citadel. It is here that they learn their trade, forging the links of the neck chains they'll wear until the day they die. These collars signify that the Maesters do not serve themselves but are, instead, the servants of Westeros. They also represent their mastery of certain subjects and skills. Look closely and you'll notice that the chains consist of an assortment of different links made up of every metal known to man. These links are sacred to the Maesters and each one represents a different chapter of their education. Some notable links to look out for include:

Black iron – Ravenry
Bronze – Astronomy
Copper – History
Electrum – Astrology
Yellow Gold – Economics
Iron – Warcraft
Pale steel – Smithing
Silver – Healing
Valyrian steel – Magic and the occult.

The Citadel

The headquarters for the order of the Maesters, the Citadel is one of the most popular attractions in all of Oldtown. Its popularity has been a boon for the Maesters themselves, who have used the burgeoning tourism industry to supplement the income they make through the taxation of local residents. That money goes into training the Maesters of tomorrow. It is here in the Citadel that acolytes are trained in the ways of the world, that they forge their chains and learn the skills they will one day impart in castles across the Seven Kingdoms.

A WALKING TOUR OF THE CITADEL

Founded many centuries ago, the Citadel itself is well worth an afternoon of your time. While fresh-faced Acolytes serve as guides for organised tours, the best way to explore the Citadel is under your own steam. Indeed, it is possible to take in most of the important sites on foot. The guide below serves as a rough itinerary to help you tick off the must-see sights.

Start: The Main Gates

End: Isle of Ravens

Distance: ¾ league

Time: ½ day

Exertion: Easy

Points of interest: Scribe's Hearth, Weeping Dock, Seneschal's Court

1. The Main Gates

Start your stroll at the Citadel's main gates. While here, take a moment to admire the sphinxes that sit astride the building's entrance. These green giants have the bodies of

---

lions, the wings of eagles and the tails of serpents. Though worn over the centuries, it is just possible to make out their faces, one of which is that of a man and the other a woman.

2. Scribe's Hearth

Step through the gates and you can start to appreciate the sensational structure of the Citadel. Located on the Honeywine itself, most of the towers and domes are connected by arching stone bridges, each of which houses its own buildings. The first thing you will notice is the Scribe's Hearth, the spot where Oldtown residents come to employ the skills of the Acolytes, writing and reading letters and other documents for them. The Acolytes are arranged in open stalls that spread across the courtyard. From here you can also pick up guide maps to help you find your way around the Citadel.

3. Weeping Dock

Oft used by the Maesters and Acolytes who call the Citadel home, the Weeping Dock is a transport hub, with ferries regularly carrying passengers along the Honeywine to quays across Oldtown. For visitors touring the Citadel, however, it's a great spot to stop and take in the view, as it offers commanding vistas over the Bloody Isle and beyond.

4. Seneschal's Court

After stopping to admire the riverside views of Oldtown, make your way to Seneschal's Court, the central hub of Citadel life. The Seneschal is the head of the Maesters order; the figurehead charged with governing the Citadel and its servants. Chosen each year by a democratic vote, the Seneschal is required to offer audience to lords, Maesters and lowborn Westerosi seeking their counsel. This counsel is offered in the Seneschal's Court, a grandiose audience chamber that makes up the next stop on our walking tour. Once inside, take a moment to admire the ancient stone floor and high arched windows before making your way to the dais at the end of the hall to see the spot where the Seneschal holds court.

5. Isle of Ravens

As you leave Seneschal's Court, keep an eye on your surroundings. It is here that Acolytes are punished for petty crimes and the fruit and veg aimed at the stocks can often come perilously close to unsuspecting tourists. Once you've dodged the volleys of rotten produce, make your way to the Isle of Ravens, the final stop on our brief walking tour. Once the stronghold of a pirate lord who pillaged any ships foolish enough to sail into the Honeywine, these days the Isle roosts ravens carrying messages across the Seven Kingdoms.

The oldest wing of the Citadel, the Isle of Ravens is accessed via a weatherworn drawbridge, which looks almost as old as the Seven Kingdoms themselves. Once across the rickety walkway, you're greeted by an ancient-looking keep covered in moss, vines and bird droppings. It's an inauspicious introduction to a building that is arguably the most important in all of Westeros, even eclipsing iconic structures like the Wall and the Red Keep. Why? Because it is here that ravens are dispatched to all corners of the Seven Kingdoms. The Maesters are in control of all communications on the continent and from bountiful harvests to the results of bloody battles, these black birds ferry information from castle to castle. Most of them can trace their roots back to here, where the Maesters breed and train the birds for their life in service.

The white-raven rookery is located on the isle's westernmost tower. It can get busy during peak season, with scores of tourists lining up to feed the famous birds, so be prepared to wait a while to catch a glimpse of the airborne attractions.

THE ARBOR

The Arbor is renowned for its winemaking throughout the known world but although thousands of tourists travel to the small island's shores every year in search of a glimpse into the journey Arbor gold takes from vine to cup, few choose to stay more than a few hours. However, those who do find one of the Seven Kingdoms' hidden gems: an island paradise filled with natural beauty, fascinating history and few empty cups.

After all, the temperate climate and lush soil aren't just ripe for winemaking, they're perfect for creating the kind of place where a Westerosi can kick his/her boots off. Most vineyards offer guestrooms, giving travellers an opportunity to relax and enjoy the stunning natural scenery and sea views. But beyond the vineyards there is much more to the Arbor than meets the eye. The island has a strong military history, with shipyards that have mustered fleets for generations. The islands' constant clashes with the Ironborn have also left their mark on the landscape and it's possible to tour the battlements, which are still in use to this day. Elsewhere, settlements such as Vinetown, Starfish Bay and Mermaid's Palace provide an opportunity to immerse yourself in the everyday lives of the locals, while island hopping around the area's assorted atolls, including Stonecrab Clay and Horseshoe Rock, is increasingly popular with travellers coming south from the Iron Islands.

The Vale
of Arryn

Located on the easternmost edge of the realm, the Vale of Arryn – or simply the Vale, as it is more commonly referred to – is a kingdom full of contradictions. A land of near-impassable mountains mixed with bountiful fertile farmlands, of impregnable terrain punctuated with stunning architectural marvels, this contradiction makes up much of its charm for travellers, who traverse treacherous terrain to explore this eccentric outpost.

Thanks to the Mountains of the Moon – the colossal range in which the kingdom is set – the Vale has long been cut off from the rest of Westeros. In times of war this inaccessibility has served the kingdom well, protecting it from all but the most powerful of invaders. For millennia it also restricted travel to and from the region, with only the hardiest explorers braving the perilous journey. However, the long summer has led to an explosion in tourism as more and more people decided to venture to this isolated outpost.

What they found once they arrived was a kingdom unspoilt by war, a sparsely populated territory that has barely changed since the Andals first landed, several thousand years ago. Alongside its people and practices, the Vale's landscape has also remained largely untouched. Filled with mirror-like rivers and snow-peaked mountains, it boasts some of the most stunning natural scenery in all of Westeros.

The Eyrie is, perhaps, the region's biggest draw. An impregnable castle set within the almighty spires of the Mountains of the Moon, this fearsome fortress is as spectacular as it is stout. The Eyrie is the centre of the kingdom and a basecamp from which many travellers choose to explore the surrounding area, including the Giant's Lance – one of Westeros's highest peaks – and Alyssa's Tears – the ghostly waterfall that springs from its summit. Beyond the Eyrie, travellers can explore the Vale's coast, which stretches from the Bay of Crabs in the South to the Fingers further north, taking in major harbours such as Gulltown and small port towns, including Old Anchor and Coldwater. Those looking inland can enjoy adrenaline-fuelled adventures in the Mountains of the Moon or the arts and crafts offered in towns such as Wickenden, an artisanal outpost famed for its scented candles.

HIGHLIGHTS

The Vale (page 151)

An oasis of life nestled within a vast valley at the centre of the Mountains of the Moon, the Vale is one of the Seven Kingdoms' best-kept secrets. With lush landscapes that rival the bountiful beauties of Highgarden and architecture to compete with King's Landing, it's a must-see for any traveller.

The Mountains of the Moon (page 148)

Fearsome, formidable and undoubtedly breathtaking, the mountain range that dominates the Vale has long deterred all but the most hardy of travellers. However, the lengthy summer has seen travellers flocking to the jutting granite spires to hike, climb and mingle with the rustic local clansmen who are descended from the First Men themselves.

Wickenden (page 168)

A haven for artisans, Wickenden is one of the creative hubs of the Seven Kingdoms. Small and relatively untouched by the rigours of modern Westerosi life, its reputation for embracing the arts has made it a mecca for mummers, singers, painters and anyone else with a creative bent.

The Fingers (page 169)

Barren, rocky and windswept, these peninsulas were the point where the Andals first landed on Westeros's shores. The site of one of the most important chapters in the kingdom's history, the area is awash with history buffs, who come from all corners of the known world to retrace the footsteps of their ancestors.

Getting There and Getting About

By land: Most people travel to the Vale via the High Road, which heads eastwards from the Inn at the Crossroads near the Trident. Little more than a stony trail, the High Road can be perilous, especially during winter when it is near impassable. Several days' ride over rocky terrain, the High Road certainly lives up to its name, traversing the summits of the Mountains of the Moon before descending into the Vale through the Bloody Gate. Often dangerous and always daunting, travellers are advised to employ a good guide and a sure-footed mountain pony to ensure they make it to the Vale relatively unscathed.

By sea: If you want to escape the attention of the local clansmen or the arduous journey along the High Road, consider approaching the Vale by sea. The nearby port at Gulltown is a popular stop for merchantmen as well as travellers embarking ships to and from the east.

Dangers and Annoyances

Mountain clans – While the Vale is ruled by the Eyrie, not everyone in the kingdom bends their knee to the Warden of the East. As a result, mountain clans and bands of lawless brigands stalk the Vale, preying on travellers, tourists and locals alike. Traditionally, these clansmen had remained largely in check but the mysterious death of Jon Arryn – the late Hand to the King and Lord of the Eyrie – means they have become more active in the region. A recent report received by a travelling farmer and his effeminate son suggest that the clansmen have become bolder of late and have even been spotted carrying castle-forged steel, rather than the primitive weapons and armour they have always traditionally wielded.

This is bad news for tourists, who could lose a lobe should they be unfortunate enough to stumble across one of the Black Ears during their travels. Our advice is to avoid travelling alone, especially along the High Trail, where tourists are encouraged to employ a handful of sellswords or quick wits and deep pockets in order to encourage their assailants to leave their extremities attached to their bodies.

Shadowcats – Mountain clans, brigands and thieves are not the only things you have to worry about while travelling the Vale. Shadowcats also represent an ever-present threat to travellers in this part of Westeros. These fearsome critters prowl the road, preying on tourists foolish enough to venture away from the safety of civilisation. Travellers are advised to stay in groups unless they want to find out what life is like near the bottom of the food chain.

Rockslides – Alongside the plague, sword injuries and being flung through the Moon Door for the Prince's enjoyment, rockslides are one of the biggest causes of death in the Vale. Each year several people succumb to injuries sustained while trekking along the High Road, where falling debris is an everyday threat to travellers' safety. Of course, we can't control nature but an experienced guide and a sure-footed mountain pony can help to ensure you reach the Eyrie without being pulverised.

Robin Arryn – After the death of Jon Arryn, the beloved ruler of the Eyrie, control of the Vale has passed to his only surviving son, Robin. A sickly boy, who would struggle to conquer a plate of boiled turnips, let alone an invading army, the nominal Warden of the East is notorious for his histrionics and infantile orders. Prone to fits of anger and demands to see 'bad men fly', the young lordling can be a major annoyance for travellers passing through court, especially those who find themselves on the wrong side of his petulance.

THE MOUNTAIN CLANS

There are thought to be some 3,000 clansmen operating in and around the Mountains of the Moon. Considered primitive by the local residents of the Vale, these ragtag bands of brigands and vagabonds stick to their own rules and traditions, choosing to forego the feudal values you'll find in the rest of Westeros.

The mountain residents are separated into rough clans who were first catalogued by Archmaester Arnel during his writings on the *Mountain and Vale*. The most notable of these include:

Black Ears – Named thanks to their macabre practice of cutting off the ears of their prisoners and wearing them as necklaces, the Black Ears are one of the more prominent clans operating in the Mountains of the Moon. Led by Chella, daughter of Cheyk, many Black Ears left the area after entering the employ of Tyrion Lannister during the Battle of the Blackwater, though some of their number still remain in the Vale.

Burned Men – This band of brigands' name is derived from their coming-of-age ceremony, in which they burn off a body part of their choosing to prove their honour. Though this mutilation typically involves a finger or nipple, it is believed that the more important the body part, the higher the honour, so don't be surprised to see clansmen missing all manner of extremities. The Burned Men are said to have fought bravely during the Battle of Green Fork and have recently returned to the Vale, where they've been seen wielding castle-forged steel plundered from their enemies against unsuspecting tourists.

Moon Brothers – One of the oldest clans in the mountains, the Moon Brothers can trace their lineage back to the First Men and recently became the talk of the Vale after assaulting Catelyn Stark and her party on their way to the Eyrie.

Stone Crows – Perhaps the most famous of the mountain clans, the Stone Crows are led by Shagga, a fearsome warrior who at one point was appointed as personal guard to Tyrion Lannister during his residence at King's Landing. It is a meteoric rise that began with them threatening to kill 'the imp' and ended with them playing a crucial role in defeating Stannis Baratheon during the Battle of the Blackwater.

Creatures, Flora and Fauna

Shadowcats: Most commonly found beyond the Wall, the Mountains of the Moon is one of the only remaining habitats for these ferocious feline predators in southern Westeros. Roughly the same size as a cougar, these carnivorous critters are the only remaining big cats in the kingdom after lions were hunted to near extinction. Shadowcats are easily recognisable by their black fur and white stripes alongside rows of razor-sharp teeth that will rip men's flesh from their bones as quickly as Valyrian steel.

Though Shadowcat pelts can raise a pretty penny at market, the animals continue to thrive in the Vale, where the isolated mountain tracks provide a regular conveyor belt of travellers that make easy prey for the beasts.

Wildflowers: Away from the stony expanse of the mountains, the Vale boasts some of the richest soils in the Seven Kingdoms. These fertile lands are ideal for growing all manner of crops, including wildflowers, which bloom during the summer years, carpeting the kingdom in a kaleidoscope of colours and a cacophony of scents.

Mountain ponies: A fine destrier may be prized in the rest of Westeros but in the Vale they prefer their ponies a little smaller. In fact, the region is renowned for its mountain ponies – sure-footed and shaggy-coated steeds bred specifically for life on the narrow rocky trails that crisscross the kingdom.

Travel Essentials

Travel provisions: Although the Vale isn't as vast as Westeros's other constituent kingdoms, the rocky terrain means that settlements are few and far between. As a result, tourists are advised to always travel with provisions such as salt beef, bread and hard cheese to ensure they don't go hungry on the long treks between the area's outposts.

Sellswords: If you're travelling to the Vale, consider hiring a sellsword to ensure your safety for the duration of your stay. Whether they're covering your back on the perilous journey along the High Road or fighting your corner during trial-by-combat, a wily and well-paid warrior can be an invaluable companion in this part of Westeros. In fact, it could mean the difference between life and death.

Famous Residents

Jon Arryn is among the more notable residents to have called the Vale home over recent years. The former Hand to the King was well liked across Westeros but particularly in these parts, where he was seen as a fair and firm ruler. In his place, the young Robin Arryn was, perhaps, the Eyrie's most famous resident but the celebrity *du jour* is undoubtedly Petyr Baelish. The former Fingers resident is a local boy made good, rising through the ranks after establishing a chain of salacious establishments to serve as Master of Coin for the King himself. More recently, Baelish has returned to his former stomping grounds with his niece, Alayne.

THE VALE

Though the name is commonly used to describe the entire region, the Vale itself makes up just a small portion of Westeros's easternmost lands. Located beyond the Bloody Gate, it is an oasis of life among the granite of the Mountains of the Moon; a rich tapestry of golden wheat fields, verdant green forests and glass-like rivers offering some of the most breathtaking scenery in the Seven Kingdoms.

As bountiful as it is beautiful, the Vale is the breadbasket of the region. Home to some 45,000 soldiers and countless other civilians, it is populated by a series of holdfasts and small stone keeps, which litter the valley floor some two miles below the lowest mountain peaks. Beyond the man-made marvels, the Vale is famed for its stunning natural vistas, which are dominated by the snow-capped Mountains of the Moon. These jagged peaks stick out like stony fingers reaching to the air in stark contrast to the lush lands of the Vale and the sapphire blue of the skies above.

When to Visit

The Vale is inaccessible at the best of times but during winter travelling along the High Road is about as challenging as trying to scale the Wall. In fact, the Vale's remote location means that it is almost entirely cut off from the rest of Westeros in winter, with snow and ice making the mountain trails practically impassable. As a result, the best time to visit is during summer when the crops are flourishing and the wildflowers are in bloom but remember, winter is coming, so be sure to book early to avoid disappointment.

Where to Stay

Though tourism has only recently arrived in the Vale, a number of hostels and hotels have sprung up to cater for the ever-growing influx of travellers who have started to explore the East. These were the best available at the time of writing:

The Maiden's Tower (£££)

The latest addition to the area's ever-growing array of accommodation, the Maiden's Tower is a boutique bed-and-breakfast offering opulent lodgings and an opportunity to rub shoulders with the Vale's elite, including Lady Sansa Stark herself. Located on the easternmost edge of the Eyrie, the rooms are impeccably appointed and come complete with all mod cons, including privies and your very own dressing room. Ask for a room with a balcony to enjoy your own private view of the Vale, the surrounding mountains and, on a good day, well beyond.

Drearfort (£)

Pit stop of choice for pilgrims heading to the Fingers, the mockingly named Drearfort is a flint-stone tower that sits on jagged rocks right by the water's edge. Owned by Petyr Baelish, this modest hostel is basic at best but as close as you'll come to comfort in this bleak quarter of the kingdom. Run by a ragtag crew of servants who somehow look even older than the ancient stonewalls they tend to, the keep is unpretentiously appointed but boasts a warm hearth, along with all the salt-mutton you can eat.

Sky Cells (£)

Located underneath the Eyrie itself, the Sky Cells are part of a honeycomb of gaols built to house the region's prisoners and miscreants. These days, however, you're just as likely to find adventurous tourists under lock and key as you are to find traitorous imps, after the castle opened the doors to its dungeons to create a unique and stomach-churning experience.

Unlike conventional dungeons, the Sky Cells only

have three walls, with the fourth left entirely open to the elements. Set into the side of the mountain itself, the cells are said to be the only prisons in the realm where the inmates are able to escape at will, even if it's to certain death after a 600ft fall. The cells were said to be a particular favourite of Tyrion Lannister, who slept here during his brief stay in the Eyrie. Now, brave travellers can follow in the imp's footsteps, sleeping on the rough hay floors, enjoying some friendly repartee with the dim-witted gaoler and taking in the breathtaking views offered by the open-air sleeping quarters.

But be warned: a night in the dungeons is not for everyone. Sleep comes at a premium when you're exposed to the elements, while sleepwalkers might also be advised to explore more stable surroundings to rest their heads. If, however, you want to see what life is like for the Eyries incarcerated, the Sky Cells guarantee a night you'll never forget.

Eating and Drinking

Behind its almost impregnable mountain exterior, the Vale plays host to some of the most fertile lands in all the Seven Kingdoms. Its black soils and lush farmlands breed bountiful crops, including corn, barley and wheat. In fact, it is said that not even in Highgarden do the pumpkins grow so large or the fruit so sweet. As a result, there is a burgeoning culinary scene squirrelled away in this obscure outpost with plenty of foodie fare to fill your stomach after a hard day's trekking.

Meat skewers

Served by street vendors who line the perilous trail from

the foot of the Vale to the gates of the Eyrie, these meaty, greasy treats are the perfect way to restore your energy on the long climb upwards. Originally offered to working men and women who ferried provisions and passengers to the lofty mountain battlements, the meat – often mountain goat or sometimes cattle – is slowly cooked on skewers and served fresh from the fire. The end result is inevitably messy but incredibly tasty.

Orange-scented wine

While it doesn't quite rival the legendary Arbor vines or the fine vintages brought across the Narrow Sea, the Vale has become renowned in drinking circles for its orange-scented wine, a local delicacy that's started to make a big splash on Westeros's wine scene. Enjoyed by high and lowborn alike, this fruity thirst-quencher is often quaffed during the summer years as a means of warding off the sweltering temperatures. Grab a skin to lubricate your travels or order a barrel or two to take home. You won't regret it!

Blackberries with thick cream

A favourite of the House of Arryn, this dish has spread throughout the Seven Kingdoms but nowhere is it better than in the Vale, where the cream is thick and the blackberries as sharp as a tavern wench's tongue. Visitors frequently choose to enjoy them in one of the Eyrie's many balconies, where this sumptuous dessert is served with a side order of breathtaking views. But those with lighter purses – and healthy appetites – can enjoy the classic pud anywhere across the kingdom, where it has become a staple on many a menu.

Gulls' eggs and seaweed soup

A local delicacy from the Fingers, this dish reflects the

region it stems from. It might not have the spices of Dorne or the rich meats of the Reach, but in its own way this broth is one of the best you'll find anywhere in Westeros. Full of local ingredients, the salty seaweed contrasts perfectly with the rich yolks of the gulls' eggs to create a sumptuous soup that can help stave off the stiff breezes that sweep in from the Bite.

Areas of Interest/What to Do When You're There

From outdoor exploits to exploring the region's ancient – and impregnable – defences, a trip to the Vale offers a multitude of activities for travellers to enjoy. Here are some of our favourites.

Climb the Giant's Lance

The highest peak of the Mountains of the Moon is the Giant's Lance, a colossal shaft of rock that looms above the Vale. Standing 3.5 miles high, it dwarfs the surrounding mountains and is so high that its peak stands above the cloud line. Unsurprisingly, the Lance has become popular with adrenaline junkies attempting to ascend one of Westeros's mightiest peaks.

There are several marked trails that begin from the Eyrie, which sits aside the Giant's Lance, but conquering this mighty mountain is no mean feat. Only expert climbers are advised to attempt an ascent. Even then, planning and preparation are key. If you're not a hardy climber, or if you're simply looking for a more sedate way to enjoy this stunning spectacle, the Eyrie offers unparalleled views of this geological marvel.

SER ARTYS ARRYN

The Giant's Lance is the site of the battle of the Griffin King, a children's story of derring-do that's popular across the Seven Kingdoms. The Griffin King is a legendary figure who ruled the Vale some 6,000 years ago. The last of the Mountain Kings – the First Men who ruled all of Westeros from their stronghold in the east – legend has it that the Griffin Knight was defeated by Ser Artys Arryn, an Andal warlord who flew to the top of the Giant's Lance on the wings of a giant falcon.

Though an enticing idea, in reality the tale of the so-called 'Winged Knight' is altogether more grounded. A pureblood Andal born in the shadow of the Giant's Lance, Artys Arryn was esteemed as the finest warrior of his day and a resourceful leader who inspired all those who fought beside him. It was Artys Arryn who united the Vale's Essos invaders against the First Men, who sought to reclaim their land, leading the Andal army in the Battle of the Seven Stars, a climactic conflict that secured the Arryn's dominion over the East.

His victory, however, was not secured by soaring to the peak of the Giant's Lance on the wings of a falcon. Instead, Artys led some 500 knights through an old goat track to take the ranks of the First Men in the rear, crushing the army and forcing them to bend their knee to him. Afterwards he was proclaimed King of the Mountain and the Vale, founding the Arryn dynasty that would last for centuries until the Targaryen invasion.

Alyssa's Tears

Located on the western face of the Giant's Lance, Alyssa's Tears is one of the most evocative waterfalls in all of Westeros. Running some 3.5 miles from the peak of the colossal mountain, it's the highest waterfall in the realm and a jaw-dropping spectacle that draws visitors from across the Seven Kingdoms.

The legend behind the landmark is almost as beautiful as the falls themselves for the falls are named after Alyssa Arryn, an ancient member of the noble house who watched her brothers, sons and husband butchered before her and yet she never shed a single tear. Upon her death, it is said the gods declared her weeping would not stop until her tears reached the black soil of the valley below – something that hasn't happened in the 6,000 years since records began, as the water vaporises before it can reach the Vale.

Best viewed from the Eyrie, where several balconies have been given over to eager tourists keen to catch a glimpse of this ghostly marvel, the falls are a must-see for anyone stopping at the castle. While the waterfall itself has remained untainted for millennia, the same cannot be said of the viewing spots at the Eyrie, which have become overrun by peddlers hawking tapestries and etchings to visitors. A particular favourite of the local merchants is vials said to be filled with genuine tears from the waterfall. It's a fine story and a great souvenir but in reality the vials are more likely to be filled in privies than the falls themselves.

Pony trekking through the Mountains of the Moon

The mountains surrounding the Vale not only make for a stunning backdrop to the region's rich and fertile lands, they're also a playground for tourists wanting to explore the wild scenery that makes up the Mountains of the Moon. The trails round here can be perilous for the inexperienced and are especially dangerous, thanks to the increased activity of mountain bandits.

Therefore, the best way to explore the peaks is in the company of an official tour party. These groups depart daily from the Bloody Gate and take travellers on a trek through the stunning scenery served up by the Mountains of the Moon. For a gold dragon, tourists get a guide, a sure-footed mountain pony and enough provisions to sustain them for the duration of their trek. Many of these day trips are also accompanied by sellswords, who help to ensure that tourists can enjoy the spectacular scenery without worrying about the unwanted attentions of the Mountain Clansmen.

THE BLOODY GATE

Famed throughout the Seven Kingdoms, this bloody battlement is a popular attraction for visitors to the Vale. Guarding the southwest entrance to the Eyrie, the gate is built into the very mountains themselves, with parapets and battlements carved into the rock overlooking the narrow passage leading to the fertile lands beyond.

The battlement takes its name from the Age of Heroes, where it's said that a dozen armies dashed themselves to bits attempting to breach the Bloody Gate. Originally crafted out of rough-hewn unmortared walls in the fashion of the ring forts of the First Men, the Bloody Gate has undergone many alterations over the years and was even constructed anew by King Osric V Arryn, whose design still stands today.

While the crenelments and watchtowers built into the cliff face immediately draw the eye, it's the mountains themselves that give the Bloody Gate its strategic advantage. Surrounded by steep cliffs on either side, the small passage leading up to the gate is only wide enough for four horsemen to ride abreast – a bottleneck that meant the Vale's defences could pick off an armed host, one by one.

It was this strength that Sharra Arryn, Queen Regent of the Vale of Arryn, believed would protect her kingdom during the Targaryen's War of Conquest. When news of the Targaryen's host reached the Eyrie, Sharra amassed the Vale's entire army at the Bloody Gate ready to defend her borders against the oppressors. However, mounted on her dragon Vhagar, Visenya Targaryen simply flew over the defences, bypassing both the gate and Sharra's army to land in the courtyard of the Eyrie demanding the surrender of the House of Arryn.

Though still a fully functioning border post, today tourists are welcome to wander the Bloody Gate, to stand on its battlements and even pass through the passageway under the watchful eye of the Knight of the Gate and the Vale's finest footsoldiers.

Candle-making in Wickenden

Famed throughout the known world for their extravagantly scented creations, legendary candle-makers House Waxley are based in Wickenden in the southeast quarter of the Vale. From here they run a series of courses teaching the tricks of their trade to tourists. With expert tuition on everything from ingredients to the techniques used to create the candles, students will learn how to harvest their own beeswax and scent it with exotic spices such as nutmeg and cinnamon. Best of all, you get to keep your creations at the end of the day, saving you the inevitable annoyance of souvenir shopping later on in your trip.

The High Hall

No trip to the Vale would be complete without a visit to the Eyrie's High Hall. The centre of castle life, tourists can spend an afternoon enjoying an audience with the Warden of the Vale, sitting inside the blue-veined marble walls to experience the day-to-day running of the kingdom. What you'll see once you're there is purely down to chance. Sometimes it can be as menial as crop counts and the administrative running of the region and sometimes you can catch a criminal being flung out of the Moon Door or a trial-by-combat to determine a prisoner's fate.

Spaces among the galleries are offered on a first-come, first-served basis, so be sure to arrive early to avoid disappointment. It's also well worth packing some warm furs – the High Hall can be draughty and a long day spent in the Warden's company can chill even the hardiest Northman to the bone.

THE EYRIE

The stronghold of the House of Arryn – one of the oldest lineages in the known world – the Eyrie clings to the side of the Giant's Lance, several thousand feet above sea level. Considered one of the most iconic of Westeros's great castles, the Eyrie is also one of the smallest too, consisting of just seven slim marble towers, which can only hold some 500 men.

Originally built as a summer palace for the Kings of the Mountain and the Vale, over time the castle has become one of the most fearsome fortifications in the Seven Kingdoms. Its defences are said to be impregnable, thanks to the small mountain causeway that provides the only access to its gate. This causeway is just large enough for men to march single file at some points, making a massed assault impossible. It's also guarded by three waycastles, which make any attack even more unlikely.

Currently the home of Lord Petyr Baelish, the new Steward of The Vale, the Eyrie boasts scores of famous residents, including Jon Arryn, the recently deceased King's Hand. It was also here that Robert Baratheon and Eddard Stark were fostered as boys and where they first raised their banners in revolt during the rebellion against King Aerys II Targaryen.

THE CLIMB TO THE CASTLE

A trail that defended the castle against aggressors for millennia is now a popular trek for tourists, scores of whom gather every day to ascend the narrow trail to the

---

Eyrie. The going is tough, even for seasoned hikers, but the destination is worth it and the views along the journey offer a welcome distraction from weary legs.

Start: Gates of the Moon

End: The Eyrie

Elevation: 2 miles

Time: 1 day

Exertion: Hard (the altitude, thin mountain air and steep, narrow trails make the ascent up the Giant's Lance difficult for all but the hardiest of hikers)

Points of interest: Stone, Snow and Sky castles

Rest stop: Snow

1. Gates of the Moon

You start your climb at the Gates of the Moon, a small castle that sits at the base of the Giant's Lance. The home of Lord Nestor Royce, High Steward of the Vale, it's a meeting point for travellers looking to make the heady ascent to the Eyrie.

Consisting of a moat, a gatehouse, a yard and square towers, the stout castle is actually larger than the Eyrie and even serves as the Arryn's residence during winter. It is here that the climb up the Giant's Lance begins and where you'll meet your guide. The ascent to the Eyrie is not for the faint of heart. It is difficult, daunting and dizzying – some travellers are said to prefer to make the journey with their eyes closed to avoid the inevitable vertigo. As a result, a trained guide is essential to ensure your survival, as one wrong step could see you dashed on the valley floor below. Guides are easily recruited at the Gates of the Moon, where local bastards are trained from a young age to excel at the ascent. Most of them ferry several parties up a day, so be sure to sling a copper or two their way to thank them for the service.

A sturdy steed is also advised. The narrow rocky trail isn't large enough for a horse – even an eastern pony bred for such work – so a mule is your best choice. Available to rent for as little as a silver stag, these mules will safely carry you and your possessions as far as Snow, the final of the Eyrie's three waycastles.

Once you've employed your guide and corralled your mule you have to head through the postern gate, where you're greeted with a dense forest thick with the smell of pine and spruce, which stands in front of the steps that will carry you up into the clouds.

2. Stone

The trail to the Eyrie can get busy during peak season but it's not just fellow tourists that you'll find on the ride upwards. For many the trail is an everyday part of their working life as they ferry food, arms and supplies up to the castle. The route is also home to the Vale's highborn lords, who must make the long journey to the castle among the clouds in order to take their seat at court.

After rubbing shoulders with tourists and residents alike on the steep, narrow trail from the Gates of the Moon, your first stop will be Stone – a resolute tower that emerges suddenly from the gloom of the dense forest shrouding the mountain trail. Travellers will be greeted with an ironbound gate and thick studded walls that belie a fortification built to defend the trail, rather than help travellers ascend it. Beyond the defences, however, there is a little more comfort to be found, with street vendors serving hot meat skewers and cups of orange-scented wine to weary trekkers. If you want to make the Eyrie by nightfall, however, you'll have to forego the all-too-tempting provisions and continue your ascent.

3. Snow

The trail to Snow is steeper and narrower than that leading up to Stone and the castle, too, is distinctly smaller than its forebear. Made up of a single fortified tower and a stable nestled behind a low wall of unmortared rock, it is built into the side of the mountain itself so that it can command the entire pathway. Once beyond its gate, it's easy to see why this small but stout outpost has never been taken by an opposing army.

At this altitude the forest also starts to thin out, revealing breathtaking views that extend across the valley. The watchtower provides uninterrupted sightlines across the entire Vale below and is the perfect spot to rest your limbs and fill your belly with the hot skewered snacks served up by the local merchants. With bellies full and jaws left agape by the Vale's world-renowned vistas, it's time to mount your mule once again to continue the climb to Sky.

4. Sky

Difficult as it may seem, the trail to the final waycastle on the ascent to the Eyrie is even more treacherous than the road you've travelled thus far. Here, the steps grow ever narrower and are cracked by centuries of freeze and thaw alongside the constant clatter of mules' hooves. The wind here can also be perilous, with the exposed trail getting a battering from the elements, even in the height of summer.

Once you've finished the path, you're greeted with a waypoint that is less of a castle and more of a ragtag fortification. Sky is little more than a crescent-shaped wall raised against the side of the mountain; a defensive position that doesn't offer much in the way of respite for those making the climb. Beyond the wall lie a series of rough earthen ramps, which contain a number of rocks and boulders ready to drop onto any would-be attackers. There's also a cavern within the rockface that houses a hall alongside stables and supply stores. It is here that you'll leave your trusty steed, as the final leg to the Eyrie is too steep even for the Vale's mountain-trained mules.

Those unable to make the final ascent can hitch a ride on one of the six great winches used to ferry supplies to the castle's storerooms. However, be warned: arriving alongside the grain and dry goods is frowned upon by locals and while your legs might be spared the pain of the final ascent, your pride will no doubt be battered in its place.

5. The Eyrie

The final leg of your journey is a 600ft climb up sheer rock to the gates of the Eyrie. Comprised of narrow steps and handholds dug into the rock, this section of the trail takes travellers inside the mountain itself. Though you'll miss the stunning views across the Vale and beyond, you'll be thankful for the shelter the mountain offers.

Finally, after what feels like an eternity, you've reached your destination. The air up here might be rare but whether it's the absence of oxygen or the elation at reaching the end of your trek, the sense of accomplishment can feel dizzying; a light-headed rush of endorphins that (almost) makes the whole ordeal worthwhile. Visitors are traditionally greeted in the Crescent Chamber – the Eyrie's reception hall – where guests are given refreshments and warmed by the fire after making the climb up the Giant's Lance.

Castle Highlights

Built on one of the highest peaks in Westeros, the Eyrie perches some two miles above sea level astride the Giant's Lance. The exact date of construction is unknown but the history of the castle and its surrounding area dates back several millennia to the age of the First Men and the subsequent Andal invasion.

Built of glimmering white marble, the castle is almost ghostly in appearance as it sits amidst the clouds that form over the Mountains of the Moon. Though the ascent to the castle is steep, the views that await you are well worth the hike and once within the Eyrie's walls, you'll discover a treasure trove of sights. Some of our highlights include...

The Moon Door

The King's Justice is dispensed evenly across the Seven

Kingdoms but from Dorne to the Wall, nowhere conducts executions quite like the Eyrie. Those sentenced to death in the Vale aren't beheaded, instead they're flung through the Moon Door to meet their maker after the dizzying 600ft drop to the rocks below.

It's a grizzly spectacle but the door itself is incredibly ornate. Located in the High Hall between two marble pillars, the door is made of Weirwood and barred with bronze. It is also ornately carved but don't look too closely – the last thing you want to do is fall through!

The Gardens

Much like Westeros's other major castles, the Eyrie's towers are built to encircle a central garden originally intended to be a Godswood. However, no matter how many barrowfuls of black soil were brought up the rocky trail to the castle, no Weirwoods would take root on the rocky, windswept landscape. So, instead of a Godswood, today there lies a beautiful garden filled with blue flowers and ornate shrubbery.

At its centre stands a statue of a weeping Alyssa carved from white marble. Look closely and you can actually see traces of the damage caused by a recent trial-by-combat in which the sellsword Bronn defeated Ser Vardis Egen to free Tyrion Lannister from his imprisonment at the hands of Catelyn Tully.

WICKENDEN

Located a few days' ride southwest of the Vale, Wickenden is a sleepy shorefront town that is home to a bustling community of artisans. Presided over by the House of Waxley, the town is famous for its assortment of exotic scented candles – a booming industry that attracts flocks of tourists every year.

Situated on the northern shore of the Bay of Crabs, this picturesque hamlet is made up of a kaleidoscope of homesteads, keeps and shacks in attractive contrast to the stony natural surroundings. The candles here are predominantly made with local beeswax using a technique that has been passed down from generation to generation. The wax is scented with exotic spices from Dorne and the Free Cities, nutmeg and cinnamon being particularly popular with highborn lords and ladies. The candles are available to buy across the town but the picturesque alleys that criss-cross Wickenden are filled with wares designed to separate you from your hard-earned gold. A heavy purse and an eye for a bargain are highly recommended.

THE FINGERS

Lonely, cold and windswept, the Fingers are located along the shores of the Narrow Sea on the east coast of the Vale of Arryn. Made up of four slender peninsulas that extend directly into the sea, each rocky digit is divided by numerous bays, inlets and channels. A rugged landscape scattered with pebbles and barren earth, there wouldn't be much to recommend the area to tourists were it not for the rich history that marks the Fingers on many a traveller's map.

It is here, after all, that the Andals first invaded Westeros, marking the beginning of one of the most significant chapters in the continent's history. The opportunity to walk in the footsteps of the Andals who crossed the Narrow Sea makes this a popular destination for history buffs as well as pilgrims, who come to see the sites where the crusaders landed, bringing with them the Faith of the Seven. These sites, which are scattered across this barren peninsula, are marked by a series of boulders into which the Andals chiselled the seven-pointed star of their faith.

It's not just history you'll find at the Fingers, however. Though the inclement weather makes exploring the area arduous, it has helped to shape the surrounding landscape over the eons, forging the rock into wondrous crags, crenels and craters. With its diverse geological features and historic, not to mention holy, sites, the Fingers is a paradise for ramblers, history buffs and nature lovers alike.

'The Fingers are a lovely place, if you happen to be a stone.'
Petyr Baelish

The Westerlands

Oft discussed but little travelled, the Westerlands is not the largest, most fertile or most populous kingdom in Westeros; it is, however, the richest. Full of hills, mountains and rocky crags, below the unwelcoming surface lies a warren of mines plucking gold and silver out of the kingdom's seemingly inexhaustible reserves. These mineral riches have helped to shape the land alongside the people who live upon it and, despite its relatively meagre status, the Westerlands plays an important role in the running of the Seven Kingdoms.

Much of the region's mining is based in the rocky landscape to the east, with stout fortresses like Golden Tooth guarding the invaluable mines at Nunn's Deep and Pendric Hills. Farther west the realm opens out onto Ironman's Bay, with Lannisport serving as the Westerlands' central hub: a thriving community of merchants, metalworkers and fishermen. In the south the rocky mountains give way to flat rolling plains as you reach the border with the Reach. Sparsely populated save for a few holdfasts, the region is most famous for the Ocean Road, a well-travelled trail with stunning scenery that attracts scores of backpackers each and every year.

The jewel in the kingdom's crown is, of course, Casterly Rock: the region's capital and seat of power for the Lannisters. Over the past century Casterly Rock's importance to the Crown has grown considerably and its increased prominence has brought with it an influx of travellers who have helped transform the rock into a fashionable destination for the highborn, who come to feast in its halls and barter for its bullion. Nearby Lannisport is also a popular pit stop, with its well-to-do social elite and buzzing nightlife a particular draw.

It's not all gold and granite, however. There's also plenty of history to be explored at the Ruins of Castamere and outdoorsy adventures to be had at Golden Tooth. Most visitors start in Lannisport or Casterly Rock and explore the region from there. However, if you're light of purse, it's possible to base yourself at the nearby Clegane's Keep, or farther afield at Golden Tooth, which offer a more affordable starting point.

HIGHLIGHTS

The Ocean Road (page 174)
A popular walking trail offering superlative views over the Sunset Sea and the Shield Islands.

Casterly Rock (page 183)
The region's capital and seat of power for the House of Lannister, Casterly Rock is known throughout the kingdoms for its wealth and power.

Lannisport (page 186)
This busy harbour town is a hub for travellers and home to a thriving community. From fishermen to footsoldiers, it's the beating heart of the region and home to some of the most skilled goldworkers in all of the Seven Kingdoms.

Golden Tooth (page 186)
A formidable mountain fort, Golden Tooth is key to the security of the realm and the source of wealth for its ruling family.

Getting There and Getting About

By land: The Westerlands are easily accessible from the rest of Westeros. The Gold Road from King's Landing is a well-travelled trail offering safe passage to tourists. A pipeline for gold, silver and merchantmen, the trail is a financial lifeline for the Crown and one of the most well-guarded routes in the realm, thanks to the nearby garrison at Deep Den. Those travelling north from the Reach can reach the Westerlands via the Ocean Road, a picturesque thoroughfare that traces the line of the Sunset Sea from Highgarden to Lannisport, while the Riverroad, which connects the Westerlands with the Riverlands, is also a busy artery for transport and well travelled by tourists looking to make their way northeast to Riverrun and the Vale of Arryn.

By sea: Lannisport is one of the biggest port towns in the Seven Kingdoms. Home to the Lannister fleet, the harbour is also a hub for travel, with merchants ferrying goods and passengers to and from every corner of the Seven Kingdoms and beyond.

THE OCEAN ROAD

One of Westeros's classic walks, the Ocean Road runs from Highgarden in the Reach to Lannisport in the Westerlands tracing some of the most spectacular coastal scenery in the Seven Kingdoms. It's no Sunday stroll but nevertheless the road has become a popular destination for travellers looking to soak up the cliff-top views over the stunning Sunset Sea.

Originally a trade route between the two Kingdoms – the road still bustles with merchants ferrying farmed fare from the Reach to trade with the gold-rich Westerlands – it has become popular with backpackers, who have steadily been growing in number over recent years.

Starting out along the banks of the Mander, the trail moves towards the coast, where it hugs the Sunset Sea, offering views of the Shield Islands and the reaving Iron Born aboard their longships. From there it passes through the historical town of Old Oak, complete with ancient tapestries depicting the House's battle against the Dornish. It then descends into the dense forest around Crakehall before once again proceeding northwest along the shoreline all the way to Lannisport.

Practicalities: Pre-planning is essential if you're going to travel along the trail. While it's possible to re-supply at Old Oak, walkers must have adequate equipment, provisions and a fair level of fitness before setting out from Highgarden. Most people camp where they can, setting up along the side of the road and sharing fires with their fellow explorers, so be ready to sleep under the stars and to share your fire (and a few stories) with your fellow walkers.

Weather: Although the road is easily traversed during summer, it is most popular in autumn when the changing leaves in Crakehall Forest and the beautiful dusks on the Sunset Sea attract an avalanche of tourists. If you're looking for more of a challenge – alongside some inevitable isolation – travel in winter, when the harsh winds whipping in from the sea tend to deter all but the most hardy of holidaymakers.

Dangers and Annoyances

Politics – Since helping to elevate Robert Baratheon to the throne, the House of Lannister has been at the centre of Westerosi politics, providing funding, figureheads and fighting forces to help rule the realm. As such, the lands from which they take their wealth are often in a constant state of flux. Whether they are amassing forces to take on Northern armies or funnelling wealth into the King's coffers, the events of King's Landing affect the Westerlands more than anywhere else in the Seven Kingdoms.

Conflict – Though well protected, the recent War of the Five Kings brought battle to the Westerlands' door, with Robb Stark's daring assault on Oxcross, alongside battles in Ashemark, Nunn's Deep and the Crag. Since the Stark rebellion was crushed, a sense of calm has returned to the region. However, war is never far away in Westeros and tourists are advised to send ravens for news before setting out.

THE BATTLE OF OXCROSS

One of the most daring victories during the War of the Five Kings, Robb Stark's defeat of the Lannister host at the Battle of Oxcross would be the stuff of legends had the Lannisters not acted to snuff out the Stark threat during the Red Wedding.

Fresh from his victory at Whispering Wood, the Young Wolf entered the Westerlands through a previously unknown trail said to have been discovered by his pet Direwolf. The trail led the Northmen beyond the Westerlands' border forts and allowed them to descend on Oxcross, where Ser Stafford Lannister was raising a new host.

Thinking himself safe in his own lands, Stafford did not bother to set sentries. This error would prove fatal as Robb Stark and his men descended unseen on the camp and spooked the host's horses, causing them to run amok

---

among the camp. The ensuing battle was more a rout than a real encounter. A black eye for the Lannisters, the daring raid forced Lord Tywin Lannister to leave his garrison at Harrenhal and march west to face the Northern threat.

The Battle of Oxcross remains one of the most famous chapters in the short-lived conflict and one that's since been made famous by Rymund the Rhymer's song, 'Wolf in the Night'.

Famous Residents

The Lannisters are, without doubt, the biggest name in town, having governed over the region for generations. While the late Lord Tywin used to be the biggest draw, the prodigal twins, Cersei and Jaime, are now undoubtedly the most iconic residents of the Westerlands – although both now spend more time in King's Landing than they do at Casterly Rock.

When to Visit

The Westerlands is an all-season kingdom. Unlike the North, where the rolling plains are ravaged during the cold winters, the weather is much milder in this part of the realm. The region's wealth also goes a long way to ensuring it is habitable in all seasons, with the rich deposits of gold and silver ensuring some of the finest infrastructure in the Seven Kingdoms. Despite this, autumn is a popular season for travellers who flock to Lannisport for the spectacular show of colours on display when the sun dips below the horizon on the Sunset Sea.

Where to Stay

From high end to budget, there is plenty of accommodation to be found in the Westerlands and the kingdom's seemingly inexhaustible wealth means that new hostelries are cropping up faster than we can write about them.

Casterly Rock (£££)

Pretend you're one of the most powerful men in the realm by staying among the well-to-do at Casterly Rock. The place to be seen for noble-born travellers – the Martells are among the more famous guests to have stayed at the castle – the Lannister Castle is richly appointed (as you might imagine) with spacious rooms that are decadently furnished and ornately decorated. The privies are equally well appointed – though those looking to see if there's any truth in the tale that the Lannisters shit gold will be quickly disappointed.

Lannisport (££)

There are plenty of inns available to spend a night during your stay in Lannisport but for the real experience consider renting out one of the port town's numerous fishing cabins. These heritage buildings have long been used by the town's fishing fleets, but thanks to the efforts of enterprising locals, a few have been refurbished to house travellers.

Lined with local paraphernalia, these craftsmen cottages have a homey feel – think wood-planked floors, well-worn furniture and copper bathtubs – with decks looking out westwards across the Sunset Sea. A three-night minimum stay belies their popularity with travellers, so be sure to book ahead to avoid disappointment.

Clegane's Keep (£)

Cheap and not so cheerful, Clegane's Keep offers some of the most affordable accommodation in the Westerlands. However, cheap lodgings often come with a hidden cost and that's true of those who wish to rest their head at Gregor Clegane's keep. Located a short ride southeast of Lannisport, the keep's reputation is almost as fearsome as its owner.

With comfortable beds, a roasting hot hearth – just ask Sandor Clegane – and a nearby village offering all the amenities you require (even a toymaker), Clegane's Keep is well appointed. However, travellers report that there is an unnerving air to the place. 'Accidents' are a common occurrence, servants are said to unaccountably disappear in the night and the keep is supposedly so grim that even the dogs are seemingly too afraid to enter the Great Hall when their master is in residence. Still, a bargain is a bargain and given that Gregor Clegane is currently confined to his bed in King's Landing, travellers might want to roll the dice on staying under the Mountain that Moves' roof.

Areas of Interest/What to Do When You're There

If you like gold, you're in the right place. Famed across the Seven Kingdoms for its riches, the Westerlands is a mecca for shoppers looking to buy their bullion from the local merchants and miners. If you haven't brought your wealth with you, however, you can also head for the hills and try to find a fortune for yourself.

Gold panning

Given the riches that lie beneath the Westerlands' surface,

it is perhaps no surprise that travellers flock to mining towns in the hope of finding their own fortune. These tourist traps offer little in the way of an authentic mining experience but what they lack in historical accuracy they more than make up for in fun, as visitors get to learn about the tools of the trade and put them to good use as they pan for their own precious metals. The few flecks of dust on offer are hardly enough to worry the Lannister treasurers but they do offer a memorable keepsake of an enjoyable day's adventure.

Tours and panning experiences at mining towns including Nunn's Deep and the Pendric Hills run regularly during the summer season. Entry is a few coins and covers equipment rental, instruction and all of the gold that participants can pan for.

Shopping

The Westerlands are home to some of the finest metalwork in the Seven Kingdoms, with exquisite armour, jewellery and weapons on offer in just about every single street, square or castle. The best bargains can be found in the mining towns themselves, where enterprising smiths knock the local quarry into serviceable souvenirs. But if you're after something a little more spectacular, head for Lannisport, which is renowned across the Seven Kingdoms for its goldwork.

Here you'll find expert craftsmen who fashion the local gold into stunning accessories and armaments. From gilded plate to embossed swords and jewel-encrusted necklaces, rings and brooches, there's something to suit every taste and just about every budget besides. Be sure to look for gold inlaid with the Lannister Lion – the hallmark of Westerland craftsmanship – and make sure you haggle over the price as a few minutes negotiating can save you a small fortune.

THE REYNE-TARBECK REBELLION

One of the most infamous chapters in the region's history, the Reyne-Tarbeck rebellion is the name given to a 261 AC uprising that challenged the rule of the House of Lannister over the Westerlands.

Unconvinced by Tytos Lannister's rule, those from the House of Reyne and the House of Tarbeck had repeatedly challenged his command, even going so far as to kidnap and imprison three Lannisters. Robb Reyne was an experienced warrior and when he once again rose up against his more inexperienced overlord with the help of Lord Tarbeck of Tarbeck Hill, many suspected the Lannisters would be overthrown and control of their lands pass into the hands of their aggressors.

However, Tytos's eldest son, Tywin Lannister, took it upon himself to take control of his father's armies and marched upon the upstart Houses. Not only did Tywin defeat them in the field, he also put a torch to their lands and obliterated their lineage so that they might never raise arms against his House again.

This bloody and brutal chapter in the family's history is immortalised in the song 'The Rains of Castamere'. Tywin's cold-bloodedness also landed him a spot as the Hand of the King alongside a reputation as one of the

> most ruthless leaders in all of Westeros. It's a reputation
> that is well deserved, as anyone who has spent any time in
> his company will readily tell you.

Ruins of Castamere

Lord Tywin Lannister didn't leave much left after exterminating the House Reyne in 261AC but that doesn't stop tourists from making the macabre journey to see the ruins of Castamere, their once fine castle. Razed to the ground during the Reyne-Tarbeck rebellion, today Castamere is a sombre site that attracts military enthusiasts and history boffs looking to relive one of the bloodier chapters in the Westerlands' history.

Battle re-enactments take place daily, giving tourists the opportunity to safely experience the blood-curdling thrill of combat. For a few coppers you can also employ a local guide, who'll tour you round the remaining ruins as well as the nearby mine from which Castamere's former wealth was sprung.

Merling spotting tours

The fisherfolk at Lannisport have long claimed to have spotted Merlings off the harbour town's coast – a point backed up by none other than Tyrion Lannister himself. It's perhaps no surprise that a small but burgeoning trade in Merling-watching tours has sprung up around the harbour. Though tourists are unlikely to spot the elusive creatures these tours are a great way to explore the harbour as well as an ideal opportunity to catch a glimpse of Casterly Rock from the sea.

THE RAINS OF CASTAMERE

One of the most loved or loathed songs in the Seven Kingdoms – depending on whether or not you're a Lannister – 'The Rains of Castamere' famously immortalises Tywin Lannister's destruction of the House of Reyne, who once had the folly of opposing his family's rule in the Westerlands. Today, it's little more than a reminder of the great House's history and a popular – if foreboding – ditty that is regularly heard at noble weddings.

'And who are you, the proud lord said,
that I must bow so low?
Only a cat of a different coat,
that's all the truth I know.
In a coat of gold or a coat of red,
a lion still has claws,
And mine are long and sharp, my lord,
as long and sharp as yours.
And so he spoke, and so he spoke,
that lord of Castamere,
But now the rains weep o'er his hall,
with no one there to hear.
Yes now the rains weep o'er his hall,
and not a soul to hear.'

CASTERLY ROCK

The capital of the region, it's easy to see why this great castle is often simply referred to as 'The Rock'. Carved out of a great stone hill overlooking Lannisport, the fortress stands high above the surrounding area, dominating the landscape for miles around. Imposing in every sense of the word, Casterly Rock is the second largest fortification in the realm after Harrenhal and one of the few never to have fallen in combat – although Lann the Clever is said to have tricked it away from its original incumbents during the Age of Heroes.

The rooms and halls are quarried directly into the rock itself, while additional structures including keeps and defences sporadically constructed over the centuries appear to perch precariously atop of it. The rock on which Casterly is built is not just an excellent strategic setting but also one of the primary sources of the family's wealth due to the fact that it houses an active goldmine. The belly of the rock also hides other secrets, including rooms where exotic animals like lions are kept and dungeons where the likes of Aeron Greyjoy were once held after the Iron Islanders' short-lived rebellion.

Although wealthy in rare metals, the castle itself isn't as rich in history as other fortresses in the Seven Kingdoms and so many travellers forego the sightseeing to enjoy the luxurious surroundings at Casterly Rock. However, there is still plenty to entertain those tourists who are curious to know more about the infamous capital.

KEY SIGHTS

Some of the key sights for visitors to explore during their stay at the castle include…

The Golden Gallery – Famed throughout Westeros, the Golden Gallery is the centre of court life at Casterly Rock. Where other castles' social spaces are forged from stone or marble, the Lannisters' lust for precious metal led to them plating their gallery entirely in gold. The end result is nothing short of exquisite: a decadent space that positively shimmers with light from the sun.

The Lion's Mouth – Forged in the shape of a lion's head – the sigil for the House of Lannister – the Lion's Mouth is the gate by which visitors must pass to enter the Rock. Ferocious as the giant-sized feline it depicts, it is a popular stop for tourists, who flock to have their portraits painted by artists in front of this iconic landmark.

The Hall of Heroes – This is where the Lannisters and their close kin who've died a valiant death are interred. Filled with the sepulchres of iconic kinsmen like Tommen II Lannister, Tytos Lannister and, most recently, his son Tywin, the mausoleum is located in the belly of the Rock itself. This leads to a peculiar acoustic quirk for the marble-filled hall echoes like thunder as the waves of the Sunset Sea crash on the rock below.

The Stone Garden – The castle's Godswood is far from impressive but still offers a welcome respite from the gold and granite that surrounds the rest of Casterly Rock.

LANNISPORT

Sitting in the shadow of Casterly Rock, many believe this walled harbour town to be the capital's poorer cousin but the reality couldn't be further from the truth. As one of the busiest ports in all of Westeros, Lannisport is a veritable hive of activity. From hosts being raised to merchants fetching and carrying goods and gold, there's a buzz around the town that makes it a popular stop with passing travellers.

Filled with the yellow-haired cousins of the Lannisters, the well-to-do crowd can be found enjoying the town's many taverns or supping local seafood from harbour-front eateries. The shopping is also unparalleled, with Lannisport boasting some of the finest goldsmiths in the known world.

Though the city used to be a target for raiders from the Iron Islands, the presence of the Lannister fleet, as well as Lannisport's own expertly trained City Watch, has made this harbour town one of the safest spots in the Seven Kingdoms. This safety, alongside the reserves of gold and silver in the region's mines, means that it is also one of the kingdom's most expensive towns and travellers will have to empty their purses to fully experience its delights.

GOLDEN TOOTH

Though not as popular a destination as Lannisport or Casterly Rock, Golden Tooth has enjoyed a growing reputation as an outdoor adventurer's paradise over recent years. As well as rock climbing and pot holing among the area's now exhausted mines, excellent hiking and riding are also on offer via a recently rediscovered goat path, which offers a challenging, if treacherous, expedition for adventurous visitors.

The Crownlands

Though prominent today, the Crownlands didn't truly establish their place in Westerosi history until the arrival of Aegon the Conqueror. Hailing from the Targaryen's island homeland of Dragonstone, Aegon landed his forces in the region during his War of Conquest more than three centuries ago, seizing control of the surrounding land and transforming the region into the heart of modern Westeros.

The geography of the region is dominated by Blackwater Bay, a vast inlet to the Narrow Sea that has helped shape the land over the millennia. King's Landing sits at the point where the bay meets the Blackwater Rush, the river that extends inland from the coast. A vast metropolis, the city is the beating heart of the kingdom and, indeed, the continent that lies beyond its borders. The capital is not only home to Westeros's king and ruling elite but it is also where vast swathes of the population reside, with more than 500,000 citizens, both high and lowborn, choosing to lay their heads within its walls. It's a far cry from the fishing village that stood here when Aegon and his sisters first arrived on these shores to begin their War of Conquest.

Beyond King's Landing, the nearby island fortress of Dragonstone is perhaps the region's biggest draw. Located at the mouth of the Blackwater Bay, this volcanic island is the original seat of power for the House of Targaryen – a dynasty who can trace their roots back to the old Valyrian Freehold. Built using long-forgotten techniques, the blackstone citadel is one of the most awe-inspiring sights in all of Westeros. Its role in the realm's history and the creation of the Seven Kingdoms under the rule of the Iron Throne has made it a popular destination for tourists, who brave rough seas and the island's active volcano to see the spot where Aegon first plotted his invasion.

While King's Landing and the nearby Dragonstone dominate any itinerary for travellers heading to this part of the continent, there is much more to the Crownlands than its two most famous sights. To the north, the nearby port town of Duskendale is a particular highlight and a hidden gem that provides just the tonic for travellers who've grown weary of the hustle and bustle of the continent's capital. While south of King's Landing the Kingswood – the area's royal hunting grounds – offers an oasis of nature in a region forever transformed by the actions of man.

For tourists, the Crownlands are one of the Seven Kingdoms' must-sees. Steeped in history and filled with a cross-section of cultures from across the continent, they are a melting pot of sights and experiences that you will find nowhere else in Westeros.

HIGHLIGHTS

King's Landing (page 206)
Home to the King, the Red Keep and the Iron Throne, King's Landing's iconic landmarks stand atop a warren of squalid streets and crooked alleyways filled with sights, sounds and smells from across the Seven Kingdoms.

Dragonstone (page 193)
A site of vast historical importance, this volcanic island was once home to the Targaryen dynasty, who united the Seven Kingdoms. With imposing landscapes, breathtaking vistas and jaw-dropping feats of architectural brilliance, it's a must-see for anyone travelling to the Crownlands.

Duskendale (page 204)
A thriving port town with a bustling famers' market and some of the continent's best hot crab stew, the sleepy streets of Duskendale are just the tonic for travellers who are weary of the hustle and bustle of King's Landing.

The Kingswood (page 226)
This large forest situated across the Blackwater Rush is the personal hunting ground of the King; a densely wooded oasis of nature that lies in stark contrast to the sprawling city you can still see from its fringe.

Getting There and Getting About
By land: All roads lead to King's Landing, literally – from

the Kingsroad, which runs right past it from Storm's End in the south to the Wall in the North, to the Roseroad from the Reach and, finally, the Goldroad, which links the capital to the riches of Lannisport in the west. Its easy accessibility is ideal for tourists, who can rely on cheap and efficient travel from all corners of Westeros.

By sea: It is also possible to approach King's Landing via Blackwater Bay, so long as the city's colossal defensive chain and seemingly inexhaustible supply of wildfire aren't in place to ward off unwanted visitors. Indeed, if the winds are fair, it is possible to reach the city from as far afield as Dorne and White Harbor far quicker than parties travelling over land. Travel by sea isn't just easier, it's essential if you're going to visit nearby Dragonstone, which can only be reached with the aid of an able seaman.

Dangers and Annoyances

Political upheaval – Power can be a fluid concept in the capital of the Seven Kingdoms. Political skulduggery is rife among the ruling elite, who will stab anyone in the back – even their own siblings – if it means securing their grip on the Iron Throne. The end result is a place in a constant state of flux; a city where rulers and their aides come and go at an alarming rate. You might go to bed with one king preparing for his wedding only to wake and find out that he choked on his pigeon pie, leaving his brother to rule in his stead. For travellers, it can be an uncertain experience, as you're never entirely sure who is actually in command of the city and its forces.

Food prices – The recent conflict that has ravaged the continent has led to a scarcity of food in the city, with only a trickle of produce making it through to King's Landing. The Throne's alliance with Highgarden has helped to alleviate the pressure somewhat but food prices in King's Landing remain high. A heel of stale bread, for example, will now set you back a copper, while it will cost you six coppers to buy a melon, a silver stag for a bushel of corn and a gold dragon for a side of beef or six skinny piglets.

Though those prices might take their toll on tourists' budgets, they've been disastrous for locals, who have been pushed to the brink of starvation by their rulers' quest for power. As a result, food riots are now a near and ever-present danger and even the late King Joffrey couldn't escape his starving subjects' anger when he was ambushed by rioters on the muddy track from the docks to Aegon's Hill.

Crime – Crime is rampant in King's Landing, where scoundrels, denizens and unsavoury characters run rife. The recent food riots are just the latest chapter in the city's increasingly unruly recent history. Begging Brothers are a common sight across the city, while the slums of Flea Bottom are awash with scoundrels, sellswords and cutpurses. The situation is even worse during the summer months when the cloying climate stirs men's blood, causing knife fights, tavern riots and even the occasional drunken horse race down the Street of Sisters.

Though the gold-cloaked City Watch is tasked with upholding the King's Peace, desertion and deaths from recent campaigns have seen its number dwindle to just 4,400. Many of those that remain are wet behind the ears, while corruption is rife within the established ranks, seemingly intent on bribing and embezzling their way to wealth. The city is still relatively secure for those tourists who are willing to pay off their so-called protectors. However, if you're truly looking to stay safe during your stay in King's Landing, it's advisable to travel with a personal sellsword in tow.

The smell – They say you can smell King's Landing long before you can see the city looming on the horizon. It's easy to see why. Despite being the continent's capital, the city is, in reality, a squalor where the stench of sweat, shit and some might say treachery hang thick in the air. Locals quickly grow accustomed to the familiar stink of sour wine, rotting fish, nightsoil, smoke, sweat and horse piss. But for first time visitors, it is an assault on the senses that can take a while to get used to.

When to Visit

Though the Crownlands opens its doors to tourists year-round, travellers are advised to avoid the summer months, when the hot and humid weather drives many locals towards the riverbanks in search of cool air. In terms of attractions, travellers will find that Dragonstone is similarly bleak and desolate no matter when you visit. However, if possible, it's best to try and time your trip to King's Landing to coincide with a tourney, when the city comes alive with pageantry and visitors from across the Seven Kingdoms.

Famous Residents

Without doubt, the most famous resident of the Crownlands is the King himself. After several years of stability under the much-loved King Robert Baratheon, over recent months the crown has been thrown into disarray. Though his reign was cut short by his untimely demise, King Joffrey proved to be a very unpopular regent, with rumours of incest and brutality blighting his time on the Iron Throne. The new King Tommen is better liked. However, he is still but a boy and the presence of his perennially unpopular mother, Cersei Lannister, as Queen Regent has done little to assuage the public's distrust of the Iron Throne's latest incumbent.

Other notable dignitaries you might find during your visit to the region include the King's Hand, who is second in authority only to the King himself, and the crystal-crowned High Septon, figurehead of the Faith of the Seven, who can regularly be seen at the King's Court or conducting ceremonies in the Great Sept of Baelor.

DRAGONSTONE

Its Valyrian origins make Dragonstone distinct among the Seven Kingdoms' great castles. The ancient fortress was wrought using techniques brought from Old Valyria itself when the Targaryen's ancestors made the journey across the Narrow Sea. Those techniques are more magical than masonry and it is said that the wizards of Old Valyria did not chisel the stone like modern builders but worked it with fire and magic like a potter works clay.

Upon seeing Dragonstone for the first time, it is a legend that is easy to believe. Made of jet-black stone, the castle is warped into shapes so wondrous it is impossible to imagine that they could have been created by man. As you might expect of a castle built by Valyrian Dragonlords, the winged fire-breathers play a prominent role in the design. Indeed, dragons are everywhere you look. The towers are designed as dragons hunched above the curtain walls ready for flight, the Great Hall is forged in the likeness of a dragon lying on its belly and even the kitchen is shaped like a dragon, with steam and smoke from its stoves pouring from the beast's nostrils. Bridges and staircases, too, are shaped like giant tails, while the armoury and smithy are both surrounded by a pair of giant stone wings.

There are other beasts on the battlements too. The walls are home to more than 1,000 gargoyles shaped in the likeness of minotaurs, griffins, wyveres, manticores, demons, basilisks, cockatrices and hellhounds. Standing some 12ft in height, these crenellations only add to the mystic air surrounding the castle.

Once inside, the madcap nature of the castle's design continues. There are more dragons, more exotic architecture and jaw-dropping feats of engineering. True, there are gardens, keeps and kitchens, but while Dragonstone might resemble the Seven Kingdoms' other great castles in terms of layout, aesthetically it is like nothing else you'll see in all of Westeros.

DRAGONSTONE ON FOOT

Exploring the architecture and aesthetics that make Dragonstone unique among Westeros's great castles, this walking tour will guide you around the citadel, taking in key historical sites along the way.

Start: Castle Gate

End: The Chamber of the Painted Table

Time: 1 day

Exertion: Medium (though the turnpike staircases can be tough going for the old and frail)

Points of interest: Aegon's Gardens, the Great Hall and the Chamber of the Painted Table

Rest stop: Kitchens

1. The Castle Gate

Our tour starts outside the castle gate, which takes visitors through Dragonstone's three colossal black-stone curtain walls. Take a moment to admire the carving of the gate, which is formed by two small dragons that have been etched into the oily stone.

Once you've admired the architecture, make your way across the yard (be sure to watch out for errant arrows from the morning's archery lessons) and towards the tail of the great dragon that forms the centre of the castle.

2. Aegon's Garden

In the shadow of the dragon's great stone tail lies Aegon's Garden. Feel free to stroll around this surprisingly large expanse, admiring the tall pine trees that ring its outskirts and breathing in the scent of the roses that grow within its beds and hedges. If you're willing to get your boots wet in the boggier areas, you can even find wild cranberries, which are delicious when ripe.

3. The Stone Drum

Once you've had your fill of cranberries, make your way

towards the Stone Drum, the stout keep which forms the centre of the castle. So named because of the constant booming created by the sound of storm winds crashing against its walls, the Stone Drum is where you'll find the castle's accommodation, as well as its dungeons, which are dug deep into base of Dragonmont, the active volcano on which the entire island is built.

4. The Sept

On the lower floors of the Stone Drum you will find Dragonstone's Sept, which is filled with sumptuously carved altars and exquisite stained-glass windows. It is here that Aegon is said to have knelt and prayed to the gods the night before setting out for Westeros to begin his War of Conquest. Tourists line up to kneel at the spot the King is said to have prayed at, while others mill around, examining the idols that represent the seven aspects of the Faith of the Seven. Carved from the masts of the ships that carried the first Targaryens to Dragonstone, these ancient statues are encrusted with pearls and gold. Sadly, only three (the Crone, the Father and the Stranger) of the original statues remain; the others were burned in a recent show of defiance from the followers of R'hllor.

5. The Gallery

Now make your way to the gallery: a long walkway flanked by a row of tall, arched windows that offer commanding views of the outer bailey, the curtain walls and the fishing village and port beyond. Take a moment to admire the views as you stroll along its length, including the intricate stonework, which includes dragon's claws that are used to grasp lit torches during the evening.

6. The Great Hall

At the far end of the gallery you'll find the opening to Dragonstone's Great Hall. Shaped like a giant dragon lying on its belly, the entrance is set into the jaws of the beast itself, with visitors required to pass through its razor-sharp teeth and down the red-painted gullet to reach the hall itself. Inside you will find a space that Aegon himself would have used to entertain his guests – a vast room that today seats row upon row of hungry tourists.

7. Kitchens

Just outside of the Great Hall you'll find the kitchens, which are shaped in the likeness of a dragon's head. Stop to admire the novel use of the beast's nostrils as vents for the steam and smoke from the stoves as well as views across to the armoury and smithy. Though off limits to visitors it's possible to admire the exterior of the buildings, which are protected by a pair of massive stone wings enveloping the two structures. The kitchens form our rest stop so be sure to use the privy, should you need to do so, or to grab some fish stew and black bread to sustain you during the afternoon's excursions.

8. Sea Dragon Tower

Once your strength has been restored, start to make your way towards the base of the Sea Dragon Tower and begin to climb the twisting and narrow staircase that lies at its centre. Atop this tower are the Maester's Quarters, offering stunning sea views and a chance for travellers to catch their breath after climbing the steep stairs. From here you can also admire Dragonstone's other principal tower – the Windwyrm – which is shaped like a dragon arching into the sky.

9. The Chamber of the Painted Table

The final leg of our journey takes us back down the turnpike staircase of the Sea Dragon Tower, through the black gates that guard the castle's middle and inner walls, across the gallery and back into the Stone Drum, where you'll climb even more steps to find the famed Chamber of the Painted Table.

The chamber itself isn't all that impressive – a bare black stone room with four tall, narrow windows that look out at the points of the compass. But we're not here to admire the interior; we're here for the great table that sits at its centre and from which the room takes its name.

A giant slab of carved wood, the table is more than 50ft long and almost half that broad at its widest point. Fashioned in the days leading up to his War of Conquest, it was built at the behest of Aegon Targaryen, who commanded his carpenters to build the table into a map of Westeros, sawing every individual bay, peninsula and inlet in stunning detail. On the surface was painted the Seven Kingdoms (as they had been in Aegon's day) alongside the rivers, mountains, cities, lakes and forests that make up Westeros. Though darkened by nearly three centuries of varnish, it is still possible to make out the topographical details that the Iron Throne's first owner would have used to plot his invasion.

By the table there is a single chair. Located where

Dragonstone lies in relation to the rest of the continent, it is raised on a platform in order to give its incumbent a commanding view over the table. It is from here that Aegon would have plotted his moves, planning out his invasion alongside his sisters and military commanders. Today, tourists line up for hours in order to sit in the chair for themselves and recreate that iconic moment in Westerosi history.

While the island itself has become a hotspot for tourists over recent decades, sadly the accommodation available to visitors hasn't quite caught up with the increased demand. Options range from basic to barely habitable, unless, of course, you're willing to part with a purse-full of coins and spend the night in Dragonstone itself.

Dragonstone (££)

Perhaps the most popular (and some might say only) choice for travellers is to stay within the castle itself. Well appointed and comfortable, the chambers are unseasonably warm, thanks to shafts that extend deep within Dragonmont itself, staving off the dankness you'd expect on an isle such as Dragonstone. Many travellers make the mistake of spending a sleepless night in the Stone Drum, the castle's central keep, struggling to ignore the incessant booming the ocean winds make as they hit its walls. So be sure to ask for a room in one of the citadel's many towers, where the small inconvenience of a steep turnpike staircase is more than offset by a modicum of peace and quiet.

The fishing village (£)

For those who can't afford to rest their heads in Dragonstone itself, the only other option available is the nearby fishing village, where enterprising locals rent out rooms to supplement their income. Set against the backdrop of a port that is filled with war galleys, fishing vessels, stout carracks and fat-bottomed cogs, the setting may be picturesque but the village has recently been overrun by scores of soldiers, smugglers and sailors under Stannis Baratheon's command. Look for a house on the outskirts of town to avoid the worst of the revelry, as the men-at-arms dice and drink late into the night.

Eating and Drinking

As you might expect from a castle situated on a volcanic island, Dragonstone doesn't boast the most fertile of farmlands. While tillers work on terraced farms at the base of Dragonmont, much of the island is almost entirely dependent on the outside for its provisions – a system that has become increasingly unreliable thanks to the recent conflict with the Crown. As such, the cuisine here is almost as sparse as the landscape itself and travellers should be prepared to sup for sustenance rather than pleasure.

Dragonstone (££)

By far the best food on offer on the island comes from the castle. However, don't go expecting haute cuisine. Breakfasts are a pretty basic affair, with porridge served up as a staple, often with cranberries that are grown within the castle at Aegon's Garden. The later meals at least offer some variety. Fish stew served with black bread is a particular favourite with the lunchtime crowd, while evening diners should seek out the roasted gull stuffed with peppers and onion – a speciality of the chef.

The inn at the docks (£)

Those who grow tired of the castle's restrictive menu should head for the docks, where a weathered little inn stands at the end of the stone pier. Though it has no name, the inn is instantly recognisable thanks to the waist-high gargoyle that squats out front. Though its features have been all but obliterated from centuries of rain and salt, local legend says that if you pat its head, it will bring you luck.

Whether the inn brings you a good meal, however, is another matter entirely. Once inside, you'll be greeted with a boisterous common room serving up ale and whatever produce has been purchased fresh from the docks that day. Some days it can be fish from the local fleet, others it might be exotically spiced dishes brought to the island by Lysine pirates in the Lord's employ, so be sure to ask your serving wench to find out what the dish of the day is before making a decision.

FROM OLD VALYRIA TO BLACKWATER BAY

The Targaryens who first colonised Dragonstone initially hailed from across the Narrow Sea in Old Valyria. A house of noble descent, they took possession of the island and built on it, transforming Dragonstone into the westernmost settlement in the Freehold.

Initially little more than an outpost, it became the family home twelve years before the Doom of Valyria – the

---

apocalyptic natural disaster that destroyed the 5,000-year-old dynasty. Twelve years before the cataclysm Lord Aenar Targaryen's maiden daughter, Daenys the Dreamer, had foreseen the Freehold's destruction in a powerful prophetic dream. She convinced her father to ignore the jibes of locals, who labelled him a coward, and flee the land alongside his closest allies.

Aenar listened to his daughter's pleas and set sail for Dragonstone, taking his entire family and five dragons with him. Four of those dragons died once they'd reached the volcanic archipelago. However, two eggs that the Targaryens had taken with them hatched, giving birth to the dragons that Aegon would eventually use to conquer Westeros, a century later.

After his War of Conquest, Aegon moved the household to King's Landing. Dragonstone, however, remained as the home of the heir apparent, the self-styled Prince and Princesses of Dragonstone, who remained there until driven out by Stannis Baratheon and his forces during King Robert's Rebellion.

Areas of Interest/What to Do When You're There

Though the castle itself is the island's biggest draw, there are also other activities on offer to keep travellers amused during their stay. From day trips to the nearby island of Driftmark and hikes to the peak of Dragonmont, to more sedate activities like archery or sunset bonfires, there are plenty of ways to pass the time on Dragonstone.

Climb Dragonmont

A volcano that is still semi-active to this day, Dragonmont's frequent eruptions in the past are what formed the black-stone island that now surrounds its base. It is an imposing landmark, which dwarfs the castle that clings to its face, and tourists looking to stretch their legs can spend a day scaling its peak. While it is possible to explore Dragonmont on your own, it's worth spending a handful of coppers on a local guide, who can take you to the hot vents where pale grey steam rises from below the rock and show you to the caverns that burrow deep into its core. These caves are filled with rich deposits of Dragonglass, which is perhaps not surprising, seeing as how they were once home to a flourishing community of wild dragons.

Visit Driftmark

Once you've explored every inch of Dragonstone itself, hitch a ferry and make for Driftmark, a small island that lies westwards in the waters of Blackwater Bay. Though smaller, the island that was once known as New Valyria on account of the number of dragons who roosted here, is very similar to its near neighbour. Damp and cramped, Driftmark is, perhaps, most famous as one of the battlegrounds of the Dance of Dragons: the name given to the civil war fought between the Targaryens, around 129AC.

That war of ascension remains the island's biggest draw for tourists today, many of whom come to stroll around the charred ruins of Spicetown, Hull and High Tide – towns and castles that were put to the torch after the hostilities had ended and have never been rebuilt.

Archery

Ever fancied yourself as a marksman? If so, you can put your skills to the test in one of the many classes held within the castle walls. The yard here rings to the call of 'Notch, draw, loose' as tourists try (and, more often than not, fail) to master the longbow. It's hardly what you've travelled across Blackwater Bay for, but the activities are still great fun and the perfect way to pass the time if the drizzle has poured cold water on some of your more adventurous plans.

Bonfires

Like an increasing number of places across Westeros, Dragonstone has recently rejected the Faith of the Seven and converted to the Lord of the Light. Led by the Red Woman Melisandre – an exotic priestess who originally hails from Asshai in Essos – the people here hold nightly bonfires, burning idols and infidels in honour of R'hllor. These sunset pyres are open to all comers and offer the perfect way to start your evening, so long as you don't find yourself at the heart of the flames.

DUSKENDALE

If you have time, pay a visit to Duskendale, the large port town located northeast of King's Landing. This quaint market town spreads out from the harbour, where cobbled streets snake around the Dun Fort, the stout castle overlooking the town. Home to the House Rykker, once the town's gates are opened (they're locked at night), most tourists make a beeline for the local farmers' market, which serves up some of the best turnips, corn and yellow onions you'll find this side of the Reach. Local traders also flock to the square, where they line their market stalls with surcoats, leather boots and furs (available at bargain prices if you can ignore the bloodstains), as well as plate armour and mail that is among the cheapest you'll find anywhere in the Seven Kingdoms.

Once you've had your fill of shopping, make your way through the crowds to the Seven Swords. The town's largest inn, this four-storey watering hole takes its name from a sign outside that is made of seven wooden swords fixed to an iron spike. The sign is in honour of the Seven Sons of Darklyn, who once served the Kingsguard; indeed, no other House in the realm can boast so many. Once inside, try to find a window seat, from which you can admire the beautifully painted house that sits across the street, before chowing down on some of the chef's acclaimed hot crab stew.

THE KINGSGUARD

The Kingsguard, also known as the White Cloaks or the White Swords, are the sworn bodyguards of the ruler of the realm made famous by legendary knights such as Ser Ryam Redwyne, Prince Aemon the Dragonknight and Ser Gerold Hightower.

Supposedly the finest knights on the continent, they are sworn to protect the Iron Throne with their own lives, to obey the King's commands and keep his secrets. As part of their vows, the Kingsguard are sworn to service for life and forbidden from taking a wife, fathering children or owning lands. These vows are consciously modelled on those of the Night's Watch.

Originally formed by Aegon the Conqueror as an elite bodyguard for those of royal descent, the Kingsguard was actually the idea of his sister/wife Visenya after a Dornish assassination attempt on the King in the streets of King's Landing. The Kingsguard has continually existed since that day and the Order's uninterrupted history is recorded in the Book of Brothers, an official tome maintained by the leader of the bodyguard (the Lord Commander), who records the feats and deeds of its members. That tome, alongside the Kingsguard themselves, resides in the White Sword Tower in King's Landing.

KING'S LANDING

It is hard to believe that this thriving metropolis was nothing more than a fishing village a little over three centuries ago. Though long squabbled over by the lords of the Reach and the Riverlands, the fisherfolk who lived here led relatively simple lives, residing in wooden shacks that lined the Blackwater Rush. Aegon's landing changed that forever. He built his first fortifications here and, after conquering the continent, chose King's Landing as Westeros's new capital in order to set him apart from his vassals.

In the years since Aegon's Conquest, King's Landing has grown almost exponentially. It now spreads over several miles, dominating the north shore of the Blackwater Rush for as far as the eye can see; a mass of arbours, granaries, timbered inns, storerooms and houses, all interconnected with tree-lined boulevards and a warren of narrow streets, some so small that two men cannot walk abreast down them.

Of course, the city is dominated by the three tall hills that made it a strategically important location for Aegon and his army. The tallest of these is Aegon's High Hill. Located at the southeastern corner of the city, it overlooks the bay and is crowned by the Red Keep – the imposing fortress completed during the reign of Maegor the Cruel to replace Aegon's originally wooden fort. To the west, Visenya's Hill (named after Aegon's eldest sister/wife) is topped by the seven crystal towers of the Great Sept of Baelor, built to demonstrate the Targaryens' piety and devotion to the Faith of the Seven. And, finally, to the north stands Rhaenys's Hill (so-called after Aegon's other sister/wife), on which stand the blackened ruins of the Dragonpit – a once great structure built to house the Targaryen dragons, which has fallen into disrepair over recent decades.

At the foot of Rhaenys's Hill lies Flea Bottom, an aptly named collection of slums and squalor, where the city's poorest residents reside. Famed for citizens as unsavoury as its infamous Bowl o'Brown, it is an edgy mix of winesinks and taverns that has captured the hearts of adventurous tourists. In stark contrast, the other side of the hill is dominated by the city's wealthy elite, who live in richly adorned townhouses clustered around the Old Gate in King's Landing's Northwestern Quarter.

Travellers will find that they are spoilt for choice during their trip to King's Landing. It's almost impossible to explore the city in one go; in fact, people who have lived here all their lives still haven't explored every landmark, potshop and square. But therein lies its appeal. It's an ever-changing place, a city where the architecture itself seems to shift and move with its inhabitants. It may not be as ancient as Oldtown, as exotic as Sunspear or as foreboding as Winterfell, but it's alive; a place filled day and night with the chatter of people from all four corners of the Seven Kingdoms and beyond.

The hustle and bustle is intoxicating and it's easy to see why so many tourists visit every year to take it all in, stalking the streets and gazing up at the city's iconic landmarks. But King's Landing would be nothing without its people: the melting pot of highborn and lowborn who fill every street corner, winesink and tavern common room. Fiercely protective of their home, even if they don't always enjoy living in it, they exist on a steady diet of royal gossip, so you won't have to go far to find a local who's willing to bend your ear with tales of the Queen's alleged incest or the King's adultery.

NEIGHBOURHOOD WATCH

Flea Bottom – Flea Bottom is King's Landing's skid row, a rough-and-ready district that plays host to the city's poorest inhabitants. At first glance its maze of unpaved streets might not appear to be the most appealing part of town, but if you dig beyond the squalor, the open sewers and the rampant crime rate, you'll find a vibrant community filled with stores, winesinks and potshops serving up the area's ubiquitous Bowls o'Brown.

Street of Steel – The city's smithy district begins west of Fishmonger Square and snakes its way up Visenya's Hill. Most of the smiths here have their own on-site furnaces, where they forge everything from blades to breastplates. Cheaper wares can be found around the foot of the hill, but the higher you climb, the more expensive the shops become. At the top of the street you'll find the workplace of Tobho Mott, the city's master armourer, who learned his trade in Qohor and is one of the few smiths in King's Landing able to rework Valyrian Steel. His shop is a vast emporium of arms that stretches over two storeys and is easily spotted, thanks to the ebony and Weirwood double doors adorned with a hunting scene and flanked by two stone knights clad in red plate armour.

Street of Flour – A maze of twisting alleys and narrow pathways that seem to fold in on themselves, the Street of Flour is where the sweet-toothed should head to find their sugary fix. Lined with bakeries and artisanal patisseries, the air is thick with flour and the smell of freshly baked bread. Tarts are a particular speciality on the street and you can get your hands on a lemon, apricot or blueberry treat fresh from the oven for as little as three coppers.

Street of Silk – Home to the city's seemingly ever-growing expanse of brothels, the Street of Silk is lined with ornate red-glassed oil lamps advertising establishments where tourists might enjoy an evening of pleasure. Prices range from a few coppers to a king's ransom and women regularly line the street, touting themselves to passers-by. Though the street has been notably quieter since Tyrion Lannister implemented a tax on the industry – colloquially referred to as the Dwarf's Copper – long-standing establishments like Chataya's remain a hotspot for the city's sex trade.

Street of Looms – King's Landing's textiles hub has fallen on hard times of late and today you're just as likely to see a corpse being picked apart by a pack of feral dogs as you are a fine Myrish gown.

Street of Silver – Those looking to chance their arm in the city's gambling dens should head for this cramped pathway where drunkards bet their livelihoods on games of dice and tiles.

River Row – There's a definite maritime feel to this district, which runs along the southern wall of the city by the Mud Gate. It's perhaps unsurprising given the professions of its residents, the vast majority of whom are sea captains, sailors and fishermen who work in the nearby docks. The area's biggest attraction is perhaps Fishmonger's Square, a vast, open-air market that serves up the catch of the day alongside local favourites like Lamprey Pie.

Pigrun Alley – Though the area is principally known for its butchers, the aptly named Pigrun Alley attracts hundreds of tourists every year, thanks to its architecture and the mishmash of tall timber and stone buildings, whose upper stories lean out so far over the street below that they nearly touch those sitting across from them.

Cobbler's Square – A vast plaza situated by the Gate of Gods, north of Visenya's Hill, the Cobbler's Square is home to a daily craft market, where tanners come to peddle their wares.

Northwestern Quarter – Home to the city's elite, the luxurious manses that line the well-appointed streets are a world away from the nearby squalor of Flea Bottom. The area is also known for its food, with an assortment of eateries, including the famous Lady Tanda's, serving up sumptuous meals to hungry highborn.

Waterside – The clamour of dockworkers and wharfside markets is so loud that on a clear day it can be heard by ships all the way out in Blackwater Bay. The area is a hive of activity, with ships coming and going, ferrymen poling their boats back and forth across the Blackwater Rush and off-duty dock workers cramming into the ramshackle winesinks and taverns that line the streets.

Where to Stay

King's Landing has the range of accommodation you'd expect from one of Westeros's major cities. The most desirable rooms are located in the city's Northwestern Quarter, where tourists can hobnob with the highborn, while mid-range options available in the inns that litter the city are the best all-round option. It is advisable to book early, however, especially if there's a tourney in town, as accommodation can fill up fast.

Shae's Cottage (£££)

This beautiful secluded cottage lies in the heart of the Northwestern Quarter. Originally built to house Tyrion Lannister's favourite concubine, today this one-room apartment is one of the most popular accommodation options in the city. Behind its unimposing iron gate lies a luxurious interior, a spacious chamber with a large bed, adequate solar, a bath, a dressing room and even small side chambers, which accommodate the in-house staff and guards. Attention is paid to the tiniest details and the residents' anonymity is held in the utmost confidence.

The Broken Anvil Inn (££)

Located within sight of the Red Keep's walls, a stone's throw from the Gate of the Gods, this amiable inn provides old-world-style accommodation and friendly service for as fair a price as you'll find in King's Landing. The rooms are small but many of them boast views of the Great Sept of Baelor and the crown of Visenya's Hill. The downstairs common room is one of the best around and guests can spend many an evening supping wine with the locals around its great hearth.

The Inn on Eel Alley (£)

Perfect for those on a budget, this rambling old establishment is ideal for travellers who've just made land after travelling to King's Landing by sea. Located a short walk from the waterfront, for a copper you can hire workers from the nearby docks to carry your chest up Visenya's Hill to Eel Alley. Once there, you'll find a homely inn filled with large airy rooms, each with windows that look out over the nearby rooftops. The sunsets here are wonderful and more than make up for the straw-stuffed beds. There's also a common room, where the sour old crone who runs the place serves up a fish stew that is undoubtedly one of the best in the Seven Kingdoms.

Eating and Drinking

Eating in King's Landing can be a rich experience. As people have come to the city from all four corners of the Seven Kingdoms, they've brought with them some of the best dishes and delicacies in all of Westeros. Therefore, King's Landing's streets offer a wealth of choice for the hungry – from exquisitely crafted menus served up at the numerous well-to-do establishments designed to cater to the city's elite, to well-priced street-vendors, where locals buzz around spits serving up skewers of unrecognisable meats.

Tower of the Hand (£££)

According to Tyrion Lannister – the imp who knows a thing or two about food and drink – the city's finest cook sits in the Tower of the Hand. Employed by the Hand himself, the cook's position proves that sometimes the best diplomacy involves filling your enemy's belly rather than slicing it open. When they're not serving the political elite, however, the Tower opens up its doors to average punters, who can experience the extravagant eatery that has topped just about every King's Landing restaurant poll in the past few years.

The prices aren't cheap but the best use of your gold is on the famed set menu: a culinary quest that includes starters of oxtail soup and a salad of summer greens tossed with pecans, grapes, red fennel and crumbly cheese. The mains are equally impressive, with hot crab pie served alongside spiced squash and quails drowned in butter, before finishing with some of the finest cheeses in the realm. Each dish comes with its own wine pairing, enabling you to swallow down Arbor golds and Dornish reds that are handpicked to complement each course.

Lady Tanda's (££)

Located in King's Landing's well-to-do Northwestern Quarter, this glorious manse boasts some of the city's highest-born patrons, with Tyrion Lannister, Petyr Baelish and Lord Gyles Rosby all regulars. The establishment is owned and run by Lady Tanda Stokeworth, who serves up hearty fare to locals and tourists alike. Highlights include roast haunch of venison, wild boar, goose stuffed with mulberries and some of the finest lamprey pies in Westeros, all served up with a side order of doe-eyed affection from her lovelorn daughter, Lollys.

The Queen's Ballroom (£££)

If you're looking to eat like a royal, head over to the Queen's Ballroom, where the Lannisters' own private chef cooks up sumptuous feasts for those with heavy purses and hearty appetites. Located in Maegor's Holdfast, everything about the ballroom screams luxury. From the beaten silver mirrors and wood-panelled walls to the glorious high-arched windows that sit at the south of the hall, the hundred or so diners who are lucky enough to get a table can expect to feast in the lap of luxury. The food here is every inch as fine as the décor. In the evening guests can expect to enjoy dishes including broths, crab-claw pie and mutton roasted with leeks and carrots served in trenchers of bread, all washed down with choice vintages from the Red Keep's cellars (try the sweet plum wine). The Ballroom also caters to the breakfast crowd with an impressive spread that includes honeycakes baked with raisins and nuts, gammon steaks, fried fingerfish in breadcrumbs and a Dornish dish made with onions, cheese and chopped eggs cooked with fiery southern peppers.

The Maester's Apartments (££)

This breakfast hotspot, located within the walls of the Red Keep, has been serving hungry visitors great food with a side order of rambling advice for more than forty years. Run from the private chambers of Grandmaester Pycelle, highlights include boiled eggs, plums, sweet porridge and crisp fried fish.

The Maidenvault (££)

If you've got an afternoon to spare, be sure to take in afternoon tea at the Maidenvault. Located in the Red Keep, this long slate-roofed building was originally built to house the sisters of King Baelor the Blessed but today opens its doors to visitors who come to take tea and enjoy the on-site entertainment. Filled with trestle tables and sweet-smelling rushes, pots of tea are served alongside a sumptuous assortment of cakes – including some of the best lemon cakes about – while guests enjoy the entertainment of Butterbumps, the immensely fat fool who's famed for his rendition of 'The Bear and the Maiden Fair'.

Winesinks and taverns (£)

The city is filled with winesinks, dive bars and taverns where locals go to drown their sorrows and gossip over the latest happening inside the Red Keep. You won't have to go far to find a drink in the continent's capital but some of the best places are located at the foot of Visenya's Hill, where the warren of streets is filled with subterranean winesinks with low ceilings, rough plank bars and live entertainment from acclaimed singers, such as Symon Silver Tongue.

BOWL O'BROWN

While Winterfell has its blackberry preserves and Dorne has its firepeppers, much as the highborn locals would like you to believe otherwise, if King's Landing does have a signature dish, it's the Bowl o'Brown. A ubiquitous source of nourishment for this city's impoverished residents, Brown is served up from the scores of potshops that line the streets of Flea Bottom.

A stew made up of barley, carrots, onions, turnips and whatever pieces of meat its cooks can get hold of, Brown is simmered in vast pots that have been on the boil for years at a time. This low and slow cooking process produces the dish's distinctive colour, alongside a depth of flavour you wouldn't normally expect from such a culinary stalwart. The meat that's used in the dish varies from establishment to establishment, with everything from pigeon to rats, cats and even the occasional murdered singer filling it out.

For the poor, this is their only meal of the day, but for tourists, it is an opportunity to experience the unique and often peculiar charms that Flea Bottom offers. True, the sanitary conditions are as dubious as the origins of the meat but a Bowl o'Brown is a rite of passage for travellers to this part of the world. Part of its appeal also comes from the dish's variety. No two Bowls o'Brown are the same, partly because most peasants pay for their meal using vegetables and meat, which eventually become the ingredients of the next batch.

The potshops themselves are, perhaps, as much of a draw for tourists as the dishes they serve up. Though they can be dangerous and at times intimidating for outsiders, they are also a chance to get a genuine feel for what life is like in the capital's poorest district; an opportunity to rub shoulders with locals as they share stories and bawdy jokes over the city's favourite food.

Areas of Interest/What to Do When You're There

Most tourists spend their time in King's Landing taking in the city's many sights. From the Red Keep to the Dragonpit, its storied structures are an understandable draw for visitors who had previously only heard about them in songs and tall tales. There is so much to do, in fact, that your biggest problem is going to be trying to fit it all in.

THE IRON THRONE

The seat of power for the Seven Kingdoms, this monstrous metal throne was constructed by Aegon I Targaryen after he returned to King's Landing following his successful War of Conquest.

A grisly tangle of spikes, jagged edges and twisted iron, the throne was forged out of the blades Aegon's enemies laid down during battle. It is said that more than a thousand swords make up the chair, which took fifty-nine days and the dragon breath of Balerion the Dread to forge. The throne is every bit as uncomfortable as it looks and rulers are known to occasionally cut themselves on the blades, which are still sharp after centuries of use. That, however, was part of Aegon's design, as the Conqueror believed that a king should never sit easy in front of his subjects.

The Iron Throne is currently located in the Red Keep, where the King, his family or his Hand hold court.

Red Keep

The highlight of any trip to King's Landing is undoubtedly the Red Keep, the royal castle that takes its name from the pale red stone used during its construction. Built to replace the Aegonfort – a wood-and-earth structure built by Aegon's forces on their initial landing on these shores – construction on the Red Keep started a few years after Aegon conquered the Seven Kingdoms and wasn't complete until during the reign of Maegor the Cruel, some forty years later. After the project was complete, Maegor immediately ordered the execution of every carpenter and stonesmith who worked on the site in order to protect the castle's secrets. Even today the castle's exact layout remains unknown, with many new hidden rooms and passageways being discovered each year.

Formed of seven stone-drum towers crowned with iron ramparts, the Red Keep may be small – it's roughly equivalent to Winterfell in the North – but it's a ferocious fortress designed to protect the King from all attackers. That is immediately apparent when you glance up at the thick stone parapets that protect the outer edge of the keep's colossal curtain wall.

Beyond its numerous gates and portcullises lies a cobbled square alongside several small yards and outbuildings, including barracks, granaries and dungeons. The keep is also home to the Throne Room, where the King holds court, and the Small Council Chamber, where affairs of the realm are discussed, alongside historical buildings such as the Tower of the Hand and White Sword Tower. There are also gardens, ballrooms and a Godswood, all of which are open for tourists to explore when the King has opened his gates to visitors.

THE RED KEEP IN A DAY

There is so much to see in the Red Keep that simply planning your visit can be a daunting experience. However, with some careful choreographing it is possible to explore the keep's main attractions in a single day. The itinerary below offers a practical and enjoyable tour that will guide you through the castle's greatest hits.

8.30 am – Gatehouse

Start your tour of the Red Keep at the Gate House, the main entrance in and out of the castle. Take a moment to look up at the spikes, where the heads of traitors are traditionally displayed after they've been separated from their shoulders.

9 am – The Maester's Apartments

If the spiked skulls haven't turned your stomach, make your way to the Maester's Apartments, where you can grab some breakfast (see page 215) alongside a lesson or two from Grandmaester Pycelle.

10 am – The Tower of the Hand

Home to the Hand of the King, this tower might be smaller than the King's quarters but it is every bit as important, given the Hand's role in running the continent. Once inside, you'll have time to explore the rooms, which include a small hall with high vaulted ceilings, a solar and, supposedly, a warren of secret passageways. The Tower is luxuriously appointed with fine Myrish rugs, tapestries and gold-framed windows.

11.30 am – White Sword Tower

After you've explored the Tower of the Hand, make your way across the courtyard beyond the stables and barracks to the White Sword Tower, historic home of the legendary White Cloaks. A slender four-storey tower built into the corner of the Red Keep's curtain wall, the White Sword Tower commands stunning views out over the bay. While the tower contains many armouries and chambers, by far the biggest attraction is the Round Room. This circular space is filled with tapestries, whitewashed walls and a white Weirwood table, around which the seven members of the Order meet to conduct their business.

1 pm – Maegor's Holdfast

Our next stop is Maegor's Holdfast, a massive square

fortress that sits behind walls 12ft thick and a moat filled with iron spikes. A castle within a castle, the Holdfast is home to the royal apartments, including the bedchamber where the King sleeps. While here, take time to admire the fine furnishings and the ancient suits of black armour that line the hallways – a remnant of Targaryen rule. There is always a White Cloak stationed at the entrance to Maegor's, so make sure you stop to say hello.

2.30 pm – Afternoon tea in the Maidenvault

You'll probably be ready for a rest by now, so head to the Maidenvault for afternoon tea, served alongside some of the finest cakes in all of the Seven Kingdoms.

3.30 pm – The Godswood

It's time to work off those cakes with a wander around the Godswood, an acre of elm, alder and black cottonwood trees that look out over the Blackwater Rush. Make sure you make your way to the centre of the wood, where you'll find the heart tree – a great oak whose limbs have been overgrown with smokeberry vines.

4 pm – The Throne Room

For many, the main event of any tour of the Red Keep is an opportunity to explore the Throne Room – the centre of the Seven Kingdoms. It's a cavernous space where more than a thousand people can be easily accommodated. If you're lucky, the court will be in session and you'll have an opportunity to observe as the King or his Hand attends to matters of the realm. If the room is empty, however, you'll have the opportunity to explore the fine hunting tapestries that line the walls alongside the Iron Throne itself and even the spot where Jaime Lannister struck down and killed the Mad King Aerys Targaryen during the sack of King's Landing.

5 pm – Traitor's Walk/Secret Passage Tour

Once you're finished with the Iron Throne, it's time to make your way out of Maegor's Holdfast and towards the Traitor's Walk, a squat tower that contains an entrance to the castle's dungeons. We'll save a tour of the subterranean torture chambers for another day but there's just enough time to find out a little more about the warren of secret passageways that King Maegor had built into the Red Keep so that he could make a quick escape, should his enemies ever trap him. No one knows quite how many secrets are contained within the Red Keep's walls but experts predict that there might be hundreds of hidden passageways providing ways in and out of the castle, as well as spots where you can eavesdrop on private chambers.

Great Sept of Baelor

Named after Baelor the Blessed – whose statue looks out over the vast marble plaza in which it is set – the Great Sept of Baelor is the seat of the High Septon and the centre of the Faith of the Seven on the continent. Originally constructed by Baelor to transfer the religious order from the Starry Sept in Oldtown, it's a magnificent structure with a high-domed roof and seven glinting crystal towers, which can be spotted all the way out in Blackwater Bay. The Sept is just as magnificent on the inside, where the air is thick with the scent of incense and the crystal windows dance rainbow light across the Hall of Lamps, where the faithful come to light candles in honour of their gods. It is here that the city's most important ceremonies are held, from state funerals and the marriage of its king, to the beheading of northern traitors. On most days, however, travellers are free to explore the Sept at their leisure, quietly contemplating its beauty and enjoying the colossal plaza that reaches out from beyond its steps.

Dragonpit

Originally, Rhaenys's Hill was topped with the city's first Sept. However, during the religious uprising of 41 AC, Maegor the Cruel burned the Sept with dragonfire and decreed that it would be replaced by a home for the house's royal dragons. That home was the Dragonpit, a cavernous domed structure where the Targaryens would raise and house their pets. The building was so large that thirty knights were said to have been able to ride abreast through its iron doors and the roof glowed red day and night with dragonfire. However, despite its size, it was noted that the dragons raised in the pit never reached the size of their ancestors as the confines stunted their growth.

Today the Dragonpit is a shadow of its former self. The once great structure has fallen into disrepair and ruin, blackened by fire and crumbling after decades of neglect since the last of the Targaryen dragons died out. While tourists are still able to tour the site, they are advised to do so at their own risk. The area is frequented by prostitutes, who entertain their punters in the secluded area, while the long-abandoned ruins are also a potential death trap, with floors liable to give way and unstable containers of wildfire scattered haphazardly around the site.

TAKE IN A TOURNEY

Without doubt, the best time to visit the Seven Kingdoms' capital is when there's a tourney in town. King's Landing is renowned for its contests – extravagant affairs of pomp and ceremony that attract people from all corners of the continent.

When a tourney is in town, the streets are thick with commonfolk, who come from miles around to see the games. There is also an influx of highborns, as lords and ladies arrive with their entourages, intent on either enjoying the games or participating in them in order to bring honour to their houses. This flood of visitors only adds to the pageantry of the occasion and King's Landing comes alive as tourney fever grips the city.

However, the atmosphere on the streets is nothing compared to that found on the tourney grounds closer to the Blackwater Rush. Beyond the city walls hundreds of pavilions are raised by the river in a cacophony of colours, brightly coloured banners and awe-inspiring sigils. It's a splendorous backdrop against which are set the tourney's champions – anointed knights in shining armour every inch as wondrous as the songs make out.

The crowd gathers to cheer for their favourites and place wagers on the outcome of the events, which typically include archery contests, a melee and jousting. Jousting is, of course, the main event: a ferocious spectacle of thundering warhorses and lances shattering into splinters as they dislodge an opponent.

These contests often run all the way through to dusk, when the serious business of feasting and drinking begins and continues on long into the night. The food here is often as big a draw as the on-field action. Roast auroch slowly turned on spits, snails in honey and garlic, venison soup and cinnamon pies are served alongside flagons of ale and all the iced summerwine you can stomach.

Alchemists' Guildhall

Located just off the Street of Sisters at the foot of Visenya's Hill, this imposing warren of black stone is home to the ancient order of the alchemists. A once powerful institution that was favoured by the Targaryens, the alchemists' influence has waned over recent centuries as the Maesters have gradually supplanted them across the Seven Kingdoms. Recently, they have once again risen to prominence after providing Tyrion Lannister with wildfire to defend the city during the Battle of Blackwater Bay. The perilous process of creating wildfire is just one of the things you can experience upon a visit to the Guildhall, where you'll also be able to tour the Gallery of Torches, a stunning space where emerald-green flames dance around 20ft marble columns.

The Three Whores

No, it's not an organised trip down the Street of Silk but an opportunity to get up close and personal with the site of one of the most important chapters in the city's recent history. Located by the Mud Gate facing out across Blackwater Bay, the Three Whores is the name given to the trio of giant trebuchets constructed to protect King's Landing from Stannis Baratheon's invading army. Here, you can stand on the spot where Tyrion Lannister conducted the city's defences, looking out onto the bay where Stannis's fleet was trapped and then decimated with wildfire. It's an eerie place that's made all the more atmospheric, thanks to the scars of battle still evident in the makeshift fortifications.

Hunting in the Kingswood

From white stags to wild boar, the Kingswood teems with game. No wonder the forest has become a mecca for hunters, who range out daily from King's Landing. Hunting parties can be joined on the banks of the Blackwater Rush, where you'll be able to stock up on provisions before getting poled across the water on one of the specially chartered ferries. From there, your party will be led through the forest by local trackers, who will help you to seek out and hunt down a bloody souvenir to remind you of your stay in the city.

> 'Once man has seen a dragon in flight, let him stay at home and tend his garden in content, for this wide world has seen no greater wonder.' – Tyrion Lannister

Dragon Skulls

Although they've now been extinct for more than 150 years, dragons still have the power to fascinate the public. It's hard to believe the beasts that now fill our songs and stories once flew over this land, helping the Targaryens to forge the Seven Kingdoms and rule over its people. Civil war and sickness put paid to the last of the dragons – a stunted, sick, misshapen female – in 153AC, but the Targaryens remained fiercely loyal to the beasts adorning their sigils. In fact, many spent their entire dynasty attempting to hatch petrified eggs. They also adorned the throne room with the polished skulls of nineteen legendary dragons, some of which were more than a thousand years old.

After King Robert's rebellion, these skeletons were removed and put into storage in cellars below the Red Keep. Although they're no longer on public display, tourists can still visit the dank basement, where they can see the polished skulls that have long since turned to stone after the dragons' demise. The black-onyx skulls range from 3,000 years old for the oldest to just over 150 years old for the youngest. The main attractions, however, are the colossal remains of Balerion, Meraxes and Vhagar: the dragons with which Aegon and his sisters conquered the Seven Kingdoms, killing thousands of people along the way. The dragon-skull tours are understandably popular. However, continued anti-Targaryen sentiment means that there is little desire to move the skulls to a more sizeable home, which means tourists should be prepared to wait – often for hours – for a glimpse of the gargantuan remains.

Dungeon Tour

If you're feeling particularly brave, why not take a walk through the subterranean dungeons that snake below the city's streets? Originally built by Maegor the Cruel, there are four levels of cell built to house and torture both high- and lowborn alike. The dungeons are still in use to this day and travellers can experience life in incarceration, thanks to organised tours that guide you through the catacombs, allowing you to explore the cells and even meet and man-handle some of the current inmates.

Watch a knight get anointed

No matter what corner of Westeros you hail from, the chances are that you were raised on stories of brave knights and their legendary tales of derring-do. It is perhaps no wonder then that so many tourists choose to spend a morning watching a knight get anointed at the Great Sept of Baelor. Whether they've been rewarded for their bravery, their loyalty or something altogether more sinister, the newly anointed knights must first walk through the city streets barefoot in order to demonstrate their humbleness. They are then paraded in front of the High Septon, who blesses them before they pledge their fealty. For those who have grown up on the stories, it's a must-see experience, though be warned: the ceremonies are long and can take up most of the morning.

Take in a show

Entertainment isn't hard to come by in King's Landing and there are many shows on offer to keep travellers entertained during their stay. A current favourite among the common folk is a puppet show, where lions, dragons and stags play out a tale of a kingdom in chaos. The parallels with the Crown's current plight are difficult to miss and while the Small Council has reportedly taken a dim view, the show continues to play to packed audiences across the city.

Trial-by-combat

Trial-by-combat is still a popular method of justice in the Seven Kingdoms, where it is used to settle trials and grievances. These battles to the death are commonplace in King's Landing and immensely popular with the locals. Some people believe that the gods decide the fate of the criminals. However, most simply enjoy the sport and flock to the Outer Wards when a trial-by-combat is about to take place. The duels are open to the public. However, with up to a thousand people crowding the walkways in order to get a view of the action, you may have a fight on your hands yourself just to get a good vantage point.

THE CITY'S SEVEN GATES

Seven is a sacred number in Westeros, so it should come as no surprise that King's Landings' walls are home to seven gates – no more, no less. These are:

Dragon Gate – Standing by Rhaenys's Hill, the Dragon Gate leads to the Kingsroad, which continues north to Winterfell and the Wall.

Iron Gate – Though its hinges have rusted after years of neglect, the Iron Gate is still an imposing barrier, which leads to the Rosby Road – the main artery ferrying people to the nearby town of Duskendale.

Old Gate – Located on the northwestern wall of the city, the Old Gate is the nearest entrance to Rhaenys's Hill.

Gate of the Gods – One of the most visited gates, the Gate of the Gods is surrounded by intricate carvings whose eyes seem to follow you as you enter the city.

River Gate – Known as the Mud Gate by those in the city, this entrance leads south to the Kingsroad and Roseroad. Located near Fishmonger's Square, it connects the city with the wharfs on the Blackwater Rush.

Lion Gate – Leading westwards towards the Goldroad, construction is currently underway to produce a statue of the late Tywin Lannister to stand guard over the entrance for all eternity.

King's Gate – The King's Gate is currently in a state of disrepair after it was battering-rammed by Stannis's troops during the assault of King's Landing.

The Stormlands

So named for the savage squalls that batter this coastal realm, the Stormlands lie on the southeastern coast of Westeros. Surrounded by the Crownlands to the north, the Reach to the west and Dorne to the south, the borders in this part of the realm have been as turbulent as its notoriously rough seas over the course of history, although it has remained largely stable since Aegon's War of Conquest.

A relatively small kingdom made up of stony shores, foreboding mountains and rain-soaked marshes, the Stormlands is famous for its coastline and the tempestuous tides that roll into the aptly named Shipbreaker Bay. The image many people have of a desolate wind-ravaged wasteland might be accurate in parts but despite its precipitous climate, the area boasts some of the most fertile farmlands in Westeros, alongside stunning green forests,

231

with part of the Kingswood and the Rainwood resting within its borders.

Just as the land they live on has been weathered by centuries of storms, the character of the people in this corner of the Seven Kingdoms has been shaped by years of adversity. But it's not just stormy seas they've had to endure. For thousands of years the Stormlands were the first line of the defence against Dornish incursion until the region's incorporation into the Seven Kingdoms, while a long-running struggle with the Reach also helped to forge the martial society that makes up the Stormlands today.

From the weatherbeaten earth to the browbeaten residents, all in all the Stormlands might not sound like the most desirable destination for travellers heading for Westeros. After all, it has no major cities to speak of and few of the attractions that make kingdoms such as the Riverlands, the North or the Vale so popular. However, what it lacks in charm, the Stormlands more than makes up for in character. Though large areas of the kingdom remain intractable, the rough-and-ready wilderness combines with the harsh beauty of its coastline to form one of Westeros's most dramatic regions.

Although most visitors come solely for the coastal scenery, there are several castles and settlements that litter the landscape, offering a glimpse into the region's proud military past. The Stormlands' power was in terminal decline until King Robert Baratheon's rise to the throne. Storm End's most famous recent resident once again put the realm on the map, leading to a resurgent travel industry that is still pulling in the punters today.

HIGHLIGHTS

Storm's End (page 241)

Set against the swirling waters of Shipbreaker Bay, Storm's End is one of the strongest castles in the Seven Kingdoms: a stone citadel that's stood against elements and armies for centuries, thanks to the magical spells said to be woven into its foundations.

Cape Wrath (page 244)

Wet and wild, Cape Wrath is a thin peninsula that cuts out into the Narrow Sea. The region's heartland, it's filled with natural wonders including the vast rainwood and some of the finest red deer in all of Westeros.

Tarth (page 244)

The Sapphire Isle – named after the colour of its waters, not its wealth in stones – is a handsome island community that lies off the eastern coast of the Stormlands. With its azure waters, striking natural scenery and gargantuan womenfolk, it is considered by many to be among the most beautiful spots in the Stormlands and the jewel in the kingdom's crown.

The Weeping Town (page 245)

It is hard to resist this thriving port town, which handles much of the Stormlands' trade. Located on the southern coast of the Cape of Wrath along the Sea of Dorne, this amiable little market town is a hub of trade, with exotic goods brought in daily from Dorne to the south and Essos across the Narrow Sea to the east.

Getting There and Getting About

By land: The Stormlands are easily accessible from all corners of the Seven Kingdoms. Connected to the capital via the Kingsroad that runs all the way to Storm's End, the region is a relatively short ride from King's Landing. For those travelling from the west, it is best reached via the Roseroad – a popular and well-protected route used by everyone from farmers to flowered knights. Though slightly more arduous, the best way to journey north from Dorne is via the Boneway, a major pass that runs through the Red Mountains. The Martell banners have recently been called to the rocky mountain pass, but travellers are still assured of a safe passage across the border.

By sea: With its far-reaching coastlines, travellers might be tempted to travel to the Stormlands by sea, rather than make the trip via land. However, while the fares can be cheap, the journey is often perilous, with the infamous Shipbreaker Bay and its snarl of rocks regularly living up to its name by dashing passengers and their possessions along the coast. Although it's tempting to take a more direct route, travellers are advised to look for ships that circumnavigate the Cape of Wrath and put into port along the Stormlands' southern coast, where the Sea of Dorne provides a much easier – not to mention safer – ride.

Crossing the Narrow Sea: Due to its location on the continent's easternmost coast, travellers regularly use the Stormlands as a launchpad to cross the Narrow Sea and explore the Free Cities of Essos. Safe passage can be bought from port towns like the Weeping Town, where merchants regularly take on passengers in place of cargo for the right price.

Dangers and Annoyances

Shadow assassins – Recently, there has been string of mysterious deaths in the region, which has taken the lives of high-profile figures including Renly Baratheon and Ser Cortnay Penrose. Both were killed while surrounded by their men, with Renly protected by his Rainbow Guard and Ser Cortnay safely ensconced behind the walls of Storm's End.

Reports have been conflicting at best, with some stories suggesting that the men were killed by Brienne of Tarth and others stating they were murdered by shadows that bore the likeness of Stannis Baratheon, who had created them with the help of his Red Queen Melisandre. Whatever you choose to believe, travellers are advised to monitor the situation before making their journey.

Hunting accidents – Hunting is a popular pursuit in these parts, with high and lowborn alike heading to the Kingswood to stalk everything from game to wild boar. However, the recent high-profile death of King Robert Baratheon, who was mauled by a wild boar while hunting in the area, has shone a spotlight on the safety of one of the region's favourite pastimes. Wine has always been part and parcel of the hunting experience but after King Robert's death, campaigners have sought to persuade hunters to keep their wits about them while in the Kingswood. As a result, travellers who do intend to hunt during their stay in the Stormlands are encouraged to exercise restraint, lest they follow in the late King's fateful footsteps.

Creatures, Flora and Fauna

Wild boar: The boar that killed Robert Baratheon is not the only wild boar in the Stormlands. The fearsome beasts are renowned in these parts and some say they can even grow to the size of an Auroch. Though their numbers are dwindling, thanks to years of hunting, populations are still present in both the Kingswood and Rainwood. Travellers are advised not to get too close, lest they wind up on the wrong side of a murderous mauling.

Famous Residents

The Baratheons are undoubtedly the biggest name in these parts, with the stag-sigiled house ruling over the kingdom from Storm's End for generations. King Robert was roundly loved, thanks to his larger-than-life attitude, while Renly, too, was a popular figure up until his death. Stannis – the only surviving sibling – is altogether less popular, though the stern-jawed pretender to the Iron Throne is still a renowned figure across the Stormlands.

A more popular figure can be found in the form of Davos Seaworth, the smuggler-turned-Ser who is oft referred to as the Onion Knight on account of his efforts to feed Stannis Baratheon and his starving garrison during the Siege of Storm's End. Though originally from Flea Bottom in King's Landing, Davos became an adopted son of the Stormlands after Stannis granted him lands in the Cape of Wrath to thank him for his bravery.

When to Visit

The weather here can be bleak no matter when you decide

to visit, though travellers should check the tides if they wish to make the passage across the Narrow Sea as the shipping can change throughout the seasons.

Where to Stay

Despite its bleak landscape and foreboding weather, tourists will find a warm welcome in the Stormlands, where locals are all too happy to open their doors to visitors. Unlike the land in which it sits, the accommodation here is warm and hospitable – after all, the people have been sheltering from the storms for generations and, after a millennia or so, are getting quite good at it.

As a result, there are accommodation options to suit every taste and almost every budget. From rooms fit for a king – or a wannabe king – in Storm's End to hunting lodges in Bronzegate and boltholes in Stonehelm, you won't be short of a spot to lay your head.

Storm's End (£££)

Many people choose to lodge at Storm's End during their stay in the kingdom and for good reason. Built to defend its occupants from storm winds and besieging forces, the stout fortress is the largest in the realm and rooms are readily available for those willing to part with their purse. Those with gold to spend should reserve a room in the Lord's Dwelling. Richly appointed and crammed full of creature comforts, they're the ideal place to shelter from the region's squalls, though don't expect sea views as the rooms are windowless to help bar against the constant battering that the castle receives from the elements.

Those looking for a more affordable option can spend a

night under canvas in one of the many tents that are set up beyond Storm's End's walls. The remnants of a recent siege by Stannis Baratheon, these pavilions were originally intended to house a host of armed men but have been converted to accommodation by enterprising locals.

Bronzegate (££)

Supported by a smattering of small towns that have sprung up in the lands surrounding this small castle's walls, Bronzegate is located a short ride north of Storm's End. A more affordable option for those who don't want to pay a king's ransom for a room at the kingdom's seat of power, Bronzegate is ideal for tourists looking to explore the nearby Kingswood.

Griffin's Roost (££)

Perched high on a lofty crag jutting out from the shores of Cape Wrath, Griffin's Roost is set among stunning scenery with accommodation offering unspoilt views across the countryside and the stormy waters of Shipbreaker Bay. Filled with faded tapestries and stunning stained-glass windows crafted out of white-and-red diamond panes, the rooms here are richly appointed, boasting canopied beds and velvet linens.

Top tip: Try to book the east tower to make the most of the spectacular countryside views.

Stonehelm (£)

Overseeing the Slayne – a major river route through the Stormlands – this black-and-white-stone keep is little more than a rest stop for passengers travelling to and from the kingdom. The rooms here are basic – think hay-filled beds and reed-covered floors – but comfortable, with early check-out options for those eager to catch an early-morning ship across the Sea of Dorne.

Areas of Interest/What to Do When You're There

The land here provides much of the entertainment, with locals and visitors alike making the most of the fertile soils and stunning natural vistas on offer in the Storm Lands. Whether it's the lush forests that teem with challenging game or the savage coastline, where millennia of erosion has opened up a playground for cavers, there's a lot more to the Stormlands than you might expect.

Hunting in the Kingswood

Popularised by the late King Robert Baratheon – who used to hunt here while his wife was in labour – hunting in the Kingswood has become a widespread pursuit in this part of the Seven Kingdoms. With big game, including deer and wild boar, the quarry is almost as impressive as the verdant surroundings. Hunting parties can be joined from nearby Bronzegate, where horses, dogs and arms are also available for hire.

Caving

The Stormlands' coastline is a stony sprawl that is littered with a honeycomb of hidden caves and caverns. The most famous of these lies in Shipbreaker Bay in the shadow of Storm's End, the location where Ser Davos Seaworth smuggled onions in to feed the castle's starving garrison during King Robert's rebellion. However, similar sites are dotted across the coastline and further south by the Sea of Dorne. Exploring these caves has become a resurgent activity in recent years, with tourists looking to follow in the footsteps of the famous smuggler and explore sub-terranean sites that have remained largely untouched for decades. Tours operate regularly from major castles including Storm's End and Stonehelm, where equipment, guides and even onions are in bountiful supply.

Explore the Dornish Marches

For more than a thousand years the Marches, which spread for a hundred leagues in the southwest corner of the kingdom, have been a constant battleground between the Stormlands, the Reach and Dorne. However, the relative peace of recent generations has led to something of a regeneration for this long-neglected habitat. Today the Marches is an area of outstanding natural beauty, with its grasslands, moors, plains and mountains playing host to countless species of birds and wildlife. It is open to tourists to explore under their own steam or via one of the organised tours that forage out of Summerhall, a small town that's become the focal point of the area's tourism industry.

Eating and Drinking

True, the cuisine here isn't going to trouble the Reach, Dorne or King's Landing any time soon – in fact, its critics might suggest that even the Mountain Clans could teach the Stormlands a thing or two about cooking up a feast – but while the dishes are rustic, they're not short of flavour, nor history, as tourists will quickly discover.

Onions

Since they were smuggled into Storm's End by Ser Davos Seaworth during King Robert's Rebellion, onions have become a much-loved crop in the Stormlands. Several crops were said to have been planted in the Onion Knight's honour and today the region boasts some of the sweetest onions in all the Seven Kingdoms, with recipes from soups to stews crafted in the smuggler-turned-Ser's name.

Roast rat

The protein that was once the last resort for Stannis Baratheon's starving garrison at Storm's End is now served up to tourists looking to experience what life was like in the besieged castle. The meat is surprisingly tasty and if you can overlook its origins, probably not the worst thing you'll digest during your stay in the Seven Kingdoms.

STORM'S END

A formidable fortress overlooking Shipbreaker's Bay, Storm's End is one of the strongest castles in the Seven Kingdoms. Ancient as the land upon which it sits, the castle was razed during the Age of Heroes by Durran, the first Storm King. Legend has it that he had earned the love of fair Elenei, daughter of the Sea God and Goddess of the Wind. Durran angered both deities by taking the girl as his wife. In their wrath, her grieving parents sent winds and waters to batter down Durran's hold, crushing his friends and guests beneath the savage storm. But Elenei protected her betrothed and the next morning he declared war on the gods themselves, vowing to rebuild his keep.

Rebuild he did. In fact, five castles were raised only to be battered down by even more savage storms. Lords and Maesters pleaded with Durran to move his castle inland, where it would be sheltered from the storms. The Storm King refused, however, building ever-more formidable fortresses until, on his seventh attempt, his castle stood. Some say he was aided by legendary Northman Bran the Builder, others that the castle walls were carved with the help of ancient magic from the Children of the Forest. But, whichever way the story starts, it ends the same, with Durran defying the gods and living out his days with his bride behind the castle walls.

Whether or not its evocative history is true remains to be seen but what cannot be questioned are the castle's defences. Surrounded by a massive curtain wall standing 150ft high and 80ft thick on its seaward side, Storm's End is an architectural marvel. Made out of a double course of stones filled with an inner core of sand and rubble, the curtain wall is formidable. It's also smooth as a Summer Islander's skin, with its stones so well placed that the wind cannot find any purchase. It is perhaps no wonder then that Storm's End has never been breached during its long and chequered history.

Unlike Highgarden or Winterfell, there's not much to endear this defiant outpost to tourists and yet they still come in the hundreds to see the castle renowned across the known world for defying the gods. Many choose to stay within its colossal curtain walls, enjoying the relative comforts offered by its accommodation. Others decide to spend a day here, exploring the grounds for themselves and learning about the architectural quirks that have helped to shape Storm's End over the centuries.

THE SIEGE OF STORM'S END

Without doubt, the most famous chapter in the castle's recent history is the siege that Stannis Baratheon and his garrison endured during King Robert's rebellion. After taking the majority of the Stormlands' strength with him for his assault on the Seven Kingdoms, King Robert left his younger brother Stannis with just a small contingent of men with which to hold their homeland.

However, after his defeat to the Tyrell army – who'd remained loyal to the Targaryens – at the Battle of Ashford Robert's forces were cut off from their home, leaving Stannis to stand alone against the full force of Highgarden. With the Tyrell host surrounding Storm's End and Lord Paxter Redwyne cutting it off by sea, the castle was left isolated from the rest of the Seven Kingdoms. The siege lasted almost a year, with the garrison growing so desperate that they were forced to eat their horses, dogs and even the rats to stay alive.

Fortunately, Davos Seaworth – a notorious smuggler – managed to slip through the Redwyne blockade, using a ship with black sails and a black-painted hull to sail via cover of darkness to deliver onions and saltfish to the starving men of Storm's End. The provisions enabled the defenders to stand long enough for Lord Eddard Stark to ride south and lift the siege. Though no sword was swung in anger, the victory played a crucial role in Robert's ascension to the throne, as it engaged a Tyrell host who could have tipped the scales of the Battle of the Trident.

After the war, Robert pardoned the lords of the Reach for their part in the siege. To his brother Stannis he awarded Dragonstone, former seat of power of the Targaryens. He, in turn, knighted Davos Seaworth for his efforts to alleviate the garrison's struggles, granting the so-called Onion Knight his own lands, alongside a war galley for him to command.

CAPE WRATH

This beguiling peninsula boasts everything from stormy coastal headlands to plunging forested valleys, all set against the foreboding backdrop of the region's northwest mountain range. The savage beauty of its scenery has enchanted visitors for centuries and even today hundreds of tourists choose to visit the region to explore its fertile lands and rugged coastlines. The area is dominated by the Rainwood, alongside a string of strategically placed keeps and castles designed to repel the attention of invaders.

TARTH

Situated across the Straits of Tarth, a few leagues northeast of Shipbreaker's Bay, Tarth is the jewel in the Stormlands' crown. Known as the Sapphire Isle on account of the striking blue seas on which it sits, the land is full of mountains, waterfalls and shadowed vales. Renowned for its stunning scenery and stout womenfolk, it is a popular day trip for travellers, who make the short ferry ride to experience the area's outstanding natural beauty. Ferries depart daily from Storm's End and put tourists ashore at Evenfall Hall, home of the House of Tarth, which has become the de facto starting point for daytrippers and holidaymakers.

THE WEEPING TOWN

Furs from the North, spices from Dorne and exotic items from across the Narrow Sea adorn the stalls in this bustling market town. Located on the southern coast of Cape Wrath, the Weeping Town sits along the shores of the Sea of Dorne. The relative calmness of the surrounding waters – especially in comparison to the rest of the kingdom's treacherous coastline – has made it the Stormlands' busiest trading post. Once there, travellers will be amazed at just how busy Weeping Town is, especially in comparison to the rest of this sparsely populated corner of Westeros. The docks here are a hive of activity, with scores of able-bodied men helping to unload the cargo holds of the merchant vessels, ferries and trading barges lining up beyond the harbour wall.

Despite its name – the town earned its teary moniker after the body of the then king, Daeron I Targaryen, was first brought here after his murder in Dorne – Weeping Town is likely to put a smile on the most stalwart visitor's face. The markets here are among the best in southern Westeros and tourists with heavy purses and an appetite for a bargain will find some great deals on everything from Auroch skins to Oldtown wooden harps.

Dorne

Dorne is a world apart from anywhere else you'll find in Westeros. Located on the southernmost peninsula of the continent, the kingdom remains largely cut off from the rest of the lands ruled by the Iron Throne, thanks to the Red Mountains: an imposing range that has long been the first line of defence along its borders.

Dorne is hot, arid and rocky, and upon entering and for the first time travellers might feel as if they've made the trip across the Narrow Sea and not just south of the Reach. The kingdom is the hottest in all of Westeros, with a scalding southern climate that has helped to shape the land over the centuries. It is perhaps unsurprising then that Dorne plays host to the only desert in the Seven Kingdoms: an inland sea of sand, where water is almost as valuable as gold and wells are protected like vaults. However, along the coastline and the banks of its major rivers, the warm weather has encouraged fertile farmlands, where exotic produce flourishes.

But it's not just the climate that sets Dorne aside from the rest of Westeros, its people are markedly different too. Culturally and ethnically diverse from the rest of the Seven Kingdoms, the Dornish can trace their roots back more than a millennium to a period of mass immigration, when Rhoynar refugees landed from the east and intermarried with the local population of First Men and Andals. The end result is a population who look and act decidedly different even to their nearest neighbours to the north.

THREE TYPES OF DORNISHMEN

Thanks to their Rhoynish ancestry, the Dornish are notably different from the rest of the population of the Seven Kingdoms. However, even within the kingdom itself, the population is ethnically diverse. As the First King Daeron observed, there are three main groups within Dorne. These are:

Salty Dornishmen – Most likely to be found in Dorne's coastal regions, mainly by the Broken Arm, where the Red Mountains stretch out into the shores of the Sea of Dorne, Salty Dornishmen have the most Rhoynish heritage of the entire kingdom. Lithe and dark, with smooth, olive skin and silky-black hair, theirs is a culture of fishermen and sailors; hard men and women who make up the mainstay of the Dornish fleet. The Martells of Sunspear – the region's current ruling family – are considered Salty Dornishmen.

Sandy Dornishmen – Dornes who live in the kingdom's central region, made up of sun-soaked deserts and long river valleys, are known as the Sandy Dornishmen. Their complexion is even darker than their salty brethren's, as they have been burned dark by the unforgiving Dornish sun over the centuries.

Stony Dornishmen – The final major constituents of the kingdom's population are the Stony Dornes, who live along the passes and peaks of the Red Mountains that border the Stormlands. These mountain-dwelling Dornishmen have greater Andal and First Men blood than Rhoynish heritage and so more closely resemble the people you'll find across the rest of the Seven Kingdoms. As well as looking more akin to their Westerosi neighbours, Stony Dornes act more like them too, with a culture that more closely resembles what you'd expect to find in King's Landing or the Reach.

Dornishmen are typically lithe with smooth dark hair and olive complexions. It's not just their appearance that sets them apart from the rest of the continent, however. Culturally, Dorne might as well be Braavos for all that it resembles the rest of Westeros. The Rhoynar refugees and the region's relative isolation from the rest of the continent has fostered a strong national identity in the Dornish, who pride themselves on their individuality, in contrast to elsewhere in Westeros.

People here are different and proud of it. Rhoynish

customs are still strongly observed in Dorne. As a result, bastards in Dorne are loved and embraced by their fathers, unlike in the rest of the Seven Kingdoms. Women, too, are given the same rights as men, entitled to equal inheritance and allowed to take up arms in defence of their kingdom. The culture here is also a little different to the socially shackled constraints you'll find in Westeros's other kingdoms. Dorne is liberal, to say the least. Living in a land of wine and women, Dornishmen are known for their hot-blooded tempers and sexual licentiousness, which draws frowns from other quarters of the continent.

The rest of Westeros may view their southern neighbours with mistrust, but for travellers, Dorne is an oasis offering the kind of adventure, intrigue and exoticism you can only normally see if you make the perilous journey across the Narrow Sea to Essos. From fine wines and fiery foods to other-worldly landscapes, enchanting company and exquisite architecture, it's easy to see why visitors keep coming back to this part of the world.

HIGHLIGHTS

Sunspear (page 264)

Located on the far southeast of the continent on the coast of the Summer Sea, the kingdom's capital is a hodgepodge of mud and straw huts, which cling to the castle and its walls like barnacles on a ship's hull. Wild, exotic and alternative, a visit is one of the most unique experiences in all of the Seven Kingdoms.

Water Gardens (page 266)

Once the private residence of the House of Martell, the Water Gardens has become a popular destination for travellers since opening its doors to tourists. A palatial retreat three leagues west of Sunspear, it is an oasis of pink marble and cool water pools, where visitors can enjoy a respite from the kingdom's cloying climate.

Planky Town (page 261)

Evocatively named, with its rough-hewn houses and rickety market stalls, Dorne's principal trade hub certainly lives up to its playful moniker.

Stepstones (page 267)

This long-disputed island chain has been shaped by storms, sieges and swathes of pirates who've set sail from Essos. However, behind its tattered history lies an island paradise, with precipitous mountain peaks that seem to float weightlessly on the crystal-blue waters over which they loom.

Getting There and Getting About

By land: Separated from the rest of the Seven Kingdoms by the Red Mountains, Dorne is largely cut off from the rest of Westeros. That isolation makes travel by land difficult, with a series of narrow passageways providing the only means of access. There are two used routes through which tourists choose to travel. The Stoneway (or Boneway, as it is known to locals) is the most used, ferrying tourists and trade through steep-sided valleys to the outpost of Yronwood.

Once the shortest and easiest route through the Red Mountains, the Prince's Pass has fallen into disrepair in recent decades. However, it is still popular with tourists looking to enjoy the breathtaking scenery offered by the kingdom's rocky mountain border.

By sea: The preferred means of travel for tourists wishing to avoid the heat and heavy going of the Red Mountain passes, travelling to and from Dorne by sea is a relatively easy experience. Ferries from the Stormlands run regularly, carrying travellers across the Sea of Dorne for a modest sum. It is also possible to make it to the kingdom's coastlines from further afield, with boats carrying passengers from as far as King's Landing and the Iron Islands.

RHOYNISH HISTORY

Dorne owes much of its cultural heritage to the Rhoynish, who emigrated to the region a millennia ago. A proud, river-faring people, they originally dwelt on the banks of the vast River Rhoyne in Essos, where they built vast city-states that teemed with traders from all corners of the known world.

However, some 700 years before Aegon's Landing the Rhoynish were forced to leave their homelands after the expansion of old Valyria. The Valyrian dragonlords began to aggressively expand their borders, eventually overcoming Prince Garin and the Rhoynar army and killing 250,000 men in the process. The Valyrian aggressors proceeded to sack the region, turning the once proud capital, Ny Sar, and

---

major settlements of Sar Marell, Ar Noy and Chroyane into charred ruins that are today a testament to the once-great civilisation.

In the face of such devastation, the surviving population – principally made up of women, children and old men – set sail, taking some 10,000 ships across the Narrow Sea to the shores of Dorne. There they settled, blending their culture with that of the Andals, who called the arid region home. Today, almost 1,000 years after fleeing their homeland, many of the Rhoynar traditions still remain, including the practice of equal primogeniture, the region's tolerance for homosexuality and mistresses, as well as the practice of calling their rulers princes and princesses over kings and lords.

Dangers and Annoyances

Heat – By far the hottest kingdom in all of Westeros, Dorne's climate can be deadly for ill-prepared tourists. Every year travellers succumb to sunstroke or die of thirst in the desert lands that fill the kingdom's heartland. Therefore, it is essential to prepare for the ferocious temperatures before you depart. Standard practices such as travelling at night when it's cooler and always carrying a skin or two of water are advised. Tourists should also take their cue from the locals, who wind lengths of silk and satin around their heads to ward off the heat.

Rising Tensions – The recent death of Prince Oberyn Martell in King's Landing has escalated tensions in the region. With the Red Viper's daughters clamouring for revenge and Prince

Doran Martell seemingly reluctant to indulge them, the region has become dangerously destabilised. For a kingdom that is notorious for its population's hot-bloodedness and short tempers, the situation has the potential to turn into a powder keg and travellers should seek advice before heading for the region.

The Dornish coast – The cool waters along Dorne's coast are an understandable attraction for travellers looking for respite from the scalding climate. But while certain areas do provide temporary relief from the ever-rising mercury, the 400-league long Dornish coastline is dotted with unseen dangers, which claim the lives of scores of tourists each and every year. The sea is riddled with underwater obstacles and whirlpools, so tourists are advised to seek the help of locals, who can guide them to the few safe landings punctuating this perilous peninsula.

Pirates – Long a thorn in the kingdom's side, raiders are known to operate out of the nearby Stepstones, where hidden bays are filled with pirate dens. Though travel to and from the disputed archipelago is possible, tourists should avoid travelling alone and instead stick to organised, well-protected convoys to ensure they don't fall foul of the local bandits.

Feral sand dogs – Dorne is littered with feral sand dogs that roam the streets and alleyways of the kingdom's towns and cities. Tourists are advised not to approach or to feed the animals – which are gnarled, unkempt and occasionally dangerous – during their stay.

Travellers from the Reach – Centuries of conflict with their near neighbours to the north – including the short-lived rule from the House of Tyrell – has made the Dornish particularly unfriendly towards residents of the Reach. Therefore, if you do hail from Highgarden and its lands, it's best to keep your heritage hidden for the duration of your stay. Although outright aggression is rare, shopkeepers have been known to drive up prices, while taverners will spit in your ale should they find out your birthplace.

Creatures, Flora and Fauna

Sandbeggars – Exclusive to this part of Westeros, Sandbeggars are thorny trees that grow in Dorne's drylands. Gnarled and twisted from the heat of the sun, they are often carved into exotic shapes by local artisans. These trees are important waypoints for locals as they are said to mark nearby water.

Scorpions – If the heat of the Dornish desert doesn't kill you, crossing paths with one of these killer critters may just do the trick.

Sand steeds – Like the mountain ponies of the Vale and the fearsome destriers of the Riverlands, Dorne's infamous sand steeds are famed throughout the Seven Kingdoms. Smaller and slimmer than proper warhorses, the sand steeds cannot carry the weight of plate armour. However, what they lack in size they more than make up for in speed and stamina. It is said that a sand steed can run for a day and a night, and then another day without tiring. They are also exotically marked, with beautiful heads and coats that come in a kaleidoscope of colours, from red and gold to pale grey and black.

When to Visit

Winter never really extends its icy tendrils to this part of the continent, which makes Dorne the ideal place to escape the colder climes you'll find further north. However, most seasoned travellers will tell you that the region is at its best in autumn when the crops are bountiful and the long, warm days give way to cool, comfortable nights.

Famous Residents

Before his unfortunate and grisly demise at the hands of the Mountain in King's Landing, Prince Oberyn Martell – known as the Red Viper, thanks to his penchant for poisoned blades – was undoubtedly the most famous resident in the region. A member of the ruling Martell House, he is survived by the Sand Snakes: his infamous band of bastard daughters. Born to mothers both high and lowborn, the Sand Snakes are the product of the Prince's many trysts with septas, noblewomen, whores and Summer Isle traders. They all differ in appearance but are said to have their father's eyes. Alongside the exotic and recently incarcerated beauties, the latest addition to the Dornish court is Princess Myrcella – the middle child of the late King Robert Baratheon and Queen Cersei Lannister – who is being fostered in Dorne in preparation for her arranged wedding with Prince Trystane Martell.

WOMEN'S RIGHTS

Unlike the rest of Westeros, where men often ride roughshod over their female counterparts, equal rights are a very real part of day-to-day life in Dorne. Women's rights in this part of the continent can be traced back

---

to the Rhoynish migration, which brought with it many customs and practices that are alien to other parts of the Seven Kingdoms. That those traditions remain in place to this day is testament to the region.

Perhaps the biggest benefit for women south of the Red Mountains is the equal standing in inheritance law. Inheritances in Dorne pass to the eldest child regardless of gender. This means both power and wealth can be passed into the hands of women, creating an equal footing when it comes to Dornish affairs and economic standing.

Women are also given a greater social standing than in the rest of Westeros, with princesses known to rule holdfasts, keeps and even the entire kingdom. It is also possible for the fairer sex to take up arms, with some of Dorne's most accomplished fighters being women-at-arms. The permissive sexual culture in the kingdom also means that mistresses/paramours are valued and accepted. Although the region is often derided as hot-headed and just shy of savagery by their nearest neighbours, it seems that, perhaps, the rest of Westeros could take a lesson or two from the liberal locals.

Where to Stay

There are few stone keeps in Dorne. Instead, the architecture here employs mud and straw that is baked until hard in the hot southern sun. As a result, the creature comforts you'll find in other parts of the Seven Kingdoms can be hard to come by. There are still accommodation options available, however, with most falling into the 'basic' rather than 'boutique' category, so it's worth lowering your expectations before you set out.

Tower of the Sun (£££)

With its Rhoynish architecture and well-appointed rooms, the Old Palace is the most luxurious accommodation on offer in Dorne. Thanks to the pale marble floors and stained-glass windows, the rooms here are cool and comfortable, with furnishings fit for a king (or should that be prince?). Accessed via the Threefold Gate, which bars entrance to the Old Palace, guests can expect a boisterous reception on their arrival – a party that often carries on long into the night.

Skyreach (££)

Located at the southern entrance of the Prince's Pass, Skyreach is a popular pitstop for travellers looking to rest their weary legs after making their way through the Red Mountains. A castle has stood here since the time of the First Men – something that is abundantly clear when you set foot in the ageing accommodation. But while the furnishings have seen better days, there's still plenty to recommend the ancient castle to tourists, not least the soaring towers, which provide lofty views of the surrounding scenery. There's also an infamous dwarf jester who can bring a smile to even the most weary of travellers.

Lemonwood (£)

In contrast to the kaleidoscope of cargoes that pass through its port every day, the choice when it comes to accommodation in Planky Town is severely limited. In fact, the only place we feel comfortable recommending is the nearby Lemonwood, a comfortable keep that sits on the banks of the Greenblood.

Eating and Drinking

Though much of the Dornish landscape is scarred with drought-ravaged deserts, the region's few fertile lands are filled with a bounty of natural produce. From juicy olives to succulent citrus fruits, the sun-drenched kingdom produces some of the strongest flavours in the Seven Kingdoms. If you thought the people here were flamboyant, wait until you try their food!

Produce

If the Reach is known as the kingdom's breadbasket, Dorne is arguably its fruit bowl. The warm weather is ideal for growing bountiful produce, with olives, plums and pomegranates flourishing alongside abundant citrus fruits. In fact, the fruit here is so bountiful that blood oranges literally fall to the ground as you stroll around sun-baked streets.

Duck with lemons

Favoured by the kingdom's highborn, this local speciality is served throughout Dorne, with every establishment worth its salt offering its own take on the time-honoured recipe.

Street food

No trip to Dorne would be complete without sampling some of the kingdom's famed street food. The best places to visit are the ramshackle stalls set up around Sunspear, serving crisp grilled snake spiced with mustard seeds and dragon peppers. Many stalls cook the charred critters in their own venom – a fearsome concoction that carries quite a kick.

Breakfast

A Dornish dish that has grown popular throughout

Westeros is the spiced eggs that are ubiquitous on breakfast tables throughout the kingdom. While the rest of the Seven Kingdoms may purport to replicate the recipe, you can't quite appreciate this spicy fast-breaker until you've tried it in Dorne itself, where the local firepeppers mean the dish is at its mouth-burning best. Like their customs, Dornish palates differ a little from the rest of Westeros, so prepare to have your your taste buds scalded. You have been warned!

Wine

Since most grape varieties are drought-resistant, Dorne long ago formed a reputation for being a formidable wine-growing region. Indeed, Dornish wine is among the most prized in all of Westeros, standing second only to the Arbor golds that adorn the tables of the continent's upper classes. The warm weather and dry soils are perfect for fruit-forward reds with dried-berry tones as well as fortified sweetwines, which are unique to this part of the Seven Kingdoms.

THE CONQUEST OF DORNE

Despite sweeping all of the kingdoms before him during his invasion, Aegon's War of Conquest proved unsuccessful when it came to Dorne. In spite of dispatching his wife Rhaenys and an army to conquer the kingdom, they could not break the local forces, who used the land itself to their advantage, waging a guerrilla war that eventually drove out the Targaryen invaders.

Upon his ascension to the Iron Throne in 157AC, young King Daeron I Targaryen considered the conquest of

Dorne to be unfinished business and vowed to complete the job his ancestor had started a century and a half before. He amassed an army and marched south, defeating the Dornish legions and forcing the submission of Sunspear.

Dorne, however, proved harder to rule than it was to conquer. Rebellions rose across the land and after Lord Tyrell of Highgarden (who'd been left to rule in Daeron's place) was killed when a hundred red scorpions were left in his bed, the kingdom broke out into an open rebellion that would eventually claim the young king's life. Some fifty years after Daeron I's death, Dorne was finally absorbed into the Seven Kingdoms, with the combined efforts of Baelor I and Daeron II ensuring Dorne's allegiance to the Iron Throne through marriage in 197AC.

Areas of Interest/What to Do When You're There

Though sparsely populated, there is still plenty for travellers to see and do during a trip to Dorne. The region's relative poverty in contrast to the rest of the Seven Kingdoms also makes activities more affordable, meaning many tourists choose to indulge themselves during their stay. From pillow-house dalliances to shopping in Shadow City's famed bazaars, there's something to suit every taste. And in a kingdom where almost everything goes, you may find that you develop entirely new appetites along the way.

Visit Planky Town

This trading post located at the mouth of the Greenblood in southeast Dorne is famed for the cornucopia of goods stocked by its market stalls and storehouses. A popular port for traders from across the Narrow Sea, the goods on sale here come from as far afield as Myr, Volantis and the Summer Isles. From fermented mare's milk favoured in the Dothraki Sea and pear brandy from Tyrosh to beard oil from Pentos, fine tapestries from Lys and exquisite velvets from Lorath, it's as close as you'll get to Essos without actually crossing the Narrow Sea.

Shopping in the Shadow City bazaars

Though more of a town than a city, Shadow City's warren of streets boasts some of the best bazaars in all of Westeros. These marketplaces are filled with the babble of traders hawking goods and haggling prices in their heavily accented drawl. The relative poverty of the region – where water is more highly prized than gold – means that tourists can strike a bargain if they're prepared to engage with the usual sales pitter-patter. Popular items include jars of local olive oil and skins of Summerwine, alongside more exotic goods such as double-curved bows carved from Dornish yew.

Those looking to expand their wardrobe in the style of the local lords and ladies can also find exquisitely embroidered silk and satin robes, cut in the Dornish fashion with flowing sleeves and often accessorised with jewelled belts.

Try your hand at Cyvasse

First introduced by Volantene traders who'd visited Planky Town to deposit the contents of their holds, Cyvasse spread like wildfire throughout the kingdom, becoming the most popular pastime in the Dornish court. Played on a board comprised of wooden squares and mountains, it uses ten pieces, each one with different powers and abilities.

A game of strategy and cunning, it takes a day to learn and a lifetime to master. Dorne is the only place in Westeros where you'll find Cyvasse Parlors, fashioned after the kind you'll find across the Narrow Sea in Volantis. These parlors are filled with boards carved out of weirwood, bone and obsidian and packed with locals exchanging wagers and bawdy taunts, but visitors are welcome to stop by and play a game or two.

Travel along the Greenblood

The region's major river, the Greenblood, stretches from Planky Town inland past Godsgrace and beyond. Formed by the confluence of the Vaith and the Scourge, it gets its name from the murky green water that runs slowly through its shallow depths. A vital artery for traders, the river is also a popular destination for travellers, thanks largely to the Orphans of the Greenblood: Rhoynish refugees who refused to assimilate with Dorne's original Andal culture.

The Orphans live on rafts, following the same practices and traditions as their river-faring ancestors. Exquisitely carved and decorated, these rafts are poled up and down the Greenblood, where their residents fish, pick fruit and perform labour for sustenance. Some are known to sell cloth and spices, while others offer healing arts, curing ailments such as warts and even acting as midwives.

At Planky Town it's possible to charter one of the low-sided ships and take a trip up the Greenblood. The Orphans are known to be impeccable hosts and while the boats pale in comparison to the pleasure barges of the Reach, a few days spent supping Summerwine and eating freshly picked blood oranges on a shaded deck can be just what the Maester ordered after a few weeks on the road.

Visit a pillow house

While prostitutes flout their flesh across the Seven Kingdoms, like many practices the act of visiting a whorehouse is more socially acceptable than elsewhere in Westeros. Dornish pillow houses are a popular destination for travellers looking to take advantage of the region's relaxed approach to affairs of the flesh. Filled with exotic paramours, a man (or, indeed, a woman) can fulfil their every desire for a handful of gold. Pillow houses are not without their dangers, though. The fiery-tempered residents are known to regularly rush to arms and it is not uncommon to see knife-wielding women battle bare-breasted in order to secure the affections of heavy-pursed punters.

Shandystone

The desert ruins of Shandystone are a popular day trip, with tours departing regularly from Shadowcity. The ruined holdfast was abandoned long ago when its well ran dry. However, the dry climate has perfectly preserved its ruins, which are almost untouched centuries after civilisation left. The colossal columns are beautiful at sunset, while the mosaics – which are still intact below the sand – offer a glimpse into the past. The area is also a nest for vipers and many tour guides will treat you to a demonstration of venom milking as part of your trip.

SUNSPEAR/SHADOW CITY

Sunspear is the ancient stronghold of the House Martell. Designed in the Rhoynish fashion, it's built principally out of mud and straw bricks that have been baked in the harsh Dornish sun. The castle stands on the easternmost end of a small peninsula of sand and stone, surrounded on three sides by the sea.

Sunspear takes its name from the marriage between the Dornish (represented by the spear) and the Rhoynish (represented by the sun) and was built to replace the squat, unspectacular keep of Sandship that had originally formed the kingdom's capital. The castle is guarded by the Winding Walls, built seven centuries ago to protect the city and its inhabitants. Within these walls lies a maze of narrow streets, hidden courts and noisy bazaars through which runs a brickroad that takes guests through the Threefold Gate into the palace itself.

The palace is the jewel in Sunspear's crown. It is comprised of three formidable towers that jut spectacularly out of the desert floor. The highest of these three is the Spear Tower, a slender sandstone battlement that stands 150ft tall and is topped by a gilded steel spear that rises a further 30ft into the air. It is joined by the equally impressive Tower of the Sun, a mighty fortification crowned with a dome of gold and coloured glass that is home to Dorne's throneroom and the Martell household. The third tower is what remains of the Sandship – an altogether duller structure that looks like a dromond turned to stone.

While the architectural attractions of Sunspear can enamour visitors, nearby Shadow City is responsible for much of the tourism that passes through this part of Dorne. Despite its name, it is more of a squalor-filled settlement than a bonafide city; a collection of mud shacks that cling to the Winding Walls like barnacles and sprawl westwards from the palace itself. It is a warren of shops, winesinks, bazaars, markets and pillow houses that seem to fold in on themselves.

The city is deserted during the heat of the day when the sun, along with the smell of dust, sweat and sand, forces its residents indoors. However, it comes alive at night, with the streets transformed into bustling sprawls of civilisation filled with performers, market stalls and street-food vendors. The party here lasts into the early hours as the locals indulge their famed appetites in an anything-goes atmosphere that is intoxicating for those tourists who can keep up the pace.

The Water Gardens

Only three leagues' ride along the coastal road from Sunspear lies this luxurious oasis of orange groves and cool, shaded fountains. Originally raised by Prince Maron Martell as a gift for his Targaryen bride, the Water Gardens are popular with the Martell family, who have opened their doors to tourists over recent years.

Sitting on the shores of the Summer Sea, this palatial retreat is paved with cool pink marble that snakes through a seemingly endless array of blooming gardens and shady courtyards. Tranquil doesn't even come close to describing the peace and isolation offered here, where the only sounds that fill the air are the lapping of water and the giddy excitement of children playing in the fountains.

The main event is, of course, the Water Gardens themselves: a stunning ornamental arrangement of exotic flowers and foliage shaded by a grove of strong-scented orange trees. The gardens are filled with pools and fountains and reached via a fluted pillar gallery leading to an ornate triple archway.

Beyond the restorative powers of the water, guests can enjoy stunning sea views and luxurious appointed sleeping quarters complete with crisp cool linens that complement the breeze rolling in off the beach in the evenings. The food here is also outstanding. Head to the terrace to enjoy a lunchtime mezze of locally sourced purple olives, flatbread, cheese and chickpea paste and be sure to enjoy the breakfast: a local speciality made of blood oranges and gulls' eggs laced with ham and fiery peppers that is every bit as delicious as it sounds.

THE STEPSTONES

Many people believe that Westeros was originally joined with Essos via a land bridge spanning the Narrow Sea. The so-called Arm of Dorne was the route through which the First Men invaded these shores some 12,000 years before Aegon's conquest. How the arm came to be broken is an area of some debate, though. Legend has it that the Children of the Forest called on ancient magic, which caused the sea to rise up and shatter the arm in a futile attempt to end the invasion. However, Archmaester Cassander contends that the shattering of the land bridge was, in fact, an entirely natural occurrence; a slow rising of the sea level taking place over a period of centuries, which was brought on by a series of long, hot summers and short, warm winters that melted ice to the north and flooded the low-lying land.

Whether you choose to believe in the evocative

legend or the scientific explanation, the end result is the same: the formation of the Stepstones – a long-disputed archipelago that stands between southeastern Westeros and southwestern Essos. The small, rocky outpost has long been a battleground, with forces from Lys, Myr and Tyrosh exchanging control of the region, or fending off aggressors from the Seven Kingdoms. Today the sheltered islands are home to scores of pirates, who use the atolls as a base to launch raids on trading routes over the Narrow Sea.

Battered by storms and swarming with pirates, the Stepstones don't exactly scream 'holiday destination'. However, centuries of isolation have helped to create an island paradise that is all but untouched by civilisation. There are no castles, keeps or cities here, no roads or ruins. Instead, the archipelago was given over to nature, with the jungles that sit just inland from the sandy shores teeming with exotic plant and wildlife. Tours regularly run from Sunspear, ferrying paying passengers along the kingdom's southern coastline and out towards the Stepstones. It is too dangerous to set foot on the islands themselves but well-armed pleasure cruises offer the perfect opportunity to experience these wild outposts from the relative comfort of a merchant cog.

Further Afield

There is enough in Westeros to keep even the most adventurous of travellers on their toes. But while the locals might like to view the Seven Kingdoms as the centre of the universe, the truth is that Westeros is far from alone. There is a whole world out there (or, at least, we assume there is) – one that starts with nearby Essos.

The neighbouring continent sits just a short boat ride across the Narrow Sea but it might as well be a world away from Westeros. From the famed Free Cities to the vastness of the Dothraki Sea and the riches of Slaver's Bay to the adventure offered by the uncharted territories to the east, it's like nothing you'll see in the Seven Kingdoms.

Perhaps that's why so many people choose to take the voyage to these foreign shores. Whether you're looking for adventure, a place to lie low after murdering your own father or simply a safe spot to raise your fire-breathing babies, there's something for everyone in Essos.

Unlike Westeros, there is no dominant power here. In fact, the continent hasn't been conquered since the fall of Valyria, four centuries ago. There is no Iron Throne here. Instead, Essos is divided into many different sovereign territories and city states, a hodgepodge of power that only adds to the region's exotic allure. Like the lands on which they live, Essosi culture varies wildly from place to place. The people here have a rich and diverse history. They are the descendants of ancient cultures ranging from the Valyrian Dragonlords to the Rhoynish, the Andals and Old Ghis.

The journey to Essos is not to be taken lightly but intrepid travellers who do decide to set sail will be rewarded with a region rich in natural beauty, ancient culture and cosmopolitan cities; a place where mysticism is alive and well, where dragons still soar through the skies and where purple-lipped warlocks still ply their trade. In short, it's magical.

Getting There

By sea: The only way to and from Essos is to make the journey across the Narrow Sea. Ships travel regularly between the two continents and captains are willing to ferry anyone with a purse full of gold (or a rare Braavosi coin) across the waters. The journey can be perilous. The Narrow Sea is often stormy but strong winds and high seas are the least of your problems. Corsairs and pirates are known to hunt the southern route, while in the north, the sea is said to be haunted. Even if you avoid those dangers, giant kraken have been known to pull entire ships under the swell.

Despite its many dangers, the journey isn't without its joys, however. On a fine day the views can be breathtaking and there are few things finer than sitting on the bow of a ship watching land come into view while dolphins play in your surf.

Travel Essentials

A phrasebook: Travellers accustomed to using the common tongue will have a rude awakening when they land across the Narrow Sea. In stark contrast to Westeros, Essos is littered with different dialogues, with more than nineteen languages spoken in the lands to the east. Although skilled translators are available for hire (or to buy, over in Slaver's Bay), travellers are best advised to brush up on their language skills before they leave and at the very least to carry a phrasebook to help them with everyday discussions.

Valyrian is the most common tongue and across the continent the language of the old rulers still exists. However, four centuries without Valyrian rule has meant that in many areas the dialect has drifted from its original form. In fact, each of the nine Free Cities in Essos has developed its own bastardised version of the original Valyrian vernacular. Though colloquially referred to as Low Valyrian, there are subtle differences in vocabulary and enunciation that ground the language in each city in which it is spoken.

Beyond the Free Cities you can expect to hear the guttural Dothraki language used by the nomadic horsemen who drift across the continent's vast inland plains. You might also hear snippets of Qartheen exchanged between locals in the ancient and evocative metropolis, though the dialect is said to be so difficult for foreigners to master that locals have grown fluent in the Common Tongue.

USEFUL PHRASES

VALYRIAN

Kessa – Yes.

Daor – No.

Skoriot ñuhyz zaldrīzesse ilzi? – Where are my dragons?

Tubī daor – Not today.

Bantis zōbrie issa se ossȳngnoti lēdys – The night is dark and full of terrors.

Sīkudi nopāzmi! – Seven Hells!

Valar morghulis – All men must die.

DOTHRAKI

Sek – Yes.

Vos – No.

Me nem nesa – It is known.

San athchomari yeraan! – Thank you!

Hash yer dothrae chek asshekh? – How are you today? (Do you ride well today?)

Fini hazi? – What is that?

Aena shekhikhi! – Good morning!

Hash yer dothrae chek? – How are you?

Fonas chek! – Goodbye! (Hunt well!)

Dangers and Annoyances

Dragons – Though they were thought long extinct, recent reports have reached us suggesting that dragons are alive and well in Essos. Yes, dragons – big, fire-breathing dragons with razor-sharp teeth and hellfire halitosis. Though the three fire-breathers currently operating on the continent are said to still be in their infancy, they can pose a significant threat to tourists, who are advised to steer clear of these mythical beasts at all costs.

Blood flies – Though this breed died out long ago in Westeros, they are still a significant annoyance across the Narrow Sea. The insects feed on the blood of men and horses and lay their eggs in the dead. They are typically little more than a pest that can be carelessly swatted away. However, they can easily infect an open wound, causing serious complications further down the line. If you do suspect a wound has become infected, visit a local herb woman or Maegi, who are trained in the ways of healing. However, tourists are advised to avoid Blood Magic at all costs, lest they're prepared to pay a high price for their health.

Disease – Thanks to its sub-tropical climate, Essos is the unhappy home to some serious and, indeed, deadly diseases. Dead Eye Fever is a very real threat to those travelling on the continent and tourists are advised to seek out their local Maester before travelling to ensure they are properly vaccinated.

Counterfeiting – There is a kaleidoscope of exotic goods on offer in Essos. Whether it's Myrish lace, Tyroshi pepperwine, saffron from Yi Ti or Dragonglass out of Asshai, the markets and bazaars in cities such as Braavos, Qarth and Pentos are like catnip for souvenir hunters. However, not every trader in Essos is as good as his word. Counterfeiting is a common problem on the continent, with dragon eggs and arakhs among the 'genuine' items touted to travellers. Tourists are advised to exercise caution before emptying the contents of their purses: if it sounds too good to be true, it probably is.

SLAVERY

Abhorred in Westeros, where the practice has been illegal since the Andals landed some 6,000 years ago, slavery is commonplace almost everywhere in Essos, with the exception of Pentos and Braavos.

Much of Essos's slave trade is based in the south of the continent around the area known as Slaver's Bay. The region has long been a busy hub, with cities such as Astapor, Yunkai and Meereen boasting trade routes that stretch back millennia. For centuries Dothraki khals and corsairs from the Basilisk Isles have passed through the region, selling thousands of people into slavery at the cities' vast markets. In time, each city has developed its own slavery speciality. In Astrapor, for example, they are renowned for training soldiers – specifically the eunuch armies known as the Unsullied – while Yunkai is famed for training bed slaves, who are prized for their knowledge of the seven sighs and the sixteen seats of pleasure, rather than their skills with sword or spear.

The practice isn't just isolated in the south, however. In Myr and Tyrosh the slave trade booms. In Volantis there

---

is a particularly high population, with some five slaves for every one free man. The problem is perhaps most notable in Lys, where, thanks to a practice of tattooing the faces of their slaves, the sheer size of the issue is abundantly apparent.

Apart from the occasional exile that has attempted to swell their wealth by engaging in the barbaric practice, the trade has traditionally left a sour taste in the mouths of visitors from the west. However, all that might be about to change, thanks to the actions of Daenerys Targaryen, the so-called Mother of Dragons, who has led a rebellion against the previously all-powerful slavers. With the help of an army made up of sellswords and liberated Unsullied, she has ransacked Slaver's Bay, bringing dynasties that have stood for centuries to their knees in the process. Her actions have divided the continent. But while the economic implications remain to be seen, her systematic destruction of the slave trade has been a shot in the arm for tourism, with travellers from the west now able to enjoy guilt-free trips to the east.

HIGHLIGHTS
THE FREE CITIES

Stretched across the western shore of the continent, the nine Free Cities are individual states that share a common ancestry (aside from Braavos) as former colonies of the Valyrian Dragonlords who once dominated the region. As vast as they are varied, these cities swim in wealth as traders come from all four corners of the known world to sell their wares to locals and visitors alike.

Braavos

Perhaps the most beautiful of Essos's nine Free Cities, Braavos is a sprawling metropolis built over a series of more than a hundred interconnected isles. Located in a sheltered bay, where the mountainous surroundings historically provided its citizens with refuge from the Valyrian Dragonlords, Braavos is a sprawl of domed buildings and grey-stone houses, which seem to rise effortlessly from the waters.

With a tangle of piers, quays and bridges spanning the waterways that join its myriad of islands together, Braavos is like nothing you'll find in Westeros. The buildings here dwarf their western counterparts, while the exotic architecture that makes up the palaces, temples and towers littering the landscape is beyond even the finest masonry across the Narrow Sea. The people here reflect the city in which they live. Originally founded by slaves who'd escaped Valyrian rule, the city has always welcomed outsiders, which is easy to see as you view the vibrant and diverse cultures that fill the streets.

As well as welcoming all people, Braavos is famed for its religious tolerance. All gods are worshipped here and most command their own temples, which are located on an isle in the centre of the city. Among them is the Temple of the Moonsingers – who is said to have led the original Braavosi to these islands – the temple to the Father of the Waters, the Sept Beyond the Sea, as well as temples to the Lord of Light R'hllor and the Many-Faced God. There are also shrines to the Weeping Lady of Lys, the Lord of Harmony and the Black Goat. Even gods who have no followers are honoured in a temple called the Holy Refuge or, as the locals are wont to call it, the Warren. The best way to explore this religious ramshackle is on foot, where you can best admire the intricacies that go into the composition of each site.

In contrast, the best way to explore Braavos itself is by boat, traversing the numerous waterways that criss-cross the hundred or so islands on which it sits. The most impressive of these is the Grand Canal, which is flanked by giant stone monuments that pay homage to the city's former Sealords. The Drowned Town – an area of the city almost completely reclaimed by the lagoon that surrounds it – is also a popular destination for tourists, as are the wharfside bazaars and markets, which stock everything from fresh fish to exotic goods from as far afield as the Jade Sea and beyond.

Of course, the city's biggest attraction is the Titan of Braavos, a colossal structure that stands astride the sole channel leading into the bay. Part defensive structure, part lighthouse, you must pass through the Titan's legs in order to gain entrance to the city. A giant of stone and bronze that stands almost as big as a mountain, his hair is made of green hempen ropes that blow in the wind and the caves that form his eyes burn bright with huge fires, which are lit to guide ships safely into port. It is said that whenever Braavos stood in danger, he would wake with fire in his eyes, his rocky limbs grinding and groaning as he waded out to sea to smash his enemies with his half-broken sword. In reality, he is a fortified watchtower – the first line of many defences that make this island haven near impregnable to attack.

Do stop by the Spotted Cellar down by the gates of Drowned Town to take in an eel fight, a popular pastime of the Braavosi. If duelling congers aren't your cup of tea, head for the Ship, where the in-house Mummers are renowned for their fine enactment of Seven Drunken Oarsmen.

Don't linger by the wharves. The docks can be a dangerous place, especially for men fresh off the boats, preyed on by the local whores who rob them, kill them and then feed them to the eels.

WORLD-FAMOUS COURTESANS

Though the pillow houses of Dorne and the girls in King's Landing's Street of Silk might argue otherwise, the working women of Braavos are like none other in all of Westeros. No normal prostitutes, these are courtesans of the highest order who are famed throughout the known world for their beauty and sophistication. Singers sing for them, jewellers shower them with gifts and merchant princes have been known to spend a royal sum to have them on their arms at feasts.

Every courtesan in the city has her own barge and a carefully constructed persona to match. The Poetess, for example, always carries a book; the Moonshadow wears only white and silver, while the Veiled Lady only shows her face to her lovers. However, they say the most beautiful is the Black Pearl, who is said to descend from the old Dragonlords of Valyria.

Pentos

One of the largest of the nine Free Cities, Pentos lies on the Bay of Pentos – a stunning natural harbour dotted with the square stone towers and tiled roofs that make up the city's skyline. The first Pentoshi were merchants, traders and farmers from old Valyria; there were few nobles among them but the rich lands surrounding the city have transformed it into one of the most prosperous in all of Essos. Money talks and it's clear that the locals are listening. Gold is power in Pentos and the ability to buy or bribe your way to the top makes it a popular destination for Westerosi emigrants, who flock to the warmer climes and safer courts offered by the continent.

Once a holiday home for the Targaryens, it's easy to see Pentos's appeal to tourists, scores of whom cross the narrow sea every year to shop in the city's markets and sup pinchfire-spiced wine while enjoying the late-evening sun on one of the city's sea-facing terraces.

Do take in a Dothraki wedding. The horse lords have been known to hold their services in the fields surrounding the city and the opportunity to enjoy the ceremony is not to be missed. Dothraki weddings run from dawn until well into the night – an endless day of feasting, drinking and fighting. **Don't** let your guard down while at the service. Dothraki weddings aren't for the faint of heart. In fact, a ceremony without at least three deaths is widely considered a tame affair.

NINE DISHES YOU WON'T WANT TO MISS

Travellers can enjoy a culinary adventure during their time in Essos. The cuisine here is almost as vast and varied as the land it springs from and you can expect your taste buds to embark on a rollercoaster ride of spicy, sweet and sometimes strange dishes. Good food is relatively easy to come by, but below is our pick of nine iconic dishes you won't want to miss out on.

Horseflesh – Dothraki Sea

The horselords of the Dothraki Sea don't just ride their mounts, they eat them too. It's a practice that may seem alien to those of us who hail from Westeros but it's a natural part of life on the plains – and a delicious one at that. Though the thought of drinking unclotted blood direct from a stallion's heart (a practice observed by pregnant women in Vaes Dothrak) may turn your stomach, there are tastier ways to enjoy horseflesh. A particular favourite are horsemeat sausages, stuffed with garlic and firepeppers then grilled with onions over a hot stone – a delicious delicacy served throughout the region.

Seafood – Braavos

The waters around Braavos teem with some of the finest seafood you'll find anywhere in the known world. The clams, cockles, mussels, muskfish, leopard crabs, striped eels, lampreys and oysters are all excellent here. Best enjoyed fresh from one of the seaweed-lined barrows ferried around the city by street hawkers, they are delicious when served simply with sea salt, pepper and a strand or two of saffron. Sumptuous!

Shade of the Evening – Qarth

It won't take long for you to spot the blue-stained lips of the Qartheen people. While many people believe the pigment is a dye applied for aesthetic purposes, it's actually the result of the city's obsession with Shade of the Evening. Brewed by local Warlocks from the leaves of trees that grow wild across the city, the first taste is like ink mixed with bad meat but then it warms you and transforms into a heady concoction of anise, cream and honey. Served in small crystal vials, the drug is said to grant magical powers and no trip to the region is complete without sampling a sip or two of the perennially popular poison.

Honey duck – Pentos

Served with orange snap peppers and washed down with flagons of Myrish pepperbeer, this dish is an old favourite that has been passed down through generations of Pentoshi cooks. A common sight at feasts, the meat is so succulent that locals choose to forego their cutlery and rip the flesh apart with their bare hands instead.

Sweetgrass stew – Pentos

Unless you grew up in Dorne, Pentos's sub-tropical climate can take a while for Westerosi to adjust to. Seasoned travellers, however, will tell you that the best way to beat the heat is not with water but with a pot of sweetgrass stew: a delicately spiced dish served with lumps of frybread to mop up those all-important dregs.

Fermented mare's milk – Dothraki Sea

You'll find no beer in the Dothraki Sea. Instead, those looking to scratch their alcoholic itch will have to indulge in the local tipple of choice: a potent brew made of fermented mare's milk. Half-clotted and heavy, it's hardly Arbor gold but it does the trick.

Breakfast soup – Qarth

As you'd expect for a city that has flourished for millennia, the cuisine in Qarth is almost as sophisticated as the civilisation. Many dishes, such as this breakfast soup made from shrimp and persimmon, are designed to reflect the delicate population.

Salt fish – Meereen

You've probably tried salt fish before but nowhere is this storeroom staple more enjoyable than in Meereen, where it is served with figs, olives and a salad made of carrots and raisins soaked in wine.

Sweet-beet soup – Volantis

Volantines are fond of sweet beets, which are grown throughout the region and served as an accompaniment to almost every meal. For our money, the best dish, however, is the sweet-beet soup: a cold bowlful of brilliance that is rich, thick and tastes like purple honey.

Myr

Renowned across the known world for the skill of its craftsmen, you'll no doubt have had contact with the city, thanks to the Myrish goods that fill the highborn houses of Westeros. From fine rugs and carpets to exquisite lace gowns and hand carved far-eyes, Myrish goods are prized across the Seven Kingdoms. But nothing quite compares to a trip to the city itself, where you can watch the artisans in action and explore the many bazaars and markets.

Myr itself is as attractive as its goods – a stunning city set alongside the coast of the Sea of Myrth, with a history as rich as one of its tapestries. While certain Maesters believe the city to have originally been colonised by the Rhoynish (on account of the population's olive skin), other experts contend it was formed by Valyrian merchants, who butchered and enslaved those who lived on the site and raised their own settlement. Whatever its history, the present-day city is a modern marvel; a haven for consumers who can spend their gold on goods that would cost ten times as much across the Narrow Sea.

Do take time to shop. The famed fabrics are just the tip of the iceberg as far as goods are concerned. From crossbows and carvings to glass worth its weight in gold, there is something for everyone provided they have the gold to pay for it.

Don't engage the local Mummers' troupes, who have been known to do unspeakable things to their underage companions.

Tyrosh

Formed over 1,000 years ago, this island city at the northern tip of the Stepstones was originally raised as a military outpost designed to control shipping in the area. However, shortly after it was founded, a unique variety of sea snail was discovered around Tyrosh. When harvested, these snails secreted a substance that could be transformed into a dye that grew wildly popular with the Valyrian nobility. Soon merchants came to Tyrosh in the thousands and in a single generation the outpost flourished into one of the most bustling cities in all of Essos.

Today the city continues to flourish. A busy trade out-post with a reputation for loud and raucous behaviour, Tyrosh is known for the greed of its inhabitants – a brightly coloured bunch who use all manner of extravagant dyes to colour their clothes and hair. It is also a popular pit stop for travellers heading east from Westeros, who stop by to take in the sights, including the Bleeding Tower, the Temple of Trios and the famed Fountain of the Drunks.

Do find an inn and join the ranks of sellswords, travellers and freed slaves supping on the area's prized pear brandy.

Don't visit if you're short of stature. The recent flight of Tyrion Lannister has led to a surge in intellectually challenged criminals beheading anyone under 5ft in order to stake a claim on the generation bounty being offered by King's Landing.

Lys

A small city clinging to the storm-battered rocks on the continent's southeastern coast, Lys is known as the easiest of the Free Cities, a place crammed full of pleasure houses, winesinks and gambling dens. It is a haven for inequity, a hotbed for vice and a place that caters to every pleasure, no matter how peculiar. Many men lose themselves in Lys, living so long as they have enough coins – even the currency here is bawdy, having been adorned with the naked figure of a local goddess – or until they've fallen foul of their debtors.

Those who don't wish to while away their days in a wine-sink or lie with one of the city's world-famous courtesans can pay a visit to the Weeping Lady of Lys, a stunning marble statue dedicated to a Lyseni goddess. You might also want to take in one of the city's many markets, where you can find rich tapestries, perfumes and sweet wines for a fraction of the cost you'll have to pay in the Seven Kingdoms.

Do check out one of the city's famed pleasure houses, which are filled with some of the finest companions in the known world.

Don't forget to pay your debts. Unless, of course, you want to find out about Lys's other speciality (see below).

CHOOSE YOUR POISON

Alongside its burgeoning trade in bedslaves, Lys is famous for another altogether deadlier export. We are, of course, talking about the cornucopia of poisons that the city's infamous alchemists have been cooking up here for centuries. The most famous concoctions are the Strangler and the Tears of Lys: vicious venoms that you wouldn't wish on your worst enemy – unless, of course, they happen to be a brattish boy king with a penchant for torture.

The Strangler is made using leaves from a plant found only in the Islands of the Jade Sea. The leaves have to be aged and soaked in a wash of limes, sugar water and rare spices from the Summer Isles. After fermentation, the potion is thickened with ash and turned into crystals that can be mixed into a cup of wine. The effect is deadly and

---

deeply disturbing, closing off a man's windpipe and turning his face purple – hence its name.

In contrast, The Tears of Lys is an altogether subtler toxin – a rare and incredibly expensive elixir that is clear, sweet as water and leaves no trace. Its effects, however, are abundantly clear as the poison causes a sickness of the belly, eating away at its victim from the inside out.

Lorath

An isolated archipelago on the western coast of the continent, Lorath is said to be the poorest of the nine Free Cities, thanks in no small part to its isolation. However, what it lacks in economic importance it more than makes up for in diversity. The city was originally populated by the Mazemakers, who have left their indelible mark on the islands, thanks to the stone warrens littering Lorath. It was then populated by the Andals, who were followed by Valyrians. In more recent times, however, the city's strict anti-slavery laws have made it a haven for runaways from the rest of Essos. This injection of outsiders has made Lorath one of the most ethnically diverse regions in the known world, a melting pot of cultures far richer than its economic state might suggest.

Do stock up on some new fabrics. The city's powerful textile merchants specialise in fine velvets that can be picked up for a song.

Don't get lost in one of the city's many mazes – once inside, you might never find your way out.

Volantis

Located in southeastern Essos at the mouth of the Rhoyne and the Summer Sea, Volantis is the oldest and proudest of the nine Free Cities. Located close to Slaver's Bay, this vast city – you could fit the hundred isles of Braavos within the bay along which it stretches – was the first daughter of Old Valyrian, the grandest and most populous of its expanded territories. However, ancient wars have depopulated the city – it is said that there are five slaves for every one Volantene today. That depopulation has led to disrepair. The once vibrant streets have gone quiet, the fountains have run dry and nature has begun to reclaim much of the city's once magnificent temples.

While there, be sure to visit the Old City – an oval area cut off from the rest of Volantis by a 200ft black-stone wall originally raised by Valyrians. You should also take a stroll across the Long Bridge, an architectural marvel that joins the two halves of Volantis across the mouth of the Rhoyne. Formed of the same black stone as the Old City, it is topped with scores of stone-carved sphinxes, manticores and dragons alongside spikes containing the hands and heads of the city's criminals.

Finally, stop by the Temple of the Lord of the Light, an enormous structure forged out of yellow, orange and gold stone and adorned with towers that stretch into the sky like tongues of flame. The mass of pillars, buttresses, domes and bridges was built on the site of a great plaza and has become a popular destination for pilgrims who flock to worship R'hllor, the god who is growing in popularity across the Seven Kingdoms.

Do visit the Merchant's House – the finest inn in all Volantis. This four-storey monstrosity is home to a common room that must be seen to be believed. A colossal social space that's larger than the halls you'll find in some of Westeros's greatest castles.

Don't enter the Old City without permission. Foreigners aren't allowed inside the Black Wall without the express invitation of those who live within it.

Qohor

This vast inland empire was originally founded by Valyrian dissidents who abandoned the old Freehold to set up their own civilisation at the foot of one of Essos's great forests. Known as the City of Sorcerers, it is a truly magical place where the dark arts – including divination, blood magic and necromancy – are still openly practised. It's not just the sorcerers who are enchanted either, the swordsmiths here are pretty magical too. Qohor is one of the only cities in the known world whose residents can still reforge Valyrian steel, melding it with paints and pigments during the smelting process to create wonderous weapons. The arms on offer in its numerous markets and bazaars are some of the truest, sharpest and, indeed, deadliest on the continent. In fact, most experts will tell you they're far superior to anything forged in Westeros.

Make time during your stay to visit the Black Goat, a vast monument dedicated to the deity worshipped by locals. Though recently ransacked by followers of R'hllor, the Black Goat is still the site of daily sacrifices, with calves, bullocks and horses brought before the altars.

Do visit the markets and bazaars. As the gateway to the

east, Qohor is where caravans stop to trade after their journeys to Vaes Dothrak and the land beyond the Bones. As such, visitors can pick up some real bargains, with everything from Valyrian steel to exquisite, yet disturbing carvings forged out of the much-prized local wood.

Don't break the law. On holy days it is condemned criminals, not livestock, who go under the knife in sacrifice to the Black Goat.

THE BATTLE OF QOHOR

Four hundred years ago, during a period known as the Century of Blood, the Dothraki first rode out of the plains to the east, sacking every town and city in their path.

With 50,000 men at his back, Khal Temmo had set his sights on Qohor as his next target and so the city set about readying its defences, strengthening its walls, doubling its garrison and hiring two companies of sellswords. They also sent word to Astapor to purchase 3,000 Unsullied – the spear-wielding eunuch soliders for which the slave city is famed.

It is a long march from Astapor to Qohor and by the time the Unsullied arrived, the city's heavy horses had been defeated and the sellswords – as they are prone to do – had fled with their tails between their legs. All that stood between the city and the Khalasar's advance was the Unsullied. Under the flag of the Black Goat, 3,000 Unsullied stood against 20,000 Dothraki. Eighteen times the horsebound warriors charged and thrice the archers rode by and rained arrows on the spear-wielding slave soldiers.

By the end of 3 days of bloodshed only 600 defenders remained. However, at their feet were the corpses of some 12,000 Dothraki, including Khal Temmo, his Bloodriders, his Kos and his sons. On the fourth day the Dothraki advanced again, only this time the new Khal led his people by the Unsullied ranks in stately procession, cutting off their braids and laying them at the feet of their opponents in order to show their respect. Since that day, the city guard of Qohor has been made up entirely of Unsullied, every single one of whom carries a tall spear from which hangs a braid of human hair.

Norvos

Known as Great Norvos by its people, Norvos sits in Essos's interior among the Hills of Noyne. The city is a popular port of call for caravans and merchants heading east to west on the ancient Valyrian roads that line the continent. Norvos itself is set on two great hills. The High City, which occupies the upper altitudes, is host to the bearded holy men who rule over the people. The Lower City is filled with rivermen's haunts, brothels and taverns, which eventually give way to terraced fields, rolling hills and small walled villages supporting the population.

Here, the people are almost as picturesque as their home. The Holy Men wear fine beards, while both high- and lowborn choose long sweeping moustaches often coloured by dyes. In contrast, women are shaved bare, though noblewomen are known to don wigs, especially in the company of men from other lands.

Do visit during the city's annual Holy Festival, which features bears dancing down a path known as the Sinner's Steps.

Don't visit one of the city's brothels, the basements of which are said to be full of slave girls being forced to mate with wolves.

THE DOTHRAKI SEA

Home to the legendary horsemen who spread nomadically across this inland empire, the Dothraki Sea is a vast plain located east of the Free Cities, north of Slaver's Bay and west of the Bone Mountains. Its size is almost unfathomable, an enormous expanse of grass that extends as far as the eye can see. These grasses are key to Dothraki culture: an inland sea made up of more than a hundred different varieties. From Ghostgrass, with its milky pale stalks that stand taller than a man to a variety of green grass which blossoms blood red during springtime, it's an oasis of flora and fauna at the very heart of the continent.

The only way to truly experience the Dothraki Sea is on horseback, joining a Khalasar on its meandering journey across the plains and stopping only to hunt elk or sack the occasional village.

Vaes Dothrak

At once Essos's largest city and its smallest, Vaes Dothrak is the capital of the Dothraki lands. Though more than ten times the size of Pentos, the city looks more like a squalor, made up of grass tents, manses of woven grass the size of castles and carved stone pavilions. This is the home of the horselords; a vast city without walls that is a sacred spot for the Dothraki people. Though large enough to house every man and horse from every Khalasar on the continent, Vaes Dothrak is positively deserted for most of the year when its only full-time residents are the Crones of the Dosh Khaleen: the head of the Dothraki nation and spiritual leaders of its people.

On your way into Vaes Dothrak, stop to admire the vast Horse Gate: an archway made of two gigantic bronze stallions, which guards the entrance to the city. Beyond this impressive structure is a road lined with ancient monuments. These kings and queens are not Dothraki, however. Instead, they are the spoils of war; loot pillaged from the countless peoples and civilisations defeated by the horsemen over the centuries.

At the centre of the city is the Mother Mountain, a sacred place where only Dothraki men are allowed to go and give sacrifice to their gods. Take a moment to admire the stunning landmark before turning your attention to the Great Bazaar, a colossal marketplace that people flock to from across the continent and beyond.

The eastern end of the market features caravans from as far afield as Yi Ti, Asshai and the Shadow Lands. Here you'll find more traditional Dothraki fare, including wondrous horsemeat sausages alongside genuine Dothraki arakhs, grass vests and medallion belts. The eastern market is also alive with all manner of exotic animals, including manticores, elephants and striped black-and-white zorses of Jogos Nhai.

In contrast, the western side of the market caters to more

common tastes, with caravans coming from Free Cities like Pentos by way of Norvos. A great square of beaten earth surrounded by animal pens, drinking halls and store rooms dug into the cool earth, it's an assault on the senses, an overload of smells, sights and sounds. Here you can trade (currency means nothing to the Dothraki) in anything from Myrish Lace and scented oils to feathered cloaks from the Summer Isles that are fit for a Khaleesi. The food here is also outstanding – especially for tourists weary of the steady diet of horsemeat they will have endured during their journey across the Dothraki Sea. There are Honeyfingers from Tyrosh and wines ranging from Andalish sours to pear brandies, pepperwines and smokeberry browns.

Do stop by the Mother Mountain, where pregnant women come to participate in the stallion-heart ceremony. It's an ancient tradition that dates back millennia and sees the expectant woman consume the heart of a stallion under the watchful eye of the Dosh Khaleen. Due to the strict prohibition on bearing steel within the city, these women are forced to tear apart the heart with their teeth and fingernails. It's a gruesome spectacle but it is said that if a woman eats the entire organ, she will bear a son who is strong, swift and fearless. If, however, she chokes on the blood or brings up the flesh, the omens are altogether less favourable.

Don't bring your weapons. Even the Dothraki are forced to unladen themselves of their arms before entering the city. Outsiders can travel within the city unharmed as long as they keep the peace and bring traditional gifts of salt, silver and seed to the Dosh Khaleen.

SLAVER'S BAY

Built from the ashes of the Ghiscari Empire – the oldest civilisation in the known world – Slaver's Bay has blossomed into a wealthy hub of the slave trade. Located on the southeastern coast of the continent in the waters of the Gulf of Grief, a constant supply of slave ships ferry fresh meat into the area.

The three cities of Astapor, Yunkai and Meereen have risen to prominence in this region. It is an area of incredible wealth, excess and high culture; a place where you can enjoy every manner of opulence so long as you can stomach the slaves on whose shoulders the cities have been built.

Astapor

Once little more than a poor colony, Astapor has flourished into a hub of the slave trade and home to the Unsullied: the legendary eunuch warriors who can only be found in this part of the continent. Built from blood-red brick that has started to crumble with centuries of wear and tear, Astapor is filled with a thick red dust that swirls around its deserted streets during the heat of the day.

At night, however, the city comes alive, with silk lanterns casting a kaleidoscope of colours over the architecture. The most impressive structures are on the shoreline, where steep stone pyramids rise more than 400ft into the sky. Taller than any castle in Westeros, these stepped monoliths are covered in all manner of vines and boast commanding views over the Worm River, along which pleasure boats ferry the pampered local elite.

For tourists, the most popular attractions are the city's

colossal plazas. The Plaza of Pride is an open market where slavers take customers to view their wares. At its centre is a red-brick fountain on which stands a hammered bronze version of the Astapori harpy: a woman's torso with the wings of a bat, the legs of an eagle and a scorpion's tail. This ghastly spectre hails from Old Ghis and is a common sight across Slaver's Bay.

Those looking for a more macabre spectacle should head to the Plaza of Punishment, where rebellious slaves are tortured and killed, or the city's numerous Fighting Pits in which the imprisoned are forced to duel to the death.

Do take a pleasure barge up the Worm River.

Don't forget to check for up-to-date information before you travel. Recent reports suggest that the city has succumbed to the Bloody Flux, while Daenerys Targaryen's recent liberation of the local enslaved population has left a political void that is sure to be exploited by Astapor's many unsavoury characters.

Yunkai

Known as the 'Queen of Cities', Yunkai is renowned for its bed slaves and its wealthy arrogant lords, who call themselves the Wise Masters. Everything here is golden, from the yellow bricks that make up the high-steeped pyramids lining the city streets to the beaten masks worn by the locals. The people here are also known for their extravagant appearance and the ornate shapes and bizarre twists in which they wear their hair.

Do take some time to explore the beautiful birchwood forest that stands some three leagues south of Yunkai.

Don't forget to check before you travel. Since it was freed by Daenerys Targaryen's army, the city has become a swarm of sellswords and wannabe soldiers looking to exact their revenge on its one-time liberator.

Meeren

Meereen is as large as Yunkai and Astapor combined – a colossal city that stands on the northeast coast of Slaver's Bay at the mouth of the River Skahazadhan. A phantasmagoria of coloured bricks, it is a jumble of winding streets, brick boulevards, temples and granaries. The skyline is dominated by the Great Pyramid – the imposing 800ft high monument at its centre. At its peak there stands a giant bronze harpy of Ghis. There is also a stunning garden, which provides an excellent view of the surrounding area. Filled with figs, fresh dates and olives, it's a jaw-dropping space that will make you feel like a god as you look down on the city below.

Beyond the Great Pyramid, travellers will also want to take in the Temple of Graces, a huge structure topped with colossal golden domes that could make an entire city rich beyond its wildest dreams. And don't forget the famed fighting pits in which the city's slaves are forced to duel for their masters' amusement.

Do take a tour of the city's sewers. While not exactly pleasant on the nostrils, they are exquisitely ornate and play an important part in Meereen's recent history.

Don't eat the spiced locusts – though delicious, they are often poisoned by the locals.

FIVE MUST-HAVE SOUVENIRS

Essos's markets and bazaars are famed across the known world for their extravagant goods and great prices. Travellers will almost be spoilt for choice as they arrive across the Narrow Sea and with exchange rates continuing to stand in Westeros's favour, it's perhaps no surprise that so many tourists come in search of a bargain. To help you plan what to spend your purse on, here's our guide to the five must-buy souvenirs.

Dothraki Medallion Belts

The bronze belts worn by almost all Dothraki men are increasingly popular with tourists. The roughly forged metal is rustically hewn together with horse gut to form a fabulous item that will provide an enduring reminder of your time wandering the grasslands of the Dothraki Sea.

Myrish Fabrics

Famed across the known world, Myrish Fabrics can be picked up for a fraction of the cost you can expect to pay back in the Seven Kingdoms. From velvet and lace to rugs and tapestries, the attention to detail is nothing short of impressive and the quality unparalleled. All you have to worry about is how you're going to get it home!

Dragonglass out of Asshai

A rare item that is increasingly sought after – especially by those who live near the Wall – Dragonglass can be found in markets and bazaars across Essos. Shipped all the way from the distant port-city of Asshai, it doesn't come cheap.

But then can you put a price on your personal safety, should you one day be confronted by a White Walker?

Steel from Qohor

The Qohorian smiths are said to be able to rework Valyrian steel itself but even if you cannot get your hands on one of these ancient swords, their bog-standard blades will still surpass anything you'll find in the Seven Kingdoms.

Tyroshi Dyes

Brilliant and bountiful Tyroshi dyes can brighten the dullest of rooms. Though they fetch a high price back in Westeros, they can be picked up for a song in Essos.

QARTH

They say that Qarth is the most beautiful city that ever was or ever will be. Its residents will tell you it's the centre of the world and they might just be right. After all, it's the gateway between north and south, the bridge between east and west, so ancient that it goes beyond the memories of man and so magnificent it is said that Saathos the Wise plucked out his own eyes after gazing on Qarth for the first time because he knew everything he saw after that would be squalid and ugly by comparison.

Though, hopefully, your reaction will be a little more reserved, it's easy to see why old Saathos was so moved. From the trio of defensive walls that encircle the city – all intricately adorned with carvings and banded metal – to the towers snaking skywards from almost every corner, every inch of Qarth is testament to its vast wealth. Elaborate fountains fill every square, wrought in the shape of griffins, manticores and dragons. Beyond them lies the great arcade, lined with white-marble statues of the city's ancient heroes that stand three times the height of a normal man. And then there's the cavernous Great Bazaar with its intricate latticework ceiling, which houses 1,000 gaily coloured species of bird.

Qarth also boasts one of the finest ports in the entire world: a sheltered harbour full of colours, with large stone quays reserved for spice ships as big as palaces and humble merchants' cogs from further afield. Dockside travellers will find a frenzy of winesinks, warehouses, gaming dens, brothels and temples to peculiar gods you'll probably never have heard of. This warren of buildings is littered with all manner of locals, from cutpurses and cutthroats to spellsellers and moneysellers. Here, you'll also find the city's best bargains, with the waterfront serving as a never-closing marketplace, where stolen goods are available at knockdown prices.

Known as the Milk Men on account of their pale complexions, the Qarthian people pride themselves on their sophistication. Elaborately dressed in jewels and silks – don't worry about feeling exposed, it's the fashion for women here to bare one breast – they consider weeping to be a mark of a civilised people. They're also irredeemably corrupt. Bribery is rife, so don't expect to accomplish anything without a purse full of gold or a mouthful of kind words.

Do take in some street performances. The boulevards here are filled with exotic attractions, including jugglers, singers, harpists and tumbling monkeys. You can even pay to see real-life dragons if recent reports are to be believed. By far the most popular performers are the city's fire mages, who create ladders out of crackling flame up to 40ft high and can make blooming wildfire roses appear out of thin air.

Don't get lost in the House of the Undying: home to Qarth's legendary warlocks.